Trista... ...her more... ...life.

He would carry her to the bed and...

His eyes opened wide, his gaze flying to the bed. To the heavy blue coverlet on which his child slept, oblivious to his madness. Dear God, did he have no control over himself where this woman was concerned?

As abruptly as he had taken Lily into his arms, Tristan released her. He looked down at her, her lips that were swollen from his kisses, her eyes that were heavy with passion. And wanted her still, in spite of knowing how very wrong it was.

Lily's eyes darkened with confusion even as he watched, her hand coming up to cover her swollen lips as she whispered, "Dear heaven, help us."

A bitter laugh escaped him. "I do not think there is any help for us, Lily—either in heaven or hell...!

Dear Reader,

This month we're celebrating love "against all odds" with these four powerful romances!

Winter's Bride by longtime Harlequin author Catherine Archer is the first book in her terrific new series, SEASONS' BRIDES. Keep a hankie close by while reading about Lily and Tristan, whose love, planted years past, blossoms again. Their long-ago secret affair produced a child, but a carriage accident tore them apart, as Lily was thought to have died. But fate intervenes, and the now amnesiac Lily is hired as the nursemaid of Tristan's daughter—*her* daughter. Lily's memory dawns slowly as Tristan's actions trigger the sweet echoes of a love too strong to be forgotten....

Barbara Leigh's *The Surrogate Wife*, set in early America, is about the struggle of forbidden love. Here, the heroine is wrongfully convicted of murdering the hero's wife, and is sentenced to life as his indentured servant.... And don't miss *The Midwife* by Carolyn Davidson, about a midwife who must care for the newborn of a woman who dies in labor. She and the child's stern father marry for convenience, yet later fall in love—despite the odds.

On the heels of a starred review from *Publishers Weekly* for *Midsummer's Knight*, Tory Phillips returns with *Lady of the Knight*, the frolicking tale of a famous knight and courtier who buys a "soiled dove" and bets that he can pass her off as a lady in ten days' time.

Whatever your tastes in reading, you'll be sure to find a romantic journey back to the past between the covers of a Harlequin Historicals® novel.

Sincerely,

Tracy Farrell
Senior Editor

Please address questions and book requests to:
Harlequin Reader Service
U.S.: 3010 Walden Ave., P.O. Box 1325, Buffalo, NY 14269
Canadian: P.O. Box 609, Fort Erie, Ont. L2A 5X3

WINTER'S BRIDE

CATHERINE ARCHER

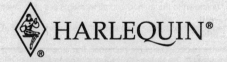

TORONTO • NEW YORK • LONDON
AMSTERDAM • PARIS • SYDNEY • HAMBURG
STOCKHOLM • ATHENS • TOKYO • MILAN • MADRID
PRAGUE • WARSAW • BUDAPEST • AUCKLAND

ISBN 0-373-29077-2

WINTER'S BRIDE

This edition published by arrangement with Harlequin Books S.A.

® and TM are trademarks of the publisher. Trademarks indicated with ® are registered in the United States Patent and Trademark Office, the Canadian Trade Marks Office and in other countries.

Visit us at www.romance.net

Printed in U.S.A.

CATHERINE ARCHER

has been hooked on historical romance since she read *Jane Eyre* at the age of twelve. She has an avid interest in history, particularly the medieval period. A homemaker and mother, Catherine lives with her husband, three children and dog in Alberta, Canada, where the long winters give this American transplant plenty of time to write.

This book is for my daughter Rosanna. She introduced me to Tristan and made me fall in love with him as she had.

This book is also for Elaina, who, like Lily, is finding her way out of the sadness of the past.

I would like to say a word of thanks to my editor, Patience Smith, for her amazing work ethic and her gratifying directness.

Prologue

England 1458

Benedict urged his mount to a faster and still faster pace, even though the heavy snowfall made doing so extremely unwise. He had to reach his brother—and his brother's mistress—before it was too late.

Tristan could not be allowed to tie himself to the wench, whose family supported Lancaster. She may have convinced Tristan that the whelp she carried was his, but Benedict was skeptical. He knew the repute of her family, knew that lying to get what they wanted was not above them. And it was most likely the case with their only offspring.

Benedict had lessoned his own siblings to a higher standard, which was why Tristan held such faith in this girl. He judged her by his own intent. Benedict was less naive. He had been left to look after himself and his three brothers when their parents died, and that he would do, no matter how determinedly Tristan resisted him.

He prodded the stallion again as another wave of

trepidation took him. There was more to his haste than his desire to save his brother from such a marriage. Some time ago, he had seen the Grays' own coach approach the crossroads to Westchurch just as he himself had come from the opposite direction. Their driver had taken no notice of him, a lone rider on the darkened road. They searched for a coach.

Even though the conditions of this stormy night did not favor such haste, Benedict had been able to press his mount to a gallop and thus outdistance whomever else sought the lovers. And even resorting to such dangerous speed might not gain him enough time. He must get to his brother and away before the girl's family did. He had no wish for this folly to cost Tristan his life.

In that instant he was distracted from his thoughts by a dark shape in the road far ahead of him. His breath caught as he realized that it was an overturned carriage.

Even after telling himself that it could be anyone, he was not able to still the throb of anxiety in his chest as he approached. The Ainsworth arms on the side of the carriage confirmed his deepest fear. It was indeed his own family's conveyance. The driver lay crumpled beside it.

Benedict pulled the reins so hard he brought his mount to a rearing halt. He leaped to the ground, his hands searching for and finding no signs of life in the poor fellow. He had no time to mourn, turning to open the door of the overturned carriage even as an unfamiliar sound prodded at his consciousness. It was a weak and reedy, high-pitched wailing. The sound of a babe crying.

Grimly, Benedict raked the inside of the carriage

with his eyes. He was intent now not only on helping his brother but also in ascertaining the source of that feeble cry.

The inside of the red-velvet-lined coach was drifted with snow, and he realized the window must have broken out. His horrified gaze lit first upon his brother. Tristan lay in a crumpled heap against the opposite door, unmoving. Even in unconsciousness he kept his arms about the form of a young woman, who was clothed in a diaphanous white gown. There was no sound other than the crying of the babe, which seemed to be coming from somewhere in the area of the woman's lap.

Benedict's gaze flew back to his brother, and his heart swelled up into his throat as he noticed the spreading red color on the snow. It also darkened Tristan's gray coat and the white fabric of the girl's gown, which partially covered his brother as he held her close to him. Both of them lay far too still.

Benedict leaped inside.

As he raised Tristan's wrist, he also looked to the woman. His lips thinned as he searched the white face, which had been hidden by the folds of her gown from his previous vantage. There was no hint of color. Indeed, she was as white as the snow and her own gown.

Concentrating then on his brother, Benedict closed his eyes in relief as he felt the faint pulse of his blood. But that relief was only momentary. Such a faint pulse meant that though there was life in him yet, it hung by a tenuous thread.

All of this he realized in the space of a heartbeat, after which he quickly knelt and moved aside the girl's skirts until he found the form of the mewling child. It was so small and blue, so cool to the touch. Fear for the babe shot through him. It was not likely to last the night if he did not get it in from this storm. Even if the child were not his brother's he could not abandon it here, in the hope that the other coach would arrive in time. Lifting the little one into his arms, he then felt for the pulse of its mother. He was not surprised to find no sign of life.

Quickly he made the sign of the cross on her forehead. Though he had not wanted Tristan to be duped by her, he had wished her no such ill as this. His heart was heavy that one so young and beautiful had met such a tragic end. Then there was no more time for mourning the loss of one he had not even known, when he must certainly act now or lose his own brother.

Only moments later he was riding away, the unconscious Tristan laid across the horse before him, the still-crying babe in his arms. He cast one last glance over his shoulder toward the poor creature who had died this night, before urging his horse to a gallop.

He did feel sympathy for her and for the family who would soon mourn her loss, but he must now think about the two who had survived and keep them alive.

Chapter One

England 1461

Lady Lillian Gray looked about the common room of the inn with little interest. She awaited the head of her guard, who had disappeared through another doorway. The low ceiling was paneled with dark wood, and behind her a staircase of equally dark wood rose into the shadowy corridor above. A fire was lit in the depths of the hearth at the end of the chamber, and several men occupied the tables that dominated its length. Each seemed more focused on the contents of his cup than on anything else.

The haunting sense of loss, which had been so much a part of Lily's awareness since waking after an accident some three years gone by, overshadowed all. That terrible accident had claimed her memory of all events preceding the moment she had awoken.

She nearly started as Sir Seymour spoke at her elbow. ''My lady?''

She swung around to face the head of her guard, whose face wore a respectful and distant mask. His

manner had been thus since he and the rest of her
future husband's men had arrived at her father's keep
to fetch her that very morning. While they had remained deferential, they gave no hint of welcome to
their master's intended bride. She withheld a sigh as
she replied, "Yes."

Clearly unaware of her discontent, the knight
bowed. "The innkeeper has assured me that you are
to have his very best rooms, my lady, just as my lord
Maxim instructed. There will be no need for you to
present yourself in the common room for the meal. I
have requested that food be brought to you in your
own chambers, as my lord has also instructed."

Lily nodded. "Thank you." It mattered not if she
dined alone. She would have felt alone even in their
company. Still, she was displeased at not being asked
which she would prefer. It seemed that no one ever
asked what she wanted, certainly not her parents.
They always decided what was best for her.

Sir Seymour bowed formally and turned away to
direct one of the men who stood on alert behind them.
"Bring in my lady's light baggage."

That man, also a stranger to her, hurried out.

Maxim had insisted that only his own men were to
be entrusted with bringing her to his home keep of
Treanly.

Treanly. The name seemed so foreign to her still,
even though she knew it was to be her new home.
Her wedding to Maxim on her arrival there would
settle that irrevocably.

She looked toward Sir Seymour's back with unconscious regret. If only she knew more about where
she was going, about what she would find there! But
the knight seemed an unlikely source of information.

He maintained that mask of deference at all times and certainly would share nothing about his master, whom he referred to with the gravest of formality. Quickly she told herself that it hardly mattered.

What could matter when her own parents seemed near strangers to her at times? Any of the deep love she must once have felt toward them had been wiped from her mind, though their dedicated care had left her with a debt of gratitude that could never be repaid.

She could not deny that there was also some relief in going away from Lakeland Park. The strain of trying to remember a past that she did not recall, her parents' obvious hurt that she no longer felt the bond of their common experience, were more painful to her with each passing day.

Lily did not want to think about that now. She wanted to look ahead, to concentrate on the new life she was about to begin. Even though she could not dispel the ever-present lethargy that gripped her, some small part of her did hope she would be accepted by her husband's folk, that her new lord might come to have some care for her.

The marriage to Maxim had been arranged by her father after only one actual meeting between the couple. Although she knew him not at all, Lily had agreed without demur. Her father had been so eager for the match. Lily felt that even if she could not recall her love for her sire, surely she owed him her obedience. She was afraid that she had not, in the past, been as dutiful a daughter as she should have been. She did, at times, feel a sense of rebellion against her father's wishes, even when she knew he was right in deciding what was best for her.

If Maxim had seemed distant when they met, it

must certainly be his greater maturity and the weighty responsibilities of running his own lands that made him appear so. At forty-two, he was over twenty years her senior and likely not given to making youthful declarations or displays of affection. There had been a hot sort of hunger in his eyes when he thought she was not looking, and although it had made her feel slightly uncomfortable, it indicated that he was not completely indifferent to her. And had he not sent her the chestnut mare she rode to Treanly as his wedding gift to her?

Further strengthening her impression of his stalwart character, he had insisted that she journey to Treanly for the marriage, saying that he could not leave his lands unattended. Her parents had agreed with his request, though it was not possible for them to accompany her, as her mother had fallen ill only weeks before and could not risk traveling in winter.

Again, Sir Seymour spoke her name, drawing her from her thoughts. "Lady Lillian."

She swung around to face him.

He held up her bag, casting a disapproving glance over those seated beyond them in the common room. "If you are ready to go up now?" He seemed anxious to lead her away from this public room. "I will see you safely there myself."

Lily nodded, wanting to give the knight no cause for worry as to her tractability. "I am ready."

With no more conversation, Sir Seymour swung toward the stairs and motioned for her to precede him.

As Lily moved toward the steps, she pushed her sable-lined hood back slightly from her face in order to see more clearly where she was going. The lantern that hung from the wall bracket cast its light upon the bottom treads, but little reached the stairs above.

Just as she was about to start up, she heard the sound of booted footsteps moving down. Realizing the stairway was too narrow for two to pass comfortably, Lily stepped back, looking upward...and became very still as her gaze met that of a man.

A man whose face was cloaked in shadow, but who radiated an emotion so raw it held her captive. And that emotion seemed somehow to be directed at her.

Even as she watched, his gaze narrowed and he continued further into the light, his expression so intent that she felt a strange ripple of awareness course down her spine. She wanted to look away, but found that she could not. Though she could not deny that the gentleman was handsome, with his blue eyes and dark, dark hair, that was not what continued to hold her so still.

As she saw his face more clearly some instantaneous and overwhelming sense of recognition washed over her—through her. Like a sweeping wind, it seemed to penetrate flesh and bone to the very inner core of her—the core that she had been unable to access since the accident.

And then, just as abruptly, the sense of awakening was gone. Again there was nothing. She immediately experienced a numbing dizziness.

Completely disoriented, Lily swayed, putting a hand to her forehead.

Tristan Ainsworth looked down at the woman at the foot of the stairs with utter disbelief. The light was not strong, but he would know her anywhere, those wide gray eyes, the sweep of black hair that fell to either side of her fair face from a center parting. Those well-remembered and beloved features were equally patrician and delicate at one and the same time. Each was perfectly in harmony with the others and molded of milky white skin so soft to the touch that it had made him tremble to do so. Her figure, though covered by the lush and enveloping cape, was equally well-known to him. She was tall and slender, her hips and waist narrow, her breasts high and perfectly molded, with raspberry tips. From the first moment of seeing her he had felt that it was as if on that fateful day God had decided to create a woman especially for Tristan's eyes—his heart.

The woman at the bottom of the stairs was *his* Lily.

But Lily was dead. He closed his eyes and took a deep breath, telling himself that this was only another vision, another specter that would fade away as the others had. For had he not seen Lily in innumerable places, innumerable times, only to discover that she was not there?

Taking a deep breath, knowing with that sinking feeling in his gut that she would be gone when he opened his eyes, he forced himself to do so anyway. There Lily stood.

Still he could not allow himself to believe. Even as he watched, she swayed, grabbing for the railing.

Dear God, there was no mistake. No specter of his conjuring had ever fainted.

Lily.

A great cascade of longing filled him. It grew, washed over and through him as if he was standing beneath a raging waterfall. He was held completely immobile by the very force of it.

As if through a haze he saw that the man behind

Lily was moving forward to take her arm. He seemed not to notice Tristan's reaction, for he was intent upon the lady herself.

It was the man's presence that finally brought him back to reality. Tristan could not deny his own interest in any man who would be with Lily.

His Lily.

Nay, he corrected himself quickly as a sudden revelation hit him. If she was alive and had not even contacted him in these three years, she was not *his* Lily.

His tormented gaze swung back to her face. He saw her glance brush his length once again, a strange haunted look in her lovely gray eyes. But there was no sign of true recognition, which made no sense whatsoever. She had known him as well as any human being could another.

Or so he had thought at the time. Perhaps he had only been fooling himself, and she had been toying with his affections, as Benedict had said from the very beginning.

Quickly he focused on her escort, who seemed, if his manner and dress were any indication, to be a knight. The reverence in the man's voice as he took her arm and asked, ''My lady, are you unwell?'' told Tristan that he did not hold himself as her familiar.

She spoke in a whisper, and to Tristan it seemed she carefully kept her gaze away from himself. ''I...nay, not unwell. I only felt dizzy for a moment.''

The man frowned in concern. ''It has been a long day, and I ask your forgiveness for that. I have pushed you so far only because my lord bade me make haste in his anticipation of your arrival. Perhaps I have been overzealous. My master would not be pleased for you to become ill and our journey delayed.''

She raised a white hand to brush the dark hair back from her pale forehead. Even from where he stood Tristan could see that her hand was trembling as she said, ''Have no great concern for me. I am sure I will be fine. As you said, we traveled far this day. Morning will see me quite recovered.''

Tristan found himself frowning at this assurance. It was clear that she was quite delicate of constitution in spite of her words, even more so than when he had known her. For then she had been imbued with a vitality of spirit that had made her appear stronger than her physical being. He looked again at that trembling hand. The bones in it and her wrist looked as fragile as those of a dove.

The man spoke again, even as he began to draw Lily up the stairs past Tristan, whom he ignored except for a brief, disdainful glance. ''Your lord husband will be very glad of that.''

Tristan froze once more, feeling as if ice had replaced the blood in his veins. Not only had Lily forgotten him and the love they had shared, but she was married. Married to another man.

How could she just forget him, forget all they had shared as if it were nothing? How could she forget the very product of the love they had shared, their own child, Sabina?

The thought made rage flow through him with the force of the winter storms that pummeled the coast at Brackenmoore, his family home. It was too much to be borne.

He would not bear it.

* * *

That night, Lily woke with a start, realizing instantly that she couldn't breathe. There was something pushing down upon her face. The fingers pressing into her cheeks told her that it was a hand.

She made to move away, but could not. Her body was held by a heavy weight. It felt as if someone must be using his or her own body to hold her down.

Wildly she tried to think as her sleep-fogged mind attempted to make sense of what was going on. She tried to see around that large hand. The room was not as dim as it had been when she retired, for someone, surely her assailant, seemed to have opened a window, allowing the moonlight to pour inside. Briefly, she wondered if the chamber had been entered by that method, even as her desperate gaze came to rest on a man's face.

She started, her mind reeling as she realized that it was the man from the stairs, the one who had caused such a strange reaction in her. The man had seemed so familiar, though she could not understand why. She did not know him, nor why he would accost her this way in her chamber.

She moved her head from side to side, trying to free herself, wanting to ask this madman why he would do this to her. He only held her more firmly, causing her teeth to dig into her lips painfully. Without thinking, she opened her mouth, sinking her teeth into that hard hand.

''God's blood,'' he cursed in outrage.

He lifted his hand for a brief moment, barely long enough for her to sputter, ''Who are you?''

There was no reply. Immediately he forced a scrap of soft fabric between her lips and held it there, then secured it with another piece of cloth, which he tied behind her head.

Driven beyond her usual strength by fear, Lily began to struggle beneath his weight. Even in her frantic state the bedcovers hindered her greatly. Realizing that it was foolish to expend her strength in this hopeless position, Lily grew still. Glaring in frustration and confusion, she met his gaze. Those strangely compelling eyes of his, so close to hers, seemed to mock her puny efforts.

Anger made her thrash anew. Her exertions were redoubled when shame washed through her as she recalled her own folly in thinking him quite attractive, at knowing that she had not been able to forget the chance meeting on the stairs. In the long interval before she had finally been able to fall asleep, she had gone over and over that strange and unexplainable sense of recognition she had felt.

Bitterly Lily told herself not to think about that. She must certainly concentrate instead on finding out what he wanted with her.

As if her own thoughts had triggered him to act, he stood and began to roll her more tightly in the bedclothes. Horrified, she began to struggle harder.

It was of little use. His much greater strength and the fact that she was already covered in the blankets prevented her from freeing so much as a hand before she was completely immobilized from head to foot.

Then there was no more time for thought as she felt herself being lifted and draped over what she was sure was the man's shoulder.

Desperately she wriggled inside the roll of bedding. Her reward was a jarring thump as she landed on the floor. She clenched her teeth at the pain in her hip, which had hit hardest, telling herself that it was worth it if someone had heard her. But the only sound that followed was a muffled curse from her assailant. He uttered a husky-voiced warning, "Don't try that again, unless your hope is to get someone hurt. I won't be thwarted," before she was again lifted and flung over his shoulder.

This remark did nothing to ease Lily's fears or explain what was happening. It told her only that the madman was serious. Though she was not familiar with her future husband's men, that did not mean she could cavalierly put them at risk by alerting them. For whatever reasons of his own, this man clearly meant to take her no matter what the cost.

Perhaps it would be best to allow this knave to get her outside the inn, then make her escape.

With that thought in mind, Lily forced herself to acquiescence as she felt herself being carried out the door and down the stairs of the inn. No sounds came to her within the muffling folds of the blankets.

Tristan allowed himself not a moment of doubt or sympathy as he took her through the darkened inn. The common room was vacant other than for two gentlemen who snored loudly as they slept upon benches before the fire. The depth of their slumber indicated that it might be aided by drink.

He was not sorry. In spite of the cold seriousness of his warning to Lily, he did not wish to actually harm anyone. He would have taken her out the window, which was the way he had entered her room, but that would be near impossible, carrying the awkward bundle she made.

Nay, he did not wish to harm anyone—even Lily,

though his heart burned like a hot coal inside his breast at the thought of her perfidy. All he wanted...well, he wasn't sure what he wanted. He only knew that he had to confront her, tell her what he thought of her betrayal. He had to make her understand that she could not just look through him as if he did not exist, as if their daughter had never been born.

Sabina deserved better than that from the woman whom they had all thought dead—whom Tristan had mourned with an unceasing agony. Even when he had agreed to an engagement to his brother Benedict's ward, Genevieve, he had grieved that his bride would not be Lily. Each and every waking moment since his recovery from his accident—that fateful accident in which he had thought she died—had been accompanied by pain at the realization that he must go on without her.

Jagged sorrow sliced him anew, but unlike all those other times in the past three years, it was dulled by a smoldering anger. She would know just what she had done to him.

Lily would acknowledge that she had wronged him—and their daughter.

Mayhap then he would let her go. He would be glad for her to return to her husband and the new life she had made for herself without them.

The very thought of that unknown man made Tristan's lower belly twist with renewed rage. Quickly he made his way from the inn and out into the courtyard, where he had tied his horse.

He knew it would not be an easy journey to his hunting lodge, Molson, with Lily lying across the saddle in front of him, even with the full moon to light his passage. But they should be able to reach the lodge before dawn. He needed night to mask his escape. The soldiers who now slept so peacefully in their own chamber next to the one Lily had occupied, and the others in the stables, would have no witnesses to tell them where she might have gone.

Tristan was feeling as if things were going even better than he could have hoped as he laid her across the front of his patiently waiting stallion. It was then that she began to thrash about once more, and he very nearly dropped her on the ground. Roughly he whispered, "You are only going to hurt yourself if you fall. What good will that do you, Lily?"

It was as he spoke her name that she became suddenly and utterly still. This seemed odd...almost as if she were surprised that he knew it.

He shook his head, telling himself that it was impossible. She knew him. There could be no mistaking the shock on her face when she had seen him on the stairs of the inn, even though she had quickly pretended otherwise.

He swung up into the saddle behind her, urging Uriel toward Molson.

Daylight was just threading through the trees near the village as he rode up the hill to his hunting lodge. It had been built just before his parents had died ten years ago, and though not nearly as large as the castle at Brackenmoore, was more comfortable and definitely warmer in winter. That he did not make his permanent home there had more to do with his wanting to be with his family than anything else. He felt it was good for Sabina to be surrounded by those who loved her, especially growing up without a mother.

His betrothed, Genevieve, seemed quite content to remain there as well.

He did not allow himself to believe that his reluctance to live at Molson had anything to do with the fact that it was there he had been with Lily. That it was there they had culminated their love, shared their innermost thoughts, made plans for a life together. Due to its close proximity to Lakeland, it was filled with memories of their stolen moments together.

He had thought of none of these things as he had left for Molson the previous day to see his man, Wilbert, the craftsman who was making the polished metal shield for the lighthouse at Brackenmoore. It was only by chance that Tristan had stopped for the night at the very inn where Lily had chosen to take her rest. If not for that odd twist of fate he would never have seen her, would not be holding her before him at this very moment.

Tristan rode to the front entrance of the three-story lodge, which was built in the fashion of a manor house and called a lodge only because of its original intended use, and dismounted. He then reached up to take Lily down from where she had lain for the past several hours. As he did so she groaned in protest.

In spite of not wishing to feel anything but outrage, Tristan frowned in chagrin. He had been so lost in his own thoughts, in his anger, that he had given little consideration to her comfort. Of course she was stiff and sore from lying in one position for so long. He looked down and saw that the blankets had pulled away from her face during the ride. Even in the dim light he could see that she was too pale. Avoiding any eye contact, he reached out and removed the gag from her mouth. Immediately she sucked in a great breath of air, closing her eyes as if overcome by the sheer joy of doing so.

Telling himself that he was giving her no more than the same consideration that he would toward even an enemy, he eased her down slowly into his arms. Even then she gave another quickly muffled gasp of pain. He supported her there for a long moment, giving the blood a chance to begin flowing through her veins.

Obviously her discomfort was not completely debilitating, for when she spoke, her voice, though confused, was also demanding. "Who are you?"

His lips twisted in ire as he told himself his sympathy was misplaced. She did not lack the energy to continue the charade that she did not know him. "Do not try to play games with me, Lily. I am not interested in them."

She replied heatedly, "Please, sir, I play no games. I beg you explain who you are and why you have abducted me!"

He pressed his lips together in irritation at her question. "I'm sure you recall my warning about not getting someone else hurt by being foolish. You will not try to enlist aid here. No one would give it in any event." Beyond that he would not deign to answer. Once they were alone he would speak. He would not participate in this pointless questioning, which was no more than pretense. Roughly he flung her over his shoulder and moved to bang the knocker upon the oak-paneled door.

It seemed a very long time before it swung inward and Hunter poked his head through the opening. "My lord Tristan?" He pulled the door wide, even as Tristan stepped across the threshold.

The elderly servant's amazed green eyes focused

on the bundle his master carried. Tristan gave a mental shrug. He knew he could not hide the fact that he carried a body. He had not meant to. He knew the servant's loyalty was without question. Yet the man was a human being and must surely have some curiosity. Unfortunately for him, Tristan was of no mind to satisfy that curiosity.

Now that he was here, standing in the entryway of his own home in the cold light of morning, he was not sure he could explain even to himself what he had done. Tristan could not hope to escape the consequences of this act. For surely Lily would not keep silent when he let her go, after he had told her exactly how he felt about her duplicity. As angry as he was, Tristan knew he could not harm her in order to prevent her from telling what he had done. The very thought made his stomach muscles clench sickeningly.

He forced himself to focus on Hunter rather than try to understand the depth of his reaction. "Are my chambers ready?"

"Of course, my lord, as your letter requested, though we had not expected you until much later in the day."

"I...yes, there was an unexpected change of plans." Tristan raised his dark eyebrows and shrugged. "I'm sure you understand."

The poor man did not look as if he did understand. Not in the least.

Tristan's mouth twisted in a wry grimace. "Well, thank you, Hunter. I'll go up now."

"Yes, my lord Tristan." The elderly gentleman bowed. "I trust you'll let us know if you have need of anything."

"Of course." Tristan smiled, glad to have passed this awkward moment with so little commotion. He then turned and made his way up the darkened stairs at the far end of the wide entryway. Not much of the morning light had found its way through the shuttered windows above the door. But Tristan didn't require much lighting. He knew where he was going.

Upon reaching his rooms, he pushed open the door and went directly to the dark cherry-wood bed, where he deposited his burden without ceremony. As soon as she landed on the mattress, Lily began to wriggle out of the blankets.

He stood back and watched as her dark head emerged, the huge dark circles of her gray eyes finding him with fury and outrage. "Now, sir, will you tell me what is going on here?"

Tristan bent over her, feeling his anger rise afresh at her continued pretense of not knowing him. "I will tell you nothing until you stop this masquerade."

She sat up straighter on the gold brocade bedcover, clearly trying to gather the scattered edges of her dignity around her as she shook her head. He tried not to notice how the thin fabric of her diaphanous white night rail clung to the curves of her breasts, hips and thighs. Nor would he allow himself to think of the times he had pulled the heavy draperies that covered these very windows closed, undressed her in this very bed and...

As Lily began to speak, he concentrated with determination on her words. "I yield, sir, if it will please you. I have somehow perpetrated some masquerade against you. Now will you set me free?"

He frowned, seeing that she was making as if to

humor him. "I can't do that, Lily, not yet. Not until
we have discussed a few things."

She sighed, the heavy fall of her raven-black hair
spilling forward over her slight shoulders to pool
about her on the bed. "Such as?"

Tristan watched with an unexpected pang in his
chest. He had so loved the way that hair spilled across
his body when she kissed him....

He gave himself a mental shake. It had been a mistake to bring her here to Molson, where they had been
together. He would never even have met the young
maiden had he not, when visiting his own lands, decided to attend the local fair on a whim. From the
moment their eyes had met across the greensward,
Tristan had cared not what side of the war her family
might be on, nor his own. Yet he had been a fool to
forget all in her eyes. He must remember that that
time was no more, must force himself to concentrate
on how she had hurt him in allowing him to think her
dead, how she had betrayed her own babe.

His eyes narrowed on hers as he answered her
question. "Such as why you refuse to admit that you
know me even now that we are alone here. It can
serve no purpose. There is no one to hear."

She turned away from him then and shoved the
tangled blankets from her legs, as if she had decided
he were not worthy of her continued consideration.
Lily looked about the dimly lit room. His gaze followed hers over the heavy brocade draperies, the rich
dark furnishings.

She sighed and ran a trembling hand through the
hair at her temple. As when he had seen her on the
stairs the previous night, this sign of weakness stirred
his compassion for some reason.

"Well?" he demanded, his own frustration with himself making his voice gruff.

She looked at him then, her brow raised high. Her expression told him clearly that she had lost patience with him. "I tell you, my lord, I am exhausted. There was very little rest to be had upon your horse, and I had been traveling the whole of yesterday. If you insist that there are things that must be discussed between us, I must also insist that I rest first. I can make no sense of any of it at the moment."

He felt an unexpected and unwelcome sense of admiration for her bravado. Here was a hint of the Lily he had once known. He had admired her spirit from the beginning.

Perhaps that was why it bothered him so much to see the weakness she tried to hide. That weakness only served to further illustrate how much had changed, how much *she* had changed.

Yet he could not bring himself to insist that, before she rested, she stand up to the weight of what she had done. What harm could it do to allow her to sleep first?

He shrugged. "Then sleep, if that is your wish." He indicated the bed upon which she half lay.

She looked at him with a momentary relief quickly masked by hauteur.

Smiling benignly, Tristan sat down on the end of the bed and began to remove his own boots. He was somewhat tired himself. It had been a long night, and it would do no harm to have all his wits about him when he faced her with her perfidy.

When Tristan swung around to lie down on the bed, Lily was still watching him. Her eyes became rounder as she saw his intent. "You do not mean to sleep here?"

His smile widened with unconcealed amusement. "I certainly do. You do not think I would go and leave you here alone so you can escape?"

She bit her lower lip. Ah, he thought, so she had been contemplating just such a move. Well, it would do her no good. Even though the way to her own father's keep from Molson was well-known to her, she was completely in Tristan's power until he chose for it to be otherwise.

Casually he got up and went to the door. Fixing his gaze upon her own, he turned the key in the lock, then with deliberate care placed the key in the waistband of his leggings.

Her gray eyes narrowed, and she leaped up from the bed. "I will not sleep in this bed with you. I wouldst rather lie upon the floor." With that she plopped down upon the gold-and-red-patterned carpet.

He frowned. Lord, but she was obstinate, just as in the old days. Then her obstinacy had shown itself in her desire to see him in spite of her parents' wishes.

Even as another shaft of regret passed through him, tightening his throat, Tristan strode across the room and scooped her up in his arms. Her eyes grew rounder still as she gasped and tried to struggle.

Ignoring her efforts, he tossed her onto the bed and stood staring down at her for a very long time, during which she did her utmost to glare back at him. But once again he could see her fatigue in the dark circles beneath her eyes and the shallowness of her breathing.

Without another word, he turned his back on her

and went to the large overstuffed chair beside the empty hearth. Tristan settled back and closed his eyes, though he was aware of her continued scrutiny for quite some time. Only when he heard her lie back upon the bed and sigh with weariness was he able to even attempt to seek his own rest.

It was some time before he was able to sleep even then.

Chapter Two

Lily woke abruptly and to the full knowledge of everything that had transpired the previous night. She had, in fact, slept very little during the hours since she had refused to continue the confrontation with the madman who had abducted her.

A very handsome madman, came an unexpected voice inside her, as a rush of heat flamed her cheeks. Even in the vehemence of anger, those oddly compelling blue eyes of his had had the power to capture and hold her own.

As they had from the first moment, when she had seen him on the stairs at the inn.

Quickly she tossed this thought aside, for it was not comforting in any way. Lily knew she must think about what she was to do now. She certainly could not allow the madman, no matter how compelling, to confuse her. No matter how appealing he was to the eyes, with that dark hair, those strongly sculpted features and intense blue eyes...

From whence had come such thoughts? she asked herself in exasperation.

Lily could not forget the strength of his arms as he

carried her up the stairs to this very chamber. And he had left her to sleep in the bed alone. But then, he had had no right to bring her here against her will at the onset.

It had been some time after he settled himself in the large chair near the window that she was able to actually believe that he meant to leave her to her rest. The eventual slowing of his breathing had finally convinced her.

Lily found herself holding her own breath as her attention centered on him now.

A sudden prickling of awareness at her nape told her that he was awake. Unbelievably, she could feel the very force of his presence in the air. Lily lay very still, unwilling to face him as yet, wishing to give herself more time to think.

He must have been as alert to her as she to him, for he spoke from the other side of the chamber. "Well, are you ready to continue our discussion?" There was no mistaking the disdain and anger in his voice. The hours that had passed had done nothing to change his demeanor.

Lily took a deep breath and let it out in a rush as she sat up, quickly pulling the silken coverlet up to cover herself when she saw how much of her was exposed by the sheer fabric of her nightgown. She replied with equal disdain. "Only if you are now ready to come to your senses and allow me to leave." She could not be blind to the fact that he was indeed even more handsome than her eyes had told her in the dim light of their previous encounter. Those blue eyes of his were narrowed under two eyebrows that were dark as sable, as was the thick thatch of wavy hair that fell across his forehead.

As she watched, he reached up and raked it back with obvious frustration. He rose and strode toward her with the grace and menace of a stalking tiger she had once seen in an illustrated book. When he reached the bed he leaned over her. "It should not surprise me in the least that you are attempting to go back on your word."

Unexpectedly stung by the insult, Lily swallowed and replied with defiance. "Why would I be bound by my word to the blackguard who took me by force from my fiancé's men?"

She watched in surprise as his lids flickered at her words. It was almost as if he was disturbed by them.

His rebuttal only served to confuse her even further, and the emptiness in his voice reminded her of the sense of despair she had felt on the day she had woken to discover that she did not recall her own life. "Your fiancé'? So you are not yet married."

"Nay, not yet. I was on my way to be married when you took me." She glared at him. "And have as yet no explanation for why those who care for me must wait in fear of my safe return."

Two deep furrows appeared between his eyebrows as he snapped, "Lily, I have had quite enough of this. You will cease pretending that you do not know me. And you will do so now!" Yet in spite of his anger there was no mistaking the shadow of anguish that darkened his eyes.

The sudden sense that this man was acting from a place of deep pain made her pause and bite back the heated reply that sprang to her lips. Something was wrong here, for there was no mistaking that this man felt she was deliberately antagonizing him.

There must be some explanation. Perhaps he had

mistaken her for some other woman, and hearing him out would clear up the confusion. Perhaps then she could use reason to help him see that she was not the woman he sought.

A woman named Lily who bears your own likeness, said the same inner voice that had plagued her earlier. This time it had an incredulous edge.

Lily scowled. It was possible.

Unexpectedly, the memory of how she had reacted to her first sight of him on the steps at the inn rose up to haunt her. In that first brief moment it was as if he were no stranger, as if…

Could her strange reaction, that inexplicable sense of familiarity, be clouding her judgment even now? Could it be making her more willing to try to understand this disturbing man's point of view?

Nay, she would not think on it. She did not know this man. 'Twas impossible.

He interrupted her thoughts. "Well, what say you?"

She replied with more care this time, remembering her decision to use reason to help him understand that she was not the woman he believed her to be. "I know not what to say, sir. You have me at a disadvantage. I do not recall where or how we might have met." She met his angry gaze directly and openly, not wavering as he seemed to search the very depths of her soul with those all-too-adamant eyes.

What he saw in her gaze made him frown, but she glimpsed the first hint of uncertainty in his well-sculpted face. He studied her for another long moment, then shook his head with a bitter laugh as he sat down on the bed near her. She was not concerned about his sitting on the bed now. Ravishing her seemed to be the furthest thing from his mind as he replied with deliberate care, his voice filled with amazement, "At last I see. You do not know me."

Lily felt slightly encouraged by this seeming acceptance of her position. She nodded eagerly. "I do not. I can see that you are most eager to find the woman you seek, and for your sake I am very sorry that I am not she. Lily is indeed my name, but that is nothing more than an extremely unlikely coincidence."

He did not look at her, and his tone was so low she could barely hear as he said, "A coincidence."

Relief at his finally understanding made her voice brighter than it might otherwise have been. "Yes, yes, now you see."

Before she even knew what was happening he had whipped around to grasp her shoulders in his two large hands, his face so near hers she could feel the hot brush of his breath on her face. "Oh aye, I see. I see everything. You are not the Lillian Gray I met and loved with every fiber of my being, would have given the last breath in my body to spend even a mere instant with. That was not you but another woman who bears your name, whose soft skin covered fragile bones that feel as yours do beneath my fingers, whose mouth spoke to me in her sweet voice, the same voice that comes from your lips. You would have me accept that you are she in flesh and bone, but you are not my Lily."

Even as she tried to push away from the hard wall of his chest, Lily felt her own heart thud in reaction to the depth of misery and loss in his voice. Even in her trepidation she could not help thinking, *God, to be loved as this man loved his Lily.*

This man, who was not ill favored by any means himself, had been driven mad by the pain of his loss, mad to the point of wanting his Lily so desperately that he had taken another woman with the same name to replace her.

Suddenly she wondered what had befallen this other Lily. For surely something had. No woman could turn aside from such a deep and true devotion.

Unexpectedly she was overwhelmed by the depth of her own sympathy for that long lost woman. And, surprisingly, for this man.

What was she to do to help him? She had no understanding of how to do so. In the past three years it was she who had been the recipient of the devotion of others, a devotion she did not quite know how to return. Not once in that time had she ever felt that anyone truly needed her, as she felt this man did now. The sense of being needed was at once frightening and exhilarating, calling up reserves of compassion she had not even known she possessed.

Though he had not loosened his grip on her, Lily felt her fear dissipate as quickly as it had come, she knew not why. She also sensed with a strange unquestioning certainty that in spite of his seeming lack of control, he would never harm her.

Without understanding why she did so, Lily reached up and put a gentle hand to his cheek. "I am so sorry, so very sorry that I am not she."

At her touch his hold on her loosened and he slumped against her, his forehead pressing to hers. "Oh, God help me. I know not what to do, Lily. The wrong words continue to come from your lips, yet I cannot sustain my anger, not when you touch me. Not

when I thought never to be touched by you again.''
His arms closed around her.

Lily was instantly, yet utterly and completely suffused with warmth and well-being. She gasped with
shock at her own reaction. There was no denying how
right it felt to have him holding her, his hard chest
pressed to hers. This hurting man and his nearness
were more real than anything she had experienced
since waking from the long sleep that had robbed her
of her past.

How could that be? He was a stranger, totally unknown to her. Surely it was only sympathy for his
anguish that made her feel this way.

Still, she said nothing, overcome and unable to understand her own responses.

When he buried his face in her throat, drawing in
a deep breath as if taking the scent of her into himself,
she knew she should pull away. Inexplicably Lily
found she could not, for his action made a wave of
dizzying weakness sweep over her, from the tips of
her toes to the top of her head.

His breath was hot on her exposed nape as he whispered in hoarse desperation, ''Lily, Lily.''

She closed her eyes as a shudder of some indefin-
able sensation raced down her spine. The feeling was
terrifying and oh so very alluring all at the same time.

The next thing she knew, his mouth, so hot and
strange, yet achingly familiar, was pressed to the sen-
sitive flesh he had just grazed with his heated breath.
Again she gasped, even as she was racked by a shudder of reaction that left an odd heaviness in her limbs
and chest. The sound seemed to encourage him, for
his arms tightened and he shifted so that she lay more
fully in his arms.

She turned her head, trying to breathe, to think, to get hold of her scattered senses. He pressed his mouth to her own.

The moment his mouth touched hers, Lily felt herself sinking, drowning in the rise of feelings and emotions inside her, that odd heaviness spreading to her belly. From somewhere inside her, in a place she had not known existed, came an acceptance, even a welcoming of these feelings, a joyous reveling. Without conscious thought she opened her own lips, her tongue flicking out to connect with his. She found herself kissing him, plying his mouth even as he did hers with a passion that was as scorching as it was shocking. It was as if some strange woman inside her knew what to do, how to react to his caresses.

When his hand closed over her breast, she turned more fully to him. One part of her mind was appalled at her behavior, the other, the one that seemed to have taken control of her, celebrated her actions, prodded her to wrap her arms around him and draw him to her.

His mouth left hers to trace a line of heat across her throat as he whispered, "Say it—say my name. Say Tristan." His thumb raked across the tip of her breast.

Her eyes closed on the spiral of hot desire that raced through her to settle in her lower belly.

He whispered again, "Oh God, say it, Lily, say it."

Why this was so important to him she did not know, only that it was. She was past thought, past caring about anything but the rage of sensation he was creating with his touch. "Tristan, Tristan, Tristan." Even to her ears it was a caress as it escaped her lips,

lips that seemed to rejoice in making the very sound of it.

Her uttering of his name seemed to end any hold he had over himself as he shifted, groaned and laid them both upon the bed. His hands grazed her every curve, tracing over her from head to toe as if memorizing every inch of her form.

Far from being frightened by his lack of restraint, Lily felt her body respond with even more ardor. It was as if each and every bit of her welcomed and delighted in this man's touch—his unbridled passion. As if her body was privy to some knowledge of him that her mind was not. Even the fine hairs on her flesh tingled at the stroking of his hands, the heat of his breath as he pressed his face to the low neckline of her night rail.

He drew the garment down, and she did not demur, but reached to hold the back of his head. Her eager hands tangled in his thick dark hair as his hot mouth found the aching tip of her breast.

Her hips rose up of their own accord, and she sobbed with unrestrained delight. Urgently she pressed her body to him as he continued to ply first that tip and then the other with his tongue.

He whispered hoarsely against her, "I have wanted you so long. I have fought the memory of this, the way we are together, without surcease."

She had no thought of telling him that he was wrong, that she was not the woman he remembered. Her body would not allow such words to fall from her lips. Her hands tugged at his garments of their own accord, wanting to touch. Her lips murmured soft sounds of encouragement and desire.

When he reached to pull her gown up over her,

Lily still had no thought of halting him, but shifted to aid him. As he drew away briefly to divest himself of his own clothing, she found herself reaching eagerly for him, drawing his hard warm body back to hers.

She, Lily, and her powers of choice and reason, seemed to exist somewhere outside her powerful and uncontrollable reactions to this man. She wanted only to be closer to him, close enough to ease this throbbing ache that consumed her. Lily sobbed his name again, unable to give voice to the need that drove her except by murmuring, "Tristan."

He rose up over her, and without even knowing what she did, she opened her knees to admit him. And then he was inside her, gliding smoothly into the warmth of her body. Her hands found his narrow hips, clasping him to her. He rested there for a long moment, breathing raggedly above her, his lips pressed to her perspiration-dampened forehead. Only when she wriggled restlessly beneath him, knowing that somehow the relief to her frustration would come from the moving of their heated flesh, did he proceed. He started slowly, then quickened to a rhythm that Lily herself set. As the pleasure increased in the place where their bodies met, she became a mindless creature, lost in the rising waves of rapture that made her moan and toss her head from side to side.

The sensations built to a peak of unutterable ecstasy. She rose up time after time to meet the thrusting of his body, until she feared she could sustain no more pleasure and survive. And then she was awash in a shower of bright sparks and rapture that streamed through and over her, making her cry out in mindless abandon, her words an unintelligible chant of exultation.

Then slowly, as the storm quieted inside herself, for what seemed the first time since he had touched her, Lily began to realize just what had taken place. Her eyes flew open and met those of the man above her. Shock at her own behavior quickly turned to despair.

She had given herself to this stranger, when even now her own husband-to-be was very certainly wondering what could have befallen her. She felt the blood drain from her face as she raised shaking hands to cover herself.

As Tristan watched her expression change from rapture to chagrin, he felt his own face register frustration. He frowned as she pressed her hands to her face, crying, "Oh dear heaven, what have I done? I don't even know you. How could I...have let you...myself...?"

Stung to the core, Tristan rolled away, unable to face her for another moment. How could she react thus after what had just passed between them? How could she bring herself to continue to deny...? How could she...unless...?

Tristan stood up, looking down at her as she pulled the coverlet over her now visibly quaking form. He felt a wave of uncertainty, immediately followed by the painful ache that he had lived with each and every day since being told of her death. He did not want to acknowledge what he was beginning to realize, but his own feelings made him see that this was not some act that she was perpetrating. There was no way Lily would react to him as she just had and still pretend that she did not know him—unless she did not know him.

This revelation was more devastating than thinking she had betrayed him. When he had thought she had betrayed him he could feed on his anger, his desire to make her admit that she had wronged him. The connection between them was strong and clear; their feelings, though changed, were still alive. Yet if she did not remember him, was he not as good as dead to her, Lily, the woman he had known and loved?

He closed his eyes, wishing he could make it all go away, hoping that somehow when he opened them again it would not be true. That he would see that everything that had happened after the birth of their baby in the carriage had all been a terrible nightmare.

But when he did lift his lids, there Lily was, staring up at him without any hint of recognition. The misery apparent in her expression was equally difficult to behold. He found himself wanting to reach out, to comfort her, but after what had just happened that could only be a mistake.

Swinging away abruptly, Tristan gathered his scattered clothing from beside the bed, then hastily dragged on his burgundy-colored *houppelande* and black leggings. He wanted to go from this room, forget that the past day and his own mad actions had ever occurred.

Instead, Tristan sat down on the end of the bed, being careful not to put himself within easy reach of her, while at the same time making eye contact with Lily. It was important to him that she understand that he had not meant to harm her, that he had believed she did know him.

He spoke carefully. "I have only just realized that

you are not deliberately lying to me." He tried to keep the pain from his voice, but feared he failed as he went on hoarsely, "You do not know me. You actually have no memory of me or what we have been to one another."

She shook her head. "I do not, though what you must think of me...having realized that now...after we..." Obviously she could not go on, and Tristan had to look away from her guilt-filled eyes.

Even as he was trying to find the words to help her, to wipe the sorrow and shame away, she said, "I do not understand what is between us, my lord, why this happened, but I know something is wrong. I have no memory of having known you in any way, yet you do seem very familiar to me...to my body. Else..." She blushed scarlet, her gaze dropping to her hands as they clutched the coverlet against her bosom. "Else I would never..."

Taking pity for her embarrassed state, Tristan nodded. "As I said, I have realized your sincerity in thinking you do not recognize me. There is no need to convince me further." He took a deep breath and let it out slowly. "What I do not understand, though, is how you came to this state. How could I—and Sabina—have been so very effectively wiped from your mind?"

Her gaze flew to his. "How do you know that name? Sabina—"

Tristan grimaced, interrupting her. "Sabina was your maternal grandmother. You were close to her when you were quite small."

She shook her head. "How would you know that? What I know of it has been told to me by my mother. I have no actual memory of that time."

"I know because you told me, Lily, with your own lips. I do not know what has made you forget all, but you have."

"'Tis not possible. My parents have told me how I came to lose my memory. They would have told me if I had loved a man—loved you." Her eyes pleaded with him to agree with her, to put her mind to rest. "It is a mistake. I cannot be the same woman."

He shook his head, not believing there was anything to be gained in telling her exactly how he felt about her parents. "There is no mistake, Lily. It was you and no other. You said that if you were ever to have a child you would wish to call her by that name...." Tristan grimaced again, this time even more deeply, realizing that in his frustration he had given away more than was wise. How could he have been so foolish as to mention their child? His doing so could only make matters worse. Lily remembered nothing of their time together, of Sabina's birth, the accident in which he'd believed she had died.

His long pause made her frown. "Go on, finish what you were saying."

He studied her for a moment. He was tempted to ignore her directive, to make up a tale that would prevent her from knowing the depth of their bond. He knew that it would be easier for her to walk away and never look back. Yet something would not let him. No matter how deeply buried her memory of him might be, there was still a connection between them, had been from the moment they looked at one another across a greensward dotted with May revelers some four years gone by.

Even more than that, did she not have a right to

know? He took a deep breath. "Sabina is our daughter."

She gasped with shock. "Our daughter. How could we have a daughter?"

Tristan could not resist a wry but pointed glance about the rumpled bed.

Lily spoke hurriedly, clearly trying to ignore her own embarrassment, but that did not keep Tristan's attention from following the blush that graced her lovely white neck. "I know how. I mean how could I not know?"

He dragged his attention from where it had no right to stray and considered her words. How could she not know? Ah, there was the dilemma indeed. He shrugged with resignation. "That I cannot tell you. Surely you would know better than I."

She shook her head in helpless frustration. "I do not know what to make of any of this. I recall nothing of what you say, yet my reaction to you, the things I have felt this day—done this day—make me know that something is very wrong. I do realize that there could be much that is truth, but foreign to me. I recall only what has occurred in the past three years, since I woke from a terrible illness. That and what my own gentle family has told me of the past."

Without thinking, he leaned toward her, his gaze intent on hers. "You were ill three years ago?"

"Yes, dreadfully. I was struck upon the head during a carriage accident and fell into a deep and unremitting slumber for many days. My mother and father feared I would be taken from them. When at last I did awaken, I was as a child. It is only by the great love and care of my own parents that I am today able to go on with my life."

Tristan could only stare. "They told you you were hit upon the head in an accident?"

She nodded. "Yes."

He shook his head in derision. "You may very well have been hit upon the head in the accident, but they have left out some relevant details. You were with me when it happened, Lily. We were running away together. We had met at a fair at a location not far from this very hunting lodge." His eyes met hers for one long and potent moment. "We fell in…love, but your parents would not hear of a match between our families, as the Grays and the Ainsworths were on opposing sides of the war between the houses of York and Lancaster. We…met in spite of their disapproval. You became pregnant with my child in this very chamber, and when they discovered your state, they forbade any further contact betwixt us, making sure there would be none by keeping you locked in your rooms."

Taking the coverlet with her as she leaped from the bed, Lily moved to stand before him, her gray eyes flashing in outrage. "Now I know you lie, for that cannot be. They would not keep such things from me. Would never keep me locked away in that manner."

He looked at her, his gaze unwavering. "How then do you explain what has happened here? You said yourself that I seem familiar to you." Again he cast a sweeping glance over the bed. "Familiar enough that you would react to me as you did just minutes ago. If I did not know you, why would I have so overcome my own sense of decency that I would forcibly bring you here? Why would I risk my own neck to take you from the protection of several armed men? What could I gain?"

She shook her head. "That I cannot answer, and I do believe that you somehow know me, sir. That much is clear. You are simply mistaken—" she took his measure carefully as she finished "—or lying."

He looked at her with pity and a hint of anger that he attempted to disguise. "You know that is not true. I am mistaken about nothing. And I certainly have no cause to lie. Make no mistake, I know you—every inch of you, Lily. I would recognize you were I blind, deaf and dumb."

She blanched, raising a trembling hand to her face. "I do not know. I cannot explain it. I only know that my parents love me. They would never deceive me that way, would never keep the fact from me that I had a child."

He shrugged. "So be it. Disbelieve the truth of your own instincts."

Spinning away from him, she moved to the tall windows and stood staring out of them. "Please, I must think and try to make some sense of all this."

"Very well then, think away, although I do not know of what use it will be to you. I have been thinking the whole night through and have resolved nothing."

She stood very still for a long time, then rubbed a hand across her forehead as she said, "If only there was a way for me to see this child. Perhaps then—"

He interrupted her. "But that is a wonderful idea."

She spun around to face him. "You cannot mean that?"

He met her incredulity with reason. "Why not?"

Lily seemed to come to some resolution within herself. "Then you must take me to her now, before my courage is lost."

Tristan knew this was mad, that there would be complications to such a brash scheme. He knew they must think this through carefully.

Yet deep inside he felt the stirring of an emotion he could barely allow himself to acknowledge. Hope. Tristan knew he could not let himself hope.

Lily had a life that had nothing to do with him now. If he agreed to this it would be for the sake of her finding out her own truth, and not connected to him in any way. "Are you certain that you wish to do this? Your fiancé is awaiting your arrival." He was relieved that there was no hint of regret or bitterness in his tone.

Lily knew that she had to do this. It was the only way she could go on from here without the thought of it all preying upon her mind like a gnawing hound. "I will send a note to Treanly, telling Maxim—"

"Treanly," Tristan interrupted, incredulous. How much worse could this situation get, that she would be marrying Maxim Harcourt, the sworn enemy of his own family?

Lily seemed oblivious to his ire. "Yes, I must tell him that I am safe and he is not to worry. It is partly for his sake that I must discover the truth. If I go to him now without settling this in my own mind, understanding how it is that I do know you, it will not be as wholly as he deserves."

Lily thought she saw Tristan grimace at the last words, but the impression was quickly gone as he replied, "I will take you to see Sabina. But you must promise me this. You must not tell her or anyone else who you are. If it is your intent to only seek truth for your own benefit, so that you may go on with your life in peace, I will allow it. Anything else would not be fair to her, considering your commitments to your future husband. We have made a good life, and I will not have it disturbed.''

Lily listened to this very carefully. Now, though he seemed prepared to take her to the child, he appeared to wish for this to happen without disruption to his own life. His stipulations seemed odd considering that the most likely explanation for all of this was that he was making it up. What his motives might be for inventing such a tale, she had no idea.

Tristan seemed to have gained complete control of his feelings. There was no longer any hint of yearning in his voice or eyes. The only emotion she could see in him now was the irritation he tried to hide at her saying that he might be lying.

Yet though so much was unclear to her, she was not afraid of this man. Surely, had he wished to harm her, he could have done so already.

It had been her own suggestion that she see the child for herself.

Her thoughts rolled on until she took a deep breath and halted them. None of this would change anything. Enough had occurred this day to make her realize that she had to see for herself, to confirm the fact that he was indeed lying, for whatever reason, so that she could go on with her life.

She nodded. ''I will tell no one.'' She paused. ''Not that I expect there to be anything to tell. As I said before, my family loved and cared for me when I was at my most vulnerable. They would not behave as you have suggested.''

He shrugged. When he spoke, she told herself his distant tone caused her no sense of regret whatsoever.

"I will say that I have engaged you as a maid for Sabina. That way you will have just cause to spend time with her without drawing comment. Then, when you are ready to leave Brackenmoore, you can do so with as little disruption as possible."

She nodded again, calling pride to the fore in the face of his indifference. "That would be for the best. I do not know what is going on here. In the remote possibility that I am wrong—" she met his gaze directly "—and it is remote, I will do what I can to discover the truth. But make no mistake, should you wish me harm, you will face retribution for your acts. If you know of my family as you claim, you know they are not without the resources to repay you in kind."

In spite of his own reaction of ire, Tristan could not help the feelings of admiration for her as he took in her proudly tilted head and determined face. As fragile as she appeared on the outside, there were still some signs of that unshakable will that had once been so much a part of her. It was one of the things he had most loved about her.

Tristan felt an urge to warn her about Harcourt, to tell her just the kind of man he was. That her loyalty was indeed misplaced in such as he. Yet Tristan knew she would not heed him. What he had told her of her family had already been too great a stress on the locked doors in her mind. Perhaps, if things changed, if she began to recall... But he would place no hope in that. He had no hope left.

He took a deep breath and turned away, for just looking at her made him long for a time that was gone, never to return. If she had been a different woman, not the Lily he had loved from the first day they met, none of this would ever have happened. He would not be faced with losing her once more.

He told himself that he would not regret it when she returned to Maxim Harcourt. Her loyalty to her family was absolute and unlikely to change. Things were as they must be.

He drew himself up stiffly, resolutely. "I will send one of the serving women with something for you to wear. Please make ready for the journey as quickly as you can."

Rigidly, she nodded. "I will give you no cause for displeasure, my lord." She paused then for a long moment, and he saw the heat that rose in her cheeks as she took a deep breath. "I...there is one more thing. What happened here was a terrible mistake. I can only imagine that my relief at discovering that you did not mean to kill me left me completely vulnerable to my baser emotions. You must understand that I cannot allow this to occur again. Such behavior is quite unlike me, I can assure you."

Tristan watched her with both respect and consternation. He did admire her ability to overcome her own obvious aversion to even mentioning the event. Yet on another level, he was annoyed that she could so coolly explain away what had taken place between them. He could tell her that such behavior had indeed been quite like her, as far as the two of them were concerned.

But what did it matter what she thought?

He also knew they could not allow it to happen again. Though theirs was no true romantic liaison, he loved Genevieve as a sister, and she deserved better from him. He replied simply, "I agree most heartily. I also overreacted to seeing you so unexpectedly. You are the Lily I once knew. However, no matter what might happen at Brackenmoore as far as your memory is concerned, you are no longer she. I also have a new life. I must tell you that I, too, am engaged to be married—to my brother's ward, Genevieve Red-greaves. We will never speak of what occurred here again.''

Her eyes widened as he finished, then she nodded very quickly, turning her back to him. Her voice seemed bright with satisfaction as she replied, ''That is very well then. We will never speak of it again.''

Her obvious relief was unexpectedly disturbing. She did not face him as he said, ''I will have some things brought up to you so you may make ready for our journey.''

She gave a brief nod and spoke with cool indifference. ''Thank you, my lord.''

Unaccountably frustrated with her demeanor, he bowed briefly and strode from the chamber without a backward glance.

Chapter Three

Brackenmoore.

Lily's hands felt like they were carved from ice as she peered through the evening gloom toward the very dark and imposing edifice of the castle. It seemed to fairly loom over the curtain wall like an enormous coiled dragon, and the salty tang of the nearby sea aided her imagination in the creation of reptilian scales for the beast. Her numb fingers fumbled as the white mare Tristan had given her to ride seemed to balk at the sight as well.

In one of their few and extremely brief exchanges of the day, Tristan had explained that he lived here with his family. He had said that he felt it was of benefit to Sabina to be near them—and his intended bride, Genevieve.

Dear God, the name had the power to bring an ache to her chest. When Tristan had so calmly, so coolly told her of his engagement, she had felt as if he'd run her through with a dull blade. Lily told herself it was because of the fact that she, Lily, had betrayed Genevieve by lying with the man she was to marry. How would Lily face this unknown woman?

Her troubled gaze ran over Tristan's back as she thought about the note she had written for Maxim. It had said simply that she was not in danger, that he should have no concern for finding her and that she would return to him before long. Tristan had taken the missive, ensuring her that it would be delivered, and in such a way that it would not be traced.

Now she could not help asking herself how she could have had the temerity to do such a thing. What would Maxim think of her undeniably extraordinary request for him to simply await her eventual arrival?

What had come over her? Why had she come here? Why worry her future husband by listening to the wild talk of a man she did not even know?

Surely it was because she had to see the child, as she had told him. And perhaps try to learn why Tristan would fabricate such a story. Yet in the darkest part of her mind she also knew it was because she could not dismiss her own unrestrained reactions to him. Something must account for the fact that he seemed so familiar, for the fact that she had allowed him to touch her, make love to her as if he had some right.

Allowed him? an inner voice chimed mockingly. Lily knew she had done far more than allow. She had encouraged, entreated, rejoiced in him.

No matter how difficult it might be, she simply had to find out what was going on. It did not seem possible that she could have had a child, that she could have loved Tristan enough to betray her own father and mother by running away with him.

Still, he knew so much about her.

She told herself again that his story simply could not be true. Her mother and father had cared for her so tenderly since her illness. They would never do anything to harm her.

It was possible for her to come here seeking the truth without damning her own family, to discover that it was Tristan Ainsworth who lied. She would do so without a repeat of the events of that morning. She was promised to Maxim and would not again reveal her attraction to this man.

That was the only way she might eventually forgive herself for what she had done with Tristan.

"Lily."

"Yes?" she replied, looking up in surprise at hearing Tristan speak her name. Immediately she realized that, while her mind wandered unchecked, they had reached the castle gates. Drawing herself up in her saddle, she nodded. She would attend to her surroundings more fully. All in this keep, and even Tristan, were strangers to her.

"Are you feeling well?" he asked, his dark eyes studying her closely.

She nodded again quickly, her own gaze dropping to the horse's white neck. It continued to be difficult to meet that gaze after what they had done together in that big soft bed back at Molson Lodge.

She was not sorry when he turned without further comment and led the way beneath the portcullis, now raised. Her mount followed his without urging, seeming eager for their journey to end.

As they passed through the curtain wall, she realized that it must be some ten feet thick at least. The rough stone was dark, nearly black in color, and she wondered if that was caused by the structure's nearness to the salty sea. Or could it be that the builder, some long deceased Ainsworth, had deliberately fashioned his fortress from the darkest and most intimidating material available?

Her gaze returned to Tristan's broad shoulders. The sheer determination and ruthlessness he had displayed in abducting her made her think it might very well be the latter.

What would happen, she wondered, should this man again decide that he wanted her? Lily tried to still the shiver that raced down her spine, deliberately averting her gaze from the shoulders her own fingers had clung to with such desperate need.

The courtyard was nearly empty. In view of her own confused feelings, Lily was glad of this. She was very tired and beginning to feel more and more as if what was happening was some product of her imagination.

They dismounted and handed their horses over to a young serving man of whom she barely took note. All her thoughts were now centered on the fact that she was soon to meet the child that Tristan claimed was hers. He led her up the wide stone steps of the keep and opened the great oaken door, which swung inward slowly on well-oiled hinges.

The light inside the enormous, high-ceilinged hall was dim, and there were many folk already stretched out upon their bedrolls. Just before they stepped inside, Tristan bent close and whispered, ''I am sorry for any offense that you might feel due to the manner in which I must address you henceforth. We must remember to behave as if you are indeed a personal servant to Sabina.''

She bowed her head. ''Of course. I will take no offense.'' Lily wished for no one here to know of her true identity. She could act the part of servant for a few days. After that she would be going back to her own life.

What would she say to her own family—to Maxim? She would have to leave that decision until the moment arrived.

Tristan went before her, going directly to a woman who was banking the fire in the enormous hearth at the far end of the room. She turned to look at them, then dipped a curtsy when she saw Tristan. "My lord Tristan. We had not expected you home so soon."

He shrugged, even as Lily felt the woman's curious eyes upon herself. She felt them linger on the shapeless gown of faded brown, which had been the only garment Tristan could produce for her at the hunting lodge. Lily twisted self-conscious fingers in the rough fabric. It was of poor quality even for a personal maid. The serving woman who had brought it to her at Molson had informed Lily that it was a castaway of one of the kitchen girls.

Without thinking, Lily raised her chin defiantly. She frowned then at herself when the serving woman's gaze moved thoughtfully from her to Tristan.

Tristan ignored the questioning expression. "Is Benedict abed, Maeve?"

Her attention diverted, the portly woman sniffed with obvious but fond disapproval. "Nay, not that one. He's up in the records chamber working. I took him a warm drink not more than minutes gone by and told him he needed to be abed, but he would not heed me."

Tristan took a deep breath and turned to indicate Lily. "Maeve, this is Lily. Lily, Maeve is the head woman here at Brackenmoore." He swung around to the older woman again. "I have brought Lily to act as personal maid to Sabina."

"Personal maid?" Her assessing gaze swept Lily again, who had to suppress the urge to comment on such rudeness from a servant.

Again Tristan ignored the woman's reaction. "Lily, please follow me."

He started off without waiting for the "Yes, my lord," she muttered in reply. Hurriedly, she followed him to an arched opening at the far side of the hall, which led directly onto a winding stair.

As they went up, the stone stairs were lit only by the taper Tristan had taken from the wall holder at the bottom. Lily sighed, telling herself she would have to quell her resentment at the head woman's manner. Lily was not accustomed to being so summarily treated by a servant, but as a servant herself she must become used to thinking of Maeve as her superior.

At the opening to the second floor, they moved down a long hall until they reached the end. Tristan stopped abruptly before a heavy wooden door and turned to face her.

Taking a deep breath, he took Lily's arm and drew her forward with him. He seemed preoccupied and oblivious of her reaction to his odd demeanor. He opened the door, and they slipped inside as he closed it quickly behind them.

The first thing Lily noticed was the many shelves of books that lined the long narrow chamber. More books were piled in front of the shelves and atop them. There were also books piled on the desk at the far end of the room, where she now saw a raven-haired man bent over an enormous tome. He looked up just then, and as his eyes came to rest on her, they widened with what Lily could only call astonishment. It quickly became bewilderment.

Tristan felt a wave of relief that was physically weakening when he saw the look of utter disbelief and amazement on his older brother's face. The words that exploded from him as he stared at Lily could leave no one in doubt of his shock. "Dear God, is this a ghost?"

Some of the tension that had been growing in Tristan since he'd realized Lily was alive left his knotted shoulders. Clearly, Benedict had not known that she lived, which meant he had not deliberately lied to Tristan by saying that she had died in the carriage accident on that terrible day.

Tristan nearly sighed aloud in relief. He had not wanted to think that his brother would betray him in that way.

Immediately he knew that he must speak with Benedict alone. He owed his brother some sort of explanation for bringing Lily to his keep. As head of the family and baron of the lands, Benedict did have some say in her staying at Brackenmoore.

If word that Lily was here did get out, the wrath of Maxim, Earl of Harcourt, might well fall upon their heads. Tristan's lips twisted at the mere thought of the man.

It would be dangerous to rile such an enemy. Though Tristan was not fearful for his own sake, he had the welfare not only of Sabina, but of his entire family to consider. Maxim's displeasure over the king allowing Benedict to serve as warden to Genevieve, who was Maxim's own cousin, was surely little abated. The earl would certainly have difficulty in making trouble for them at court now that Edward was king, but he could attempt to do so. Harcourt had kept a hand in both camps during the war between Lancaster and York, and still had managed to continue his favor at court. Tristan felt sure that young Edward's outward friendliness toward many of those whose loyalty was uncertain had something to do with settling old angers. With his father, Richard of York, dead, he had a mammoth task ahead of him in bringing order to England.

Though the problems of state were important to all in the realm, they were not paramount in Tristan's mind at this moment.

Tristan turned to Lily quickly. "I must speak with my brother alone, please."

She looked at him with obvious unease in her gray eyes. "This man, as well, believes he knows me?"

He nodded. "Of course."

Lily was clearly unnerved by this, for she looked up at him with confusion. "I—I...don't understand."

Sighing deeply in frustration, he shrugged. "Benedict is understandably shocked. He believed you dead. But I have no intention of trying to convince you of that, nor will he. You are free to believe what you will, Lily. However, I would like an opportunity to explain this situation to my brother in private."

She raised her chin. "I will await you." Admiration for her courage made a new wave of regret wash over him. If only—

"What is going on here?" Benedict's deep voice interrupted his thoughts.

Tristan answered shortly, somewhat surprised that

his brother had managed to remain silent for so long. "Just one moment, please?"

He took Lily back out into the hall. "I will try not to be overlong."

She nodded, her gray eyes enormous in her pale face.

When Tristan concluded his explanation of everything that had occurred since he had first seen Lily at the inn—nearly everything—Benedict looked, if possible, even more amazed than when he had first seen them standing in the doorway. "Are you certain, Tristan, that she is not lying to you, simply saying that she cannot remember in order to evade your anger?"

Tristan's lips pressed tightly as he shook his head, then spoke wryly. "You sound as suspicious as Lily. But to answer your question, nay. At first, I thought as much myself, yet I am now certain that she does not lie. She was not pleased to admit that she did have some sense of familiarity with me." He recalled with chagrin just how familiar they had been. "I do not believe she would have come here if she was lying. I am sure it is only her own uncertainty in the matter that has made her come."

"You mean to try to pass her off as Sabina's maid?" Benedict asked. "How do you hope to perpetrate such a hoax? As Gray's daughter she has surely not done a jot of work in her life."

Tristan looked his elder brother directly in the eyes. "That may be so, but I—we mean to do this, Benedict. In spite of the fact that she is convinced that I have fabricated the whole tale, I feel Lily has a right to know that she has a child, that what she believes about her life is nothing more than a lie told to her by those she most trusts. If, understandably, you prefer that she not remain at Brackenmoore, I shall take her and Sabina to the hunting lodge for a time.''

Benedict raked a hand over his face. ''I still don't fully understand why you felt compelled to bring her here. If she does not believe you and has no memory of what you were to one another, why could you not just let well enough alone—walk away?''

Tristan stood in agitation. ''How could I walk away from Sabina's mother?''

''Genevieve will be the child's mother. Sabina is loved by her, myself, Marcel, Kendran—all here at Brackenmoore—and has done well enough without the woman who birthed her.''

It was true. Everyone doted on the three-year-old child. But that did not mean that Lily did not have the right to know her, to love her. It was not her fault that the past had been stolen from her.

Benedict said nothing more for a long moment, considering his younger brother. ''She is to marry Harcourt.'' The disgust in his voice was obvious.

Tristan grimaced. ''Aye, she is. And there is nothing that will stop that, unless she remembers. Surely if she does recall the truth and realizes that her parents have deceived her, she will no longer blindly fall in with their wishes in that. Marriage to that man is a fate I would wish on no woman.''

Grimly, Benedict asked, ''You are set on this?''

Though it nearly choked him to say the words, Tristan replied with conviction. ''I am. I feel I owe her this much for what we shared, no matter that it is gone.''

Benedict spoke very deliberately. ''Are you certain of your motives here, Tristan? Could it be that you hope she will remember all that happened between you, recall her love for you?''

Tristan shook his head in quick denial, though the words made him feel a strange unrest. ''Nay, 'tis not possible. As I said, what we had is gone. I will have no poor imitation. You do not understand how I feel in this. I would not want her lest she could come to me as she did before, and that is not possible now. Too much has changed.''

It surprised him no small amount when Benedict nodded his own head in assent. ''You are right. I do not understand how you feel. I have not loved like that. I could not allow myself the luxury of putting love before all else. Yet simply because duty to Brackenmoore and all who abide here will ever be foremost with me, I begrudge you nothing in your own desire for such a love. If at any time you realize that you do still want this woman, Tristan, I will accept your wishes as I did not before. You have shown yourself a man beyond your years since the accident. The decision will be yours and yours alone.''

Tristan could not but feel moved by his brother's faith in him. He decided that there would be little gain in further trying to convince him that all was over between himself and Lily. Benedict was the man he most honored and respected—not simply his elder brother, nor as one of the most influential and respected intimates of the slain Richard of York. Tristan's feelings stemmed from the fact that Benedict was the most honest, dependable and strong man he had ever known. He had taken over as head of their family ten years before at the age of eighteen, when their parents' ship had been wrecked returning from a visit to their aunt Finella in Scotland. Benedict had fulfilled his duties with both diligence and love.

Though Tristan did not say it aloud, he hoped that love would someday come to his brother. Benedict deserved no less.

Tristan bowed. "I thank you."

Benedict interrupted him gently. "There is but one matter. What of Genevieve?"

Now it was Tristan's turn to rub agitated hands over his face. "I do not know. I suppose I must tell her."

"I would advise against it. She loves Sabina so and wants to be her mother. How can you take that from her for no reason, when Lily may never remember? As you say, Lily intends to stay for only a short time, presumably merely long enough to convince herself that you have indeed fabricated the whole story. Why not give the situation some time? When you have a clearer idea of what will occur, you can explain it all to Genevieve. But again, it is your decision."

Tristan was tired—tired of thinking, tired of trying to ferret out the best course with the realization of each new disheartening complication. All he wanted was to be with Lily, to see her face, hear her voice, think about the moments they had spent in one another's arms.

Tristan recoiled from his own thoughts in horror. Lily and the way they had made love were the last things he should allow himself to dwell upon now or ever again.

What he had told Benedict about not wanting Lily *was* true. There would be no repeat of those moments at the lodge. Not when Lily did not know him—love him.

Tristan rose, feeling more weary than at any time in his life. "I will take your advice to heart. I will say nothing to Genevieve for the moment. There is no need to hurt her more than must be." But as he moved toward the door he felt an unexpected surge of energy.

Lily was waiting on the other side of that portal.

He told himself that it was because he was to introduce her to Sabina. He loved the child so, was proud of her. Perhaps seeing the little one would open the locked doors in Lily's mind as nothing else had. He could not even allow himself to consider what might happen then.

As he reached for the handle, Benedict's voice halted him. "I must add this one piece of advice out of love for you. Go carefully, my brother. I know that you believe her story of forgotten memory, but Lily may ultimately prove to be lying. Please, for your own sake, guard your heart so it is not broken again."

Tristan paused and smiled at his brother. "There is no need to worry. I know what I am doing, Benedict." Then he turned away, feeling that the words did not ring quite as true as he would have wished.

Lily was utterly and completely unnerved. Benedict Ainsworth's shocked reaction at seeing her could not have been feigned.

She spent the interminable time until Tristan returned thinking of the expression of recognition and horror on his brother's face. Something was going on here, but she knew not what.

Now more than ever she needed to see the child.

Yet when Tristan did emerge from the chamber,

doubt clasped Lily in a tight grip. She found herself studying him closely.

Tristan returned her scrutiny. "Are you ready to see her?" His eyes seemed to search her own for something....

Lily looked away. She was too numb to even try to fathom his expression. Stiffly, she replied, "Aye, I am ready."

She could see the rigidity that came over his body at her distant manner, but she could not alter her behavior. She felt as if everything was now happening at a long distance from herself. She had no more palatable reactions to give. When he motioned for her to follow him, she hung back farther and farther as he made his way down the long, dimly lit hall, then up the steps to the third story of the keep.

What would she say when she met the child? What if she did have a sense of knowing, as she had with Tristan?

As they continued down the hall, Tristan said nothing and simply matched his steps to hers. At last he came to a heavy oak door, stopped and turned, his dark gaze coming back to her. His face showed civility and possibly a hint of pity. He seemed to assess her feelings in the space of a heartbeat. "You have no need to be apprehensive about seeing her. She will be sleeping."

Lily crossed her arms over her midriff, daunted that he had read her so very easily. She knew it would be useless to try to deny his accuracy. "I do not know how I will feel, what I might recall and what it would mean to my life."

He watched her for a long moment, his gaze softening even more, then he held out his hand. "I understand."

Her heart turned over in her breast. God help her, but she responded so very quickly and on such a deep level to his gentleness. She was unable to prevent herself from moving forward and taking the offered hand.

Then, while still exhibiting that same gentle strength, he opened the door and drew her inside. The chamber was bathed in the golden glow of the fire. It was large but warmly appointed, with small furnishings and brightly colored fabrics. The heavy blue drapes, which matched the bed hangings, were pulled closed over tall windows. These windows must let in a great deal of light during the day. A narrow cot, obviously made up for an attendant, rested against the outside wall. A serving woman sat sewing near the fire directly across the room from the small, carved wooden bed. When they entered, she stood up and said, "My lord Tristan."

He nodded. "You may go now, Maggie. You will not be needed this night."

As the woman left, Lily realized that the child was obviously well cared for. She was not surprised. Tristan had made no secret of his love and devotion to his daughter.

And according to his claim, *her* daughter.

Taking a deep breath for courage, Lily forced herself to move with him across the room without hesitation. She had come this far, and for the very purpose of seeing the little girl. She would do so.

Tristan stopped just shy of the bed and moved to stand behind her. Lily looked at him in confusion.

His voice was so soft she could barely hear it. "This moment is for you."

Hesitantly, Lily nodded. It would be best if she did not have the compelling power of his presence beside her when she looked at the little one. She knew already how susceptible she was to Tristan's nearness.

She took the last steps to the bed alone. The hangings had been pulled back to let in the heat of the fire, and all she had to do was lean over....

Taking another deep breath, she did so. Lily had to put her hand up to stifle a start of shock, amazement and wonder as she looked at the little girl.

Sabina Ainsworth's straight black hair fell to either side of her smooth white forehead. Her cheeks, though rounded with baby fat, were shaped by highly defined bones. Her small mouth was pink and sweetly curved, her chin softly defiant.

Lily was frozen in place. She could not deny that she was looking down at a face that was very like her own must have been some eighteen years gone by.

But even while acknowledging this, she felt no rise of recognition, no immediate recall of how they could be so alike. Disappointment and relief swept over her in the same instant. Both were immediately replaced by consternation.

She had solved nothing. Now even more questions rolled unanswered inside her.

Slowly she backed away from the bed. She could feel Tristan's gaze upon her, but refused to meet it. Lily did not wish to talk about her feelings with this man. Somehow she knew it would make her even more vulnerable to reveal her confusion to him now.

She was not even certain she wished for Tristan to know any of what was going through her mind—

though he seemed to be able to read her easily enough that she had little hope of hiding anything from him.

Tristan moved past her, first making sure the covers were pulled up on his daughter, then tenderly bending to kiss her tiny forehead. He then turned to Lily expectantly.

Lily faced him directly, aware that she must say something. "There is no denying the resemblance."

He spoke up with surprising eagerness. "I knew you could not help but see."

She answered just as quickly, "But I did not know her. There was no sense of recognition."

Clearly chagrined, Tristan frowned. "That is not too surprising when one considers it. She was born but moments before the carriage accident, and you saw her only as an infant. I simply hoped that seeing her might help you to recall...." He shrugged, his face unreadable.

Lily shook her head. "Seeing her has answered nothing." In spite of her wishes to keep her thoughts to herself, she found herself saying, "There is very dark hair in your own family. Are there gray eyes as well?"

He shook his head, unconsciously holding it at a proud angle. "All the Ainsworth men have blue eyes. My mother's were violet."

Lily took a deep breath. "I am left even more confused than before. How could a child that I have never met be so very like me in form?"

He scowled with frustration and censure. "I have told you the answer to that."

She gave him an equally disapproving stare. "Ah, yes, you have, and I am to take your word against that of my own family. You, who are a stranger to me.''

The words seemed to awaken some slumbering beast of frustration and anger in his blue eyes. He took a step closer to her. "Not so much a stranger. Your body knows me, Lily, even if your mind does not."

She had no reply to that, for it was far too true. She chose to ignore the remark, which made her own blood rise, though not with anger. "Seeing the little one has not brought about the effect you had hoped, but neither has it settled my mind. I must try to resolve this within myself. I cannot leave here with so much uncertainty. I beg that in spite of this turn of events you allow me to stay on for some days as maid to your child, as you suggested at Molson."

He looked at her with obvious indifference. "Of course. That was my intent from the beginning."

She stared down at her folded hands. "I simply thought…" She looked up at him again. "I feared you would no longer wish to keep me here, since seeing her has not made me recall the past as you had hoped."

He raised his dark eyebrows. "I do not go back on my word. I told you you would be allowed to meet and know Sabina. That is what will happen unless you wish it to be otherwise. Benedict has given his consent as well."

She bit her lip. "Your brother…I cannot help thinking about how he thought he recognized me."

Tristan shook his head. "As I told you, Benedict does recognize you, Lily. You are the one who does not."

She shook her own head. "For reasons I have already explained, I cannot just accept your word for this. I must hold all you say suspect out of love and loyalty for my family, if nothing else.''

He frowned, but said nothing.

Finally he motioned to the cot against the far wall. ''As Sabina's personal maid, you may sleep there. That will mean that you do not have to take your rest with the other servants in the great hall.''

She watched him closely. ''You trust me to stay here alone with your babe?''

Tristan returned the look in good measure. ''And why should I not trust you, Lily? I know you. No matter what has occurred, no matter what you have forgotten, there is no possible way that you could be so changed as that.'' He paused, then continued, ''Is there some reason that you do not wish to stay in Sabina's chambers?''

Lily shook her head quickly. ''No indeed. I am very grateful for your kindness in allowing me to do so. I...'twould be difficult to spend the night in the hall.'' She had not even considered where she might be sleeping. Acting the part of a servant was more complicated than she had anticipated.

But the admission had not been easy to make. She did not wish to feel grateful to Tristan for anything. He was the one who had brought about this upheaval in her life. He was the one who had set her to wondering, doubting everything she believed about herself and her family.

Yet Lily could not make herself turn her back on him as she wanted to. That haunting voice of recognition inside her would not let her do so.

Why this was so she did not know. All she knew was that she had to remain here until that voice was quieted, at rest once more. Only then would she again be secure in her own beliefs about her life.

Tristan seemed to have nothing to add to what she had said. He shrugged. "I will leave you to your bed then. Sabina is accustomed to waking early and I will attend you in the morn."

"What if she awakens before you return?"

He shrugged. "I am certain you will manage very well indeed. I have no worries on that score."

Without looking at him, Lily murmured, "I thank you for your kindness and for your faith in me." She was not as sure of her own abilities as he professed to be, but pride would not allow her to tell him that.

"Good night then," he said softly. A hush followed the words. Their gazes locked and held for a long moment in which she was sure he was waiting in expectation of what she might say or do.

But Lily made no more reply than an even more quietly voiced, "Good night." She did not look at him, but she was infinitely aware of the tall, powerful man as he turned and walked slowly from the chamber.

Chapter Four

Lily had slept very little on the narrow bed. She could not get the image of the tiny face of Tristan's daughter from her mind.

Lily was instantly aware when Sabina awoke. She made no actual noises. It was simply as if Lily was completely attuned to the very rhythm of her breathing, the restless change in the room that marked her returning consciousness.

Just as she had been with Tristan. She brushed the thought away like an irritating gnat.

She rose immediately and went to the bed, not giving herself time to reconsider. Tristan was not the reason she was staying here at Brackenmoore. No matter that *his* motives were still unknown to her, she was determined to try to understand her own feelings and reactions. There would be no more hesitating in this, no more feeling unsure of herself.

Even having reassured herself of this, Lily was not prepared for the wave of wonder that washed over her as she looked down into the child's open eyes. If the resemblance had been startling before, it was even more so now, because those gray eyes were the exact same shade as her own.

The sheer depth of sweet, pleasurable emotion that swelled in her breast as the child smiled and held out her arms brought a weakness to Lily's knees. She held out her own arms before making any conscious choice to do so.

In the next instant the little girl was cuddled close, fitting against her as if she was meant to be there. She peered up at Lily and said, "You are so beautiful, just like a princess." To Lily's surprise there was complete acceptance in that approving gaze.

Lily was moved by the child's words and expression, for they seemed to go beyond the surface meaning to encompass all of her.

"Who are you?" the child asked.

Lily paused for a long moment. "I am Lily. Your father has brought me here to look after you."

"Da is home?" The little girl beamed, her gray eyes alight with happiness and love. What, Lily wondered, would it be like to have such adoration aimed at herself? Even while she pondered her own reactions, the child began to squirm. "I want to get up now, please, and see my Da."

Lily nodded. "Yes, you may get up now."

The little one squirmed off her lap and ran to the door.

Lily stopped her with a soft laugh. She could not help herself, the child was just so ingenuous. "We had best get you washed and dressed first, hadn't we?"

Sabina scowled at the words, but raced back to her. "Yes, I will wash and dress first."

The thought of washing suddenly made Lily aware

of the chill in the air. She smiled at Sabina. ''First a fire.''

The little one nodded, and Lily went to the hearth. Though she had not much experience with such things, it went well, mostly because the fire had been expertly banked the previous night by a servant and there were live coals in the ashes.

With that done Lily stood and made her way to the chest that sat at the foot of the bed. That was certainly where the little one's garments were kept. On opening it, she found that indeed they were. And what lovely little garments. Not only were they carefully decorated by a skilled hand with intricate embroidery and fur trim, they were also clearly cut with the comfort of a small child in mind.

Again, she found herself thinking that someone was looking after this child well. She felt an unexpected stab of resentment that it was not she who had chosen and lovingly embroidered the tiny garments. She just as quickly told herself that she was being ridiculous. In spite of their obvious resemblance, the possibility that Sabina was her child was so remote that she must not allow herself to get caught up in any emotional tug-of-war.

Lily hurriedly selected a tiny gown of pale pink with spring green embroidery around the hem and sleeves, then a pair of matching pink hose. She poured water into the basin that sat atop the table, then dug until she found a soft scrap of cloth in the chest, wet it and warmed it with her hands. Sabina, who had wandered to the other side of the room to play with some toys, came immediately when Lily called to her.

* * *

Tristan looked at the two of them sitting there on the end of the bed, Lily braiding the toddler's silky black tresses into some semblance of order. He had thought to come to the chamber early so as to help in easing the initial meeting between the two.

Though he had not known it until the moment when Lily had looked at the child without knowing her, he had hoped—hoped more than he wanted to admit—that seeing Sabina would awaken her memory.

Yet standing there at the entrance to the room, he was more than surprised to see that Sabina had taken to her mother so very quickly. Though she was a bright, sweet child, she was at times somewhat shy with strangers.

But then, Lily was not a stranger. Even the babe recognized the bond between them.

Would that Lily would do so.

Immediately Tristan stopped himself. She was here for her own sake and nothing more.

As if sensing his presence, Lily suddenly swung to face him, her expression becoming more guarded as their gazes met. Tristan could barely restrain a grimace.

"My lord," she greeted him stiffly.

Tristan moved forward with a deliberately fixed smile. He was determined to hide her effect on him. "Good morrow. I see you have met your charge."

Lily set the child down and leaped to her feet, as if the words had just reminded her of her assumed position here. She dipped a hurried curtsy. "Forgive me, my lord." She tucked a heavy strand of black hair behind her right ear.

For some reason the well-remembered gesture

made his heart lurch. More than once he had leaned forward to pull that lock free and, lost in some animated conversation, she had put it back without thinking. This would go on until she realized what he was about, then they would laugh and tumble together in that big bed and... Frustrated with himself for thinking of the past, which was irretrievably lost, Tristan forced himself to concentrate on the present as Sabina cried, "Da!"

He looked down at her, and Sabina reached out to him.

Tristan picked her up and hugged her tightly. As always, his heart swelled with love for her. She was the physical manifestation of the infinite love he had borne her mother. Today he did not find as much comfort in this as he had. Lily was no longer an idealized and distant dream from the past, but a woman whole and well, yet as remote from him as the moon.

He clasped their child even more tightly. She let him hold her like that for only a few moments before squirming to get down. At three, she was impatient with being still for long. Once on her feet, she raced back to the carpet before the hearth.

He glanced at Lily, who stood with her hands folded before her in awkward submission. It was clear that she meant to play the role of servant before Sabina with all seriousness. It was equally clear that she was uneasy with the part. He could not help feeling some sympathy for her position though a devil of mischief danced through his eyes. He said with overt graciousness, "There is no need to stand on ceremony here, girl. We are quite lax about such things."

Those lovely gray eyes narrowed and flashed silver lightning as she replied with ill-disguised resentment,

"You are too kind, my lord. You need not be so familiar with a mere nursemaid."

An unexpected smile tugged at the corner of his lips. "Oh, I assure you, I am not too kind. I am only as kind as you would have me be. And make no mistake, I am quite prepared to afford you whatever familiarity you may request."

She flipped the heavy fall of her hair back over her shoulder, her hands going to slender hips. "You may rest assured, sir, that I will make no such request."

Tristan knew that he had pushed her hard enough. Not only for her sake, but for his own peace of mind. The mere thought of being familiar with her was enough to warm his blood.

He knew that she did not wish for a repeat of what had happened in the hunting lodge. Lily had been most clear on that.

Nor did he, Tristan reminded himself. Drat the sense of humor that had made him speak so foolishly. In the past he'd loved teasing Lily with such talk, seeing her blush...kissing her...

Damn!

His voice emerged with a sharper edge than he intended as he went on. "It is time to go down for the morning meal."

Sudden trepidation clouded Lily's expression as she whispered, "The rest of your family—do they think I am the child's mother, as Benedict does?"

Tristan shook his head with a glance toward Sabina, who was paying them no heed. He replied quietly, "Nay, and I will not tell them. Benedict is the only member of my family who has seen you or even heard of you. He was the one who found us on the night we had the accident. He saw you for the first time that night, and was certain you had died. Your arrival here has come as a complete shock to him."

She grimaced. "Have you then informed your... family that a new maid has come to care for Sabina?"

He noted the hesitation and knew that Lily was far more enervated than she need be. "I have had time to tell no one. You must not be so apprehensive, Lily. As long as we have a care they will not find anything amiss."

"What of your brother, Benedict?"

"Benedict will treat you with civility, as he would any of the castle folk. He was most clear in his opinion that we should keep your identity secret from Genev—other family members for the present."

Her gray eyes grew round. "How many are there in the family?"

Tristan spoke matter-of-factly, trying to act as though it were no great matter, though he did recall that her family consisted of no more than her and her parents. "Two more brothers, Marcel and Kendran, both younger than myself. And then there is Genevieve..." he faltered only briefly "...whom I have told you about."

Lily seemed not to note his difficulty in speaking of Genevieve, which he knew was caused by his own feelings of guilt. "None of them will know me?"

"They will not know you."

She looked in no way mollified by his assurances. "Please, could we not take the meal here this morn?" He was well aware of how much the question cost her pride. Lily did not care to plead.

But her doing so only illustrated how much things had changed. His heart ached for her, and he grew even more resolved to help her find the woman she had been, no matter how painful it might be for both of them.

He shook his head with determination, though he spoke gently. "Sabina always takes her meals with the rest of the family. They would wonder at such an unexpected change. I know you do not wish for anyone to question your presence here. To deviate from the child's routine in that way would cause comment. Morning is the time when her uncles have the best opportunity to see and spoil her. They have other duties to attend throughout the day, and she is often abed when they return in the evenings."

Lily nodded slowly, though he could see that she was still not at ease with the notion of going down and facing so many strangers. He was beset by a sudden wave of sympathy. He spoke with amusement, though his voice was comforting beneath that light tone. "Have no fear. My family is kind, if somewhat overwhelming for someone who does not know them." He paused and reached out a hand to her. "And I will be with you."

Lily looked up at him, his manner obviously having moved her, for those gray eyes were suddenly misty with gratitude and another fiercer emotion that he was afraid to even name.

Her slender white hands, the ones that had run so hungrily over his heated flesh, reached toward him....

"My lord?" A voice intruded from behind him.

Barely restraining a guilty start, Tristan spun around. "Yes, Maggie?" he said, addressing the serving woman whom he had sent from the room the previous night.

She dipped a respectful curtsy. "I came to see if

the new girl had need of any aid this morn. It bein' her first day.''

Tristan waved toward his freshly washed and neatly dressed daughter. ''I believe that all is fine here, though I thank you for your concern. Lily is doing quite well. You may go down to the hall.''

The serving woman nodded and curtsied again, then went on her way. Tristan knew how fond all the servants were of Sabina, how they watched over her. He should not be surprised that Maggie would wish to make sure the newcomer was performing her duties properly.

When he looked back at Lily, he could see that the moment of communication between them was gone. Her lovely face now wore that distant expression he was beginning to dread.

How had they come to this? When his searching gaze swept her face, she would not meet it, and he knew he must stop thinking this way.

What they had once had was no more.

He walked across the room and reached down, picking up his babe from where she played on the carpet, oblivious to the tension between the two adults. Immediately she wrapped her chubby little arms around his neck. ''I love you, Da.''

He hugged her tightly against him for a moment, realizing just how many times he had done this while wishing Lily were here with them, sharing their love. Well, Lily *was* here, but she did not share their love, and it was shockingly more painful than being without her had been. Then he had had the dream of her as comfort.

Tristan was determined not to let reality destroy what he did have, his daughter's love. ''I love you, too, moppet.'' He nuzzled her warm neck, then tickled her gently, making her squirm and giggle even as he turned and led the way from the chamber.

Unfortunately, Tristan could not summon his usual feelings of happiness. He found he had none to draw on in this moment.

His heart was heavy as a stone inside his chest, aching with what might have been. He was completely aware of Lily as she followed behind them—the rustling of her heavy woolen skirts, the ragged rhythm of her breathing, which indicated that she was agitated.

Tristan forced himself to concentrate on the coming ordeal of introducing her to his family—Genevieve—without giving away the turbulent state of his own feelings.

Lily held her head high as they entered the hall. She felt a slight amount of relief at seeing the state of controlled pandemonium that existed there. No one paid the least attention to her.

She was emboldened to look about. The enormous chamber was filled to overflowing, and the sound of many voices engaged in cheery conversation created even more of an impression of chaos in her mind, giving her many things to think about besides her feelings about Tristan. Long, well-scrubbed tables had been set up along the length of the room, and many of the folk seated there had already begun to break their fast. It seemed they did not stand on ceremony by awaiting the nobler members of the household.

It was a far cry from the quiet order of mornings at Lakeland Park, her family's home. Yet rather than feeling out of place, Lily found herself drawn toward the activity.

Glancing to the far end of the room, she could see that the head table was not yet full, though there were two young men seated there. She could only assume that they must be the two younger of Tristan's brothers. Perhaps, she thought with no small degree of hope, Benedict would not make his imposing presence known this morn.

Lily paused at this last thought. She had seen the man for only the briefest of moments. Was it fair to characterize him as imposing?

She could not help admitting to herself that her desire to avoid seeing Benedict had something to do with the disconcerting fact that he, too, claimed to recognize her. Lily had as yet thought of no reason for either Benedict or Tristan to try to fool her into believing she was known to them, and the notion of seeing recognition in those blue eyes was daunting. The acknowledgment did not come without irritation toward herself.

She raised her chin, determined to face this situation with courage despite the fact that her parents had protected her from any unpleasantness or difficulty at Lakeland. She still felt slightly out of her depth here. Oddly enough it made her feel stronger to know that she had to confront this on her own.

As they made their way through the throng, Tristan was greeted by many. No one did more than glance in her direction with casual curiosity.

The anonymity of being a servant would stand her in good stead. She was accustomed to being the only daughter in a noble house. Obviously, fine gowns and adorned hair earned their own respect. For the first time in her life Lily was less finely garbed than the people she was with. She eyed Tristan's knee-length, dark brown *houppelande* with its fur-trimmed sleeves and neck. The long tan boots he wore had been cleaned and polished since the previous day and were a sharp contrast to the sturdy but much scuffed shoes upon her own feet. Yet she was more amused by this than annoyed.

Except in the case of being subservient to Tristan.

Of course, he had said that he would do all he could to ease her difficulty. He did not understand that it was he who made her situation even more difficult by displaying concern for her.

For a moment, when he had reached out to her in Sabina's chamber, Lily had felt almost as if he cared for her feelings. But that could only be a misperception on her part. If Tristan was telling the truth, his interest in her was about nothing more than proving he was right. He had been clear that he wished to maintain a distance between them.

Her gaze went to his wide back as a frown of uncertainty marred her brow. He had made other remarks that made her less certain as to his motives. If he only wanted her here to acknowledge the past, why had he indulged in the sexual innuendo that not even she could fail to recognize?

As she found her gaze lingering on the narrow curve of his hips in front of her, Lily was aware of an odd fluttering in her belly.

Their small party came to the head table, and Lily told herself that she must concentrate her energy on keeping up her pose of servant before Tristan's family. Even without his elder brother being present, the thought of playing her part before them was daunting.

Surely that was what accounted for her extreme uneasiness. It was not caused by her thoughts of Tristan.

It was only when the other two brothers—one a
man, the other a lanky but handsome lad in his ado-
lescence—looked up in surprise as they came to a halt
at the table that she really took more note of them.
Lily tried not to stare as Tristan motioned for her to
sit next to Sabina.

The two had very dark hair, like Tristan. Now that
she saw them all together in the light she realized that
Tristan's hair was not black as she had first thought,
but a rich sable. The others had darker locks, and
though he was not present, she was sure Benedict's
was the deepest black, a shade that devoured light.

They, like Tristan, seemed to prefer a longer version of the *houppelande* than the ones she had heard
were favored by many at court. Their garments were
rich in color and trimmed in fur.

The elder of the two fixed her with two very blue
eyes and said, "What have we here, Tristan?" Lily
took note that those eyes were very like Tristan's, as
were the boy's. In fact, both were quite handsome.

Though not as handsome as their brother. The
thought entered her mind before she could stop it.

Her unwilling gaze went to Tristan as he replied
matter-of-factly, "Marcel, Kendran, this is Lily. I
have engaged her to act as maid to Sabina. She will,
of course, take her meals with us in order to fulfill
her duties."

Both young men nodded. She had no notion which
was which until the younger of the two spoke. "I am
Kendran. Welcome to Brackenmoore, Lily." There
was no mistaking the flirtatious gleam in his blue eyes
as they slid over her.

Tristan drew her attention to his scowling face by saying, "There will be none of that, Kendran. Lily is here to look after Sabina—that and nothing more."

Even Lily could see that Kendran was jesting as he arched a randy brow. "Saving her for yourself then, are you, Tristan? I wonder what Genevieve will say to that."

Even as he said the words, Lily felt that now familiar tightening in her abdomen at the very idea of Tristan keeping her for himself. And even worse, she knew an unwanted sense of resentment at the thought of the other woman's claim on him.

She was wrenched from her own disturbing musings by Tristan, who seemed oblivious to the fact that he was being teased. "I am not—"

Kendran interrupted him by saying, "And here is that fair damsel now. What say you, Genevieve?"

Lily swung around to face a fair young woman of no more than eighteen years. That she was beautiful was undeniable, with her gold-streaked brown curls and wide, ingenuous green eyes. The gown she wore was made of rich ivory satin, high-waisted in the latest fashion, with a wide, gem-studded collar. Her headdress was a dainty gold cap with a soft ivory veil that only drew more attention to the soft curls at her nape.

Lily found herself fiddling with the bit of string she had used to secure her own heavy braid.

When this vision spoke, it was in a sweetly modulated voice. "What say I to what, Kendran?" There was no mistaking the familial indulgence in her tone.

"Why, to Tristan's bringing such a lovely woman home to act as personal servant to Sabina?"

For a moment there was surprise on her delicate

face as she looked to Tristan. "I had not realized that you meant to engage a personal maid. I had thought you were going to Molson in order to see how work on the metal shield for the signal tower was progressing."

He shrugged. "That is why I went, and I can report that it is going very well. It is true that I had not expected to engage a maid. But the opportunity to do so arose, what with Lily needing a position, being gently reared and well-disposed toward children. Sabina is getting of an age to need someone to begin to teach her, spend constant time with her. I hope you will welcome Lily into our home."

"Is that all you are going to tell us about how this came about then, Tristan?" Marcel asked, eyeing his brother mockingly.

"There is nothing more to tell."

Genevieve watched him for a moment, then her sea green gaze focused on Lily. She felt it move over her entire length, clearly taking in the poor garments she wore, then come back to rest on her face. For a brief moment, Lily thought she saw uneasiness in the younger woman's expression, but it was gone too quickly to be sure. If it had indeed ever been there.

"Why, then I would say welcome, Lily." There was not the least hint of anything but trust in those eyes—trust and the welcome Genevieve had extended with her words.

Immediately Lily knew a sweeping sensation of guilt. She had betrayed this woman with the man she loved. Her own gaze dropped to the floor.

Tristan addressed Lily, sounding somewhat strained to her own ears. "Lily, this is the lady Genevieve.

She is to be my bride and thus Sabina's mother and your mistress."

Hurriedly, Lily remembered to dip a curtsy. "I thank you for your kind welcome, my lady."

Genevieve waved a delicate white hand toward the laden table. "Shall we all begin then? Benedict will not be joining us this morn. I am quite famished, as I am sure is our Sabina." The child smiled widely as Genevieve ran an affectionate hand over her dark hair.

"Love you, Evie." Her tiny fingers reached toward the gentlewoman.

Genevieve bent and placed a quick kiss on her forehead before taking her place at table. "I love you, too, sweeting," she replied.

Lily felt an unexpected sense of loneliness, of yearning that brought an ache to her breast as she watched this simple exchange.

Sabina looked up at Lily with those large gray eyes, seeming somehow to sense her agitation, for she cocked her small dark head to the side and murmured, "Love you, too, Lily."

Lily's heart turned over as a wave of indescribably sweet emotion swept through her, warming her from the inside out. For reasons she could not even begin to explain, she was more moved by this childlike utterance than she would have dreamed possible. Deliberately dragging her gaze away from those beguiling eyes, so like her own, she took in a deep breath, glad that the others seemed not to have taken note of her reaction.

Then something, some inner knowing, made her look up. Tristan, who had taken a place on the other side of Sabina, was staring at her. She knew that he, too, had heard the babe's words, for his face seemed pale in spite of his sun-darkened complexion. Lily raised her head high. Clearly he was disturbed by Sabina's declaration.

He might be willing for Lily to be here—to know her child—but he did not wish for the child to love her. His displeasure was hurtful. But that was ridiculous, because Lily had no care for what Tristan thought. Yet that did not ease her misery. She began to prepare a plate of soft white bread and porridge for Sabina, unable to make a reply to Sabina's heartfelt words. It was not possible to do so past the lump of sorrow in her throat.

When Lily turned back, the babe was smiling at her, her gray eyes soft with acceptance and compassion. Again, Lily was overwhelmed by the rise of gratitude and, she could not deny it, love inside herself.

Pity the woman who had birthed this child and lost her.

And what if she is yours? that irrepressible voice whispered.

Dear God, if she was, then heaven help them all. For Lily was no longer sure she could walk away and never look back. Already the little one was getting beneath her skin, finding a place in her heart.

No matter what happened, there was nothing she could do but walk away. The role of mother to Sabina had been filled by the woman Tristan was to marry, and clearly filled very well.

As the others began to eat, Lily concentrated all of her attention on assisting her charge. Shame left her unable to look at any of the others.

Until now, Genevieve had been no more than a name, a faceless woman who seemed disconnected from the strange attraction between Lily and Tristan. Now his fiancée was all too real. And even worse, she was as kind and gentle as anyone could be. Lily realized she had made a terrible mistake by coming here. She had wanted, needed, to find out what was behind her own strange feelings. She had not thought about the people who could be hurt by her own selfish desire.

If only there were some way to turn back time, to alter her own reactions from the moment Tristan had kissed her. But she could not.

Only her desperate need to know if this babe was indeed her own, however remote the possibility, kept her from walking out the door.

Chapter Five

Tristan knew he had to say something to Genevieve. But what?

He would not tell her the truth of Lily's identity. As Benedict had said, there could be no purpose in that. What he and Lily had had was now gone.

He found Genevieve in the laundry instructing the maids about where to hang the linens to dry on such an overcast day. In spite of her youth when she had begun overseeing the household, Genevieve had always been a diligent housekeeper. She spent most of her time making sure the castle was run smoothly, with a care to the comfort of the family. She had done so since first coming to Brackenmoore some four years ago, at age fourteen.

When her parents had died, leaving her the sole heir of their holdings, she had fallen to the care of Maxim, Earl of Harcourt.

Genevieve had run away after only a matter of weeks. She had come directly to Brackenmoore, since the Ainsworths had been longtime friends of her parents. Though it had proved difficult, Benedict had become her guardian by applying to Richard of York, who was protector of the realm during one of King Henry's periods of madness. He had managed to have her named Benedict's ward. It had all been settled before Maxim had been able to determine her whereabouts.

The arrangement had been a happy one for the four brothers and for Genevieve. She was accepted into their family effortlessly.

Of her time with Maxim, Genevieve had spoken very little other than to say that he had attempted to force himself upon her, but she had escaped harm. They had wanted to avenge her, but she had begged them to leave be. She wanted only to put that time behind her, and Tristan was sure that his brothers agreed with his feeling that her wishes should be honored.

It had not been until six months past that Genevieve had come to Tristan to say that she wished to remain a member of the family for always. She already felt as if she was a mother to Sabina. Tristan could not disagree with the latter. She cared for the little one as deeply as any mother could, had done so since the child arrived at Brackenmoore, though Genevieve had been only fifteen at the time.

He had felt honor-bound to tell her truthfully that he did not love her in that way. He did not bother to add that he felt he would never love another woman as he had Lily.

Genevieve was unmoved by this declaration, assuring him that she did not expect as much. It was apparent to her that he would not love again. That was why she had chosen him—that and Sabina. She felt the other three Ainsworth men still had hearts to give elsewhere.

Though he had been somewhat taken aback, Tristan had been so affected by her forthright manner that he had replied that he would proudly be her husband. He had then asked when she would like to seal the bond.

She had kissed him on the cheek with a gentle smile and said there was no rush. She felt he must have his own time to become accustomed to the notion. With that she had simply gone on about her work, seeming to be content as things were.

As was he.

Now, looking at her, Tristan wondered at his own perfidy. Surely he could not keep such a lovely, gentle woman waiting for him indefinitely.

And he would not. Once Lily had satisfied herself enough to return to her new life, he would ask Genevieve to set a date for their marriage. He did love her, in a way that was likely more good for him than the overwhelming passion he had known for Lily.

His newly realized resolution made him say her name with more than his usual care. "Genevieve."

She swung around to face him with a smile. "Tristan. Did you wish to speak with me?"

He reached out to take her hand as she came forward. "Yes, sweet, I did." He looked at the serving women. "I would do so privately if you are not too busy."

She squeezed his fingers with her own small ones. "I am never too busy to speak to you. Let us go out into the courtyard." Genevieve released his hand to take up her cape from where she had laid it on a bench near the door.

Tristan took it from her and placed it over her shoulders, then drew her outside. He watched as Genevieve pulled her wrap close around her in deference to the coolness of the day. She looked up into the cloudy sky overhead. "Do you think there will be snow?"

He shrugged. "It may come. The air has that crispness to it. But not before night, I think."

Genevieve nodded, continuing to look up at the sky as she walked beside him.

Tristan stopped her, putting a gentle hand on her arm and meeting her gaze. "I should have told you that I was going to bring home a maid for Sabina. I meant no slight to you in that."

She nodded. "Have no concern for me on that score. I understand. You are her father and need not answer to me for every action."

He frowned gently. "I want you to know that I respect and care for you greatly, Genevieve. I wish only to treat you with the honor you deserve. At no time would I deliberately hurt you."

She smiled. "Of course you would not." She looked at him then, and he had the feeling she was seeing far more than he would have wished. But all she said was, "You are a good man, Tristan. Of that I have no question. You will do what is right."

Far from reassuring him, as he knew her words were meant to, they only served to make him feel more the knave. Tristan had to bite his tongue to keep from telling her all. Only the memory of Benedict's advice not to reveal Lily's identity for the moment kept him from doing so.

He spoke with rough emotion. "You give me too much credit." He placed a gentle kiss on her forehead, then turned and walked away before he lost the tight rein he had on his tongue, resolving as he did so to attempt to be worthy of her trust in the future.

* * *

Lily had not expected Genevieve to put in an appearance in Sabina's chambers so soon after the morning meal. Yet there she was, standing in the doorway, her arms ladened with cloth.

She seemed to almost hesitate there as Lily looked up from where she was searching for Sabina's wrap in the chest at the end of the bed. Lily was surprised at this. She was a servant here, Genevieve the lady of the castle.

Lily stood quickly. "My lady."

Genevieve nodded graciously. "How are you settling in?"

Lily glanced over at where Sabina was playing on the carpet, then indicated the open trunk. "I was looking for a cloak so that I could take Sabina out for a while. Lord Tristan had said I might before he left." Tristan had said precious little else, seeming more than eager to be away from Lily when he brought them back here after the morning meal.

Sabina smiled at the golden-brown-haired woman over her doll's head. "Lily and me are going outside?"

Genevieve smiled in return. "Of course, moppet. Your da has said as much. But would you mind if I talked to Lily for a few moments first?"

Sabina nodded. She held up the doll. "I will play with my baby. Lily lets me bring her outside."

Genevieve's expression was openly admiring. "She's lovely. Lily will be very good to you."

Sabina smiled happily, her full attention going back to the toy.

Genevieve then turned back to Lily. "A walk in

the fresh air will suit her well. Like her father, she does appreciate the outdoors.''

Lily looked at the floor at the mention of Tristan. She wished to give no hint of familiarity toward him.

Genevieve fell silent for a moment, then raised the bundle of cloth as she came forward. ''I thought you might have need of some things. Maeve did not think you had any belongings with you when you arrived last night.''

Lily blushed. Of course the head woman would think that odd. A gently reared maid turned servant would have some possessions. Hers had all been left behind when Tristan abducted her. Her fingers twisted in the rough wool of her skirt as her thoughts went longingly to all the lovely new gowns in the trunks that had been left behind at the inn.

''Lily?'' Genevieve prodded.

She blushed again, realizing that the other woman was still awaiting a reply. Stiffly, she said, ''They were correct. I brought nothing save what I am wearing.'' Her embarrassment at the admission was acute. She then said the first words that came to her mind. ''There was a fire.'' Immediately she felt like a fool. It was a poor excuse at best.

Yet Genevieve seemed to accept the lie as fact, coming toward her with a kind smile as if sensing her discomfort. ''Then these might be of some use to you.'' She laid the bundle of fabric on the bed, smoothing it out. Now Lily could see that what she had taken to be cloth was in fact several gowns. There was one of a dark blue, one of black and another of gray. Without thinking, Lily reached out and ran a hand over the fine wool. From beneath these also peeked the edges of softer colors and fabrics that must be undergowns. Though of somber hues, the garments would be much more comfortable against her skin, and could not help being more attractive than the one she now wore.

Her throat constricted with emotion at this woman's thoughtfulness. Now more than ever she felt guilt at what she had done with Tristan.

Lily spoke softly, without looking at the other woman, afraid she would give away too much of what she was feeling. "There was no need for you to go to any trouble on my behalf, my lady."

Genevieve answered hurriedly, "I have gone to no trouble, beyond taking them from the bottom of my trunk. The gowns were not in use and only gathering dust. Besides, you are Sabina's companion and should be garbed as befits your position."

Of course, Genevieve was correct. Lily nodded. She was not a scullery maid and must dress in a manner suitable for the honor of their household. How could she refuse under the circumstances? Genevieve was her mistress, a nobleman's daughter her charge.

"I thank you, my lady. You are very kind." And as she said this, Lily knew that it was true. Genevieve had offered her these garments because of her gentle heart, not because of appearances. And in spite of the fact that she must wonder at the strange manner of Lily's arriving here with Tristan. Kendran's remarks could not have helped that.

Lily was not sure she would have been as quick to heed Tristan's assurances that all was well. Yet Genevieve had believed him without question.

And well she should, Lily told herself quickly. There was nothing else to tell. That one disastrous mistake would not be repeated.

Genevieve was speaking again. "I am not of your height, thus you may have need to lengthen the gowns. I believe that will not prove difficult, as there should be sufficient fabric at the hems."

Lily nodded. "Thank you. I shall manage very well."

"I will send one of the women with a needle and thread, as well as some undergarments. She will also help you with the alterations."

Lily could only nod. There were no words that would come close to her feelings of gratitude and unworthiness at such kindness.

The other woman seemed to understand some of Lily's uneasiness, though certainly not the cause of it, for she went to Sabina, gave her a quick kiss on the head, then said, "I have much to do now, so I will leave you two to make ready for your outing."

Again, Lily found herself unable to make any reply. She curtsied deeply.

When Genevieve was gone, Lily picked up the gray gown and held it before her. It was a bit too short, but the bodice had been decorated with carefully stitched pink rosebuds and delicate leaves, strung together with a chain of the same green thread. It was also fashioned more in the manner of her own lost gowns, with a high waistline, wide skirt and long train. Searching through the pile, Lily found an underdress of the same color of soft green as the stitching that decorated the bodice of the gray gown.

Eagerly she held up the other gowns. The sleeves and bodice of the black were stitched with rows of white fleurs-de-lis. There was a snow-white underdress to wear with it. The dark blue gown, though not adorned with embroidery, had a wide V-shaped collar and could only be meant to compliment the sky blue underdress and sash of the same fabric.

Lily could hardly believe her eyes. Not until this moment had she realized how very much she disliked wearing the ill-fitting brown sack. How good it would be to change out of it.

Unnoticed, Sabina had gotten up and wandered over to stand beside her. Lily looked down as the child said, "Lily has pretty dresses now."

Yes, they were pretty, but admiring them would have to wait. Lily was determined to repay Genevieve's kindness as conscientiously as possible. First, she had to fulfill her duties as Sabina's caretaker.

She ruffled the child's hair. "Aye, very pretty. But let us not think about dresses. Let us go outside."

Her reward was a beaming smile that made her heart twist with the sweetness of it. As she left the chamber with Sabina's tiny hand in hers, Lily reminded herself anew that she had no intention of betraying Genevieve. This child and her father belonged to her.

Later, at the evening meal, Lily tried not to care that Tristan cast her no more than one brief and expressionless glance on her arrival in the hall. He seemed not to even notice the black gown, which the servant Maggie had helped her to alter during the afternoon, while Sabina slept.

Once they were all seated, Benedict's assessing gaze, however, weighed heavily on Lily, where she sat beside Sabina. "I spoke with our neighbor, Henry Langley, this morning," he announced. "He tells me that there is a rumor that the Earl of Harcourt is scouring the countryside for his missing bride. It seems the young woman disappeared from an inn even as she was on her way to marry him. Word has it that he will kill anyone who had a hand in her disappearance.''

Lily felt the blood drain from her face in a sickening rush. Her horrified gaze flew to Tristan, who was looking at his brother closely. He spoke casually, but she was not unaware of the intensity in his gaze. ''Really, Benedict. Have you any personal concern in this matter?''

''Not I.'' Benedict shrugged. ''With what is known of the man, I wish him no luck in finding the poor girl. She could not fare worse than with her own fiancé.'' Lily looked at him in shock, sure she must have somehow misunderstood him. Benedict was watching Genevieve, who, though normally fair of complexion, was now white as bleached linen. Lily could not help wondering what had caused her such obvious fear. Benedict spoke to her gently. ''Maxim Harcourt is no longer a threat to you, my dear. He would not dare trespass here.''

Even further shocked, and wondering what he could be talking about, Lily sat stunned as Genevieve nodded. There was still anxiety in her eyes as she said, ''I am not afraid. I but feel pity for the young woman who might find herself wed to such a man.''

Stranger and stranger indeed, Lily thought in confusion. She glanced to Tristan, who was watching her carefully, his gaze assessing.

Lily looked away. What reaction did he expect from her? That they seemed to hold Maxim in such low esteem was more than surprising, but meant nothing to her. She had no notion of what he might have done to make them believe thus. She knew no ill of him. Her own parents had carefully chosen him for her.

Her father had made it clear that he felt the older and more mature man would make a good and dependable husband. If he were such a poor character as to warrant the reactions seen here, her father would not have chosen him.

She could not prevent herself from asking, "Why do you speak thus of my lord Harcourt?" The others at the table turned to her as if surprised that she would join their conversation. Lily blushed, realizing it was not her place to ask questions of the nobles. Her presence at table was only for the convenience of caring for Sabina. "Forgive me, I did mean not to intrude," she said quickly.

Benedict's eyebrows rose in surprise. "You do not intrude. It is your question that causes our distress."

Tristan drew her attention to himself as he spoke deliberately. "Genevieve is cousin to the earl. When her father and mother died some four years ago, Harcourt, as her eldest living relation, offered to take her into his household. She was then fourteen. What he did not tell her when he did so was that he fully intended to avail himself of her innocence, with or without her consent. She escaped, coming directly here to Benedict, whom she knew to be her father's true friend. We took her to Richard of York himself, who consented to have her made ward to Benedict as she desired."

Lily's wide eyes met Genevieve's before the young woman blushed scarlet and dropped her head.

Lily could feel the sympathy of the four brothers as they looked at Genevieve, but it was Marcel who reached out and put his hand over hers. Lily could not help noting that that strong hand seemed to be trembling as Marcel looked at her bent head. Lily recalled that it had been Marcel who had seemed to display the most disquiet concerning Lily's arrival at Brackenmoore the previous day, though he had couched it in terms of jest.

Glancing about the table, Lily realized that none of the others seemed to show the least hint of seeing what she did in the gesture. She told herself that she was reading too much into his familial care. Surely it was her own wayward attraction to Tristan that made her see hidden agendas of a similar nature in others.

"Just so." Benedict's comment drew all gazes, including Lily's, to himself. "The man is a knave and despoiler of women. Whomever he marries will be forced to accept his philandering and cruelty, for he is a law unto himself."

Genevieve broke in. "Please, I would have us discuss anything but Maxim Harcourt. If we are to think of him in any way let it be of the poor malformed creature who is rumored to be his brother."

Lily was surprised by this, as she had not been aware he had a brother. Tristan's response gave her further pause. "As no one has ever seen him, including yourself, Genevieve, I prefer to think that it is nothing more than rumor. Another Harcourt the world may do without." He fell silent, the four brothers exchanging troubled glances.

Lily finished the meal in a daze. She began to wonder if she had indeed discovered a reason for Tristan to lie to her. Obviously they bore a grudge against Maxim.

Anger suffused her. Tristan had doubtless brought her here, left her confused and tormented about herself and her life, all in aid of revenge. She told herself the disappointment she felt at learning that there was probably no real connection between herself and Sabina—or Tristan—was sheer madness.

She must learn how he was planning to use her. And how many of the family were aware of this? Lily could not help thinking that it could only be Tristan and Benedict.

When Tristan escorted them back to Sabina's room, Lily first watched the child go to her toys. It was not the child's fault that her father was a blackguard. She then rounded on him, her voice an angry whisper. "I have finally realized what is going on, my lord knave. You may now return me to my family."

He faced her with amazement, also being careful to keep his voice low. "What has come over you?"

She glared at him. "Your giving away the fact that you bear a grudge against Maxim Harcourt has confirmed my belief that all you have said were lies. You have brought me here in order to seek revenge."

He put his hands on his lean hips, his face a mask of disbelief and anger. "And what move have I made to put this revenge into effect? By telling him that I have you?" He shook his head in disgust. "You try too hard, Lily. What you say makes no sense if you will but look at it. I would have no aversion to seeking revenge against the bastard, but we have given Genevieve our word that we will not do so. The love we bear her prevents either me or my brothers from breaking that promise."

Lily bit her lip. "But it would explain everything."

He looked away from her. "There is no explanation save the one I have given you, and it is the fact that you are becoming less and less able to doubt me that has made you come up with a ridiculous tale. I will not be insulted any longer. I am not a liar, and in the event that you are still worried about my plotting some revenge against your betrothed, you have my permission to leave Brackenmoore at your convenience. It was, if you recall, your own suggestion that you come here.''

She looked at him with haunted eyes. "I do not wish to leave.''

He was irritated beyond measure when her expression sent a jab of sympathy through him. Before she could say another word, he turned and stalked away.

Tristan was frustrated beyond any imagining. He spurred Uriel on in the darkness, grateful for the sharp chill in the salty air, though it did little to cool his agitation.

After leaving Lily, he had informed Benedict that he was going out to check on the workmen's progress at the signal tower. He had not been able to meet his brother's probing gaze. Glad that Benedict had kept his thoughts to himself, Tristan escaped without having to explain why he would wish to do so.

He had spent most of this day pretending to go over the old parchments in his chambers. In actuality he had thought endlessly of Lily and the moments they had shared at Molson.

The thoughts brought him only guilt and no small measure of impatience with himself. He pined for something that had not been real.

Lily was Lily, yet she was not. It was becoming more and more difficult to sit and look at her, to see her and know that the woman he had loved was indeed gone.

She had looked so pale and fragile when she came into the hall in the black gown, yet so incredibly beautiful that he could barely prevent himself from staring like a dumbstruck lad. He had forced himself not to reveal the hungry need he felt.

He couldn't help seeing not only that she was beautiful beyond what any mere mortal woman should be, but also that she was as gentle with Sabina as he had expected she would be. Though she had not admitted it and would surely deny the truth, she already had feelings for the little one. It was apparent in her voice when she spoke to her, in the genuine affection in her soft gray eyes.

Sabina was already beginning to love Lily. This made him feel decidedly uncomfortable, especially after the way Lily had just accused him of bringing her here to seek revenge against Harcourt.

Now more than ever he wished for Lily to regain her memory. Her coming up with this mad explanation for his actions was simply a defense against seeing reality. She was beginning to doubt what she had been told of her life, he was sure.

Lily must begin to doubt if she was to learn the truth. And the truth was something he would wish for anyone to know, not only the woman he had once loved so very much.

He would allow himself no more personal motive than that.

When he reached the site of the signal tower, which overlooked the sea, he did not feel the expected rush of satisfaction that he should have in its obvious state of near completion. He had worked for over a year on this project. Tristan felt it would save many lives during the winter months on this section of England's shore, might have saved the lives of his parents had it been in place when their ship foundered offshore. It seemed less of an accomplishment than it had mere days ago, a fact that only served to increase his frustration.

Immediately after the shipwreck he had spent hours poring over old scrolls in the library at Brackenmoore. He was shocked to find that though there had once been many signal towers in England, they seemed to have fallen into disfavor and disrepair. Perhaps like his brother Benedict, most men with the wherewithal to pay for such a structure were too busy running their estates.

It had been in the second year after Lily's death—assumed death—that Benedict had found him scouring those ancient drawings once more. When Tristan had begun a diatribe on the foolishness of forgetting such advances, and the lives they saved, Benedict had told him to stop talking about it and build one.

Tristan now realized his brother had saved his sanity with that advice. The task had helped him to go on living for his own sake rather than only because Sabina needed him.

The thought made him realize that there was more than his own pain to live for now. Sabina still needed him, and though she did not know it, Lily needed him.

He would allow her to go if that was her wish, but he hoped she would not. He knew from his own experience that fooling oneself brought nothing but heartache. He was under no delusion that Lily was the same woman he had loved. The open and joyous bonding they had shared was no longer possible for either of them. Too much pain had come to both of them.

In the event that she decided to continue on here, he would try to be kind to her—show her the patience she needed to face the locked doors in her mind.

Tristan turned his mount and saw the enormous outline of the castle, keeping guard over everything in and around it. He rode toward home.

Lily sat near the window with Sabina sleeping in her lap. After their bath they had combed one another's hair, Lily having been surprised at how gentle the child was with the comb, a light snow had begun to fall. Fetching a blanket from the bed, she had bundled the excited Sabina on her lap. The babe had been contented to watch out the window until her lids closed over her sleepy eyes.

Lily ran her hand over the soft black tresses and stared out the window, wishing for one moment that this was her life, her child. Not once in the past three years had she felt as alive as she had since that first moment of seeing Tristan, no matter how difficult he had made things. Not once had she felt as contented as she did at this moment with the soft weight of Sabina in her arms.

The snow seemed to be coming down just a bit harder now, swirling and dancing in the darkness…and suddenly the scene shifted. The window shimmered and became much smaller, the ceiling lower. The babe in her lap felt smaller, tiny and fragile in her arms, which felt heavy with exhaustion. Even as Lily tried to make sense of what she was seeing, feeling, the scene changed, the air filling with the sound of a horse's scream, the world seeming to tilt sideways.…

* * *

Tristan stood in the doorway, his heart turning over at the sight of his daughter asleep in her mother's lap. No matter how he told himself that he had no feelings for Lily, he did not seem to be able to overcome just this sort of reaction to the sight of her.

Even as these self-deprecating thoughts passed through his mind, an unmistakable expression of confusion and fear swept over Lily's face. Not knowing what had caused such a sudden change in her, he started forward, anxiety gripping his chest.

Quickly he took the sleeping Sabina from her lap and placed her on the bed. He then turned back to Lily, who seemed completely oblivious to his presence, staring off as if seeing something that he could not.

He placed his hands on her shoulders, shaking her gently. "What is it? What has happened?"

Only then did she blink rapidly, her eyes focusing on him with shock. "I... Tristan, how did you..." She put a shaking hand to her forehead. "I don't understand what is going on."

Again he asked, "What has happened? I was standing there watching you and Sabina, and you suddenly began acting very strangely—as if you were seeing something that wasn't there."

She shook her head. It was obvious that she was still not quite herself as she replied, "I was just sitting here. Sabina had gone to sleep in my lap, and I was looking out at the snow." Her gaze shifted to the window. "Then something happened. It was as if everything was the same, me holding the child, the snow falling..." she met his eyes "...but not the same. I felt as if—as if we were moving, as if...we were sliding.... And then there was the sound of a horse's scream, as the world seemed to tilt.'' Her hands moved to his forearms. ''What is it, Tristan? What does it mean?''

Amazement rippled through him as he took a deep breath. ''I believe you were remembering. Remembering the night we were in the carriage accident, as I told you. The carriage overturned and we were injured, you and I. You had been holding Sabina on your lap. I believe your body shielded her from being injured as seriously as we were.''

She shook her head. ''I don't understand. It can't be true.''

He willed her to meet his unwavering gaze. ''It is true. It happened, Lily. How else do you explain what occurred just now? Could you have conjured such images with your own imagination?''

She did look at him then, but what he saw in her gaze did not please him. A light of hope shone there. ''Yes. That could very well be what happened. You had told me of the carriage accident. I was sitting here holding the babe, thinking how sweet it would be to have Sabina for my own, and the images just came.''

''No.''

She drew away from him. ''Yes. That must be what made me see. It was that momentary wanting it to be true. The images were not clear, as one remembers events from one's life. They were clouded and gray and disjointed. Surely the very fact that you told me of what had happened and that I was thinking of how very lovely it would be to have such a child made me remember things that were not real.''

Frustration rose up to burn his insides like a raging fire. He pulled her to her feet. ''First the ludicrous tale of revenge against Harcourt and now this. Why must you do this, Lily? At last a memory has come, something to help you see, to give you something of reality to hold on to, and you pushed it away. What are you afraid of, Lily? Why do you allow yourself to hide behind the lies you have been told?''

She glared up at him. ''There is nothing that I am afraid of and nothing I am hiding from. It is you who wish for me to believe what I cannot. Though I cannot understand why, as you clearly hold me in low regard.''

His eyes grew round and his voice emerged in an incredulous whisper. ''Hold you in low regard?''

Before he knew what he was doing, Tristan had pulled her against himself, his mouth finding hers. All the tension he had known over the past days found vent in that contact.

For a moment she seemed to resist, her mouth and body stiff. Then her lips softened, her slender form became pliant and she molded herself along his length.

A deep throaty sound escaped him as he wrapped his arms around her, drawing her even closer to him. As his mouth plundered, hers bade welcome, opening to his questing tongue.

Lily's head was swimming. How she had thought about this—him! There was no resistance in her. Where Tristan was concerned it seemed not to exist.

When he deepened the pressure, she tilted her head to better receive him. When his hand traced the curve of her back, then found and came to rest on her bottom, her hips arched.

Tristan wanted her, needed her more than he had anything in his life. He would carry her to the bed and...

His eyes opened wide, his gaze flying to the bed—
on which his child slept, oblivious to his madness.
Dear God, did he have no control over himself where
this woman was concerned?

As abruptly as he had taken Lily into his arms,
Tristan released her. He looked down at her—at lips
swollen from his kisses, eyes heavy with passion. And
he wanted her still, in spite of knowing how very
wrong it was.

Lily's eyes darkened with confusion even as he
watched, her hand coming up to cover her swollen
lips as she whispered, "Dear heaven, help us."

A bitter laugh escaped him. "I do not think there
is any help for us, Lily, either in heaven or hell."
Raking an unsteady hand through his hair, he swung
around and strode from the chamber before he could
cause either of them any more harm.

Chapter Six

Tristan spurred his horse forward. He was glad to be away from the keep, away from Lily. Away from the ever-pressing knowledge of just how desperately he wished she might regain her memory. His reaction to what had occurred the previous night told him just how much he did want it.

Repeatedly Tristan assured himself that his desire for her to regain her past was solely for her sake and nothing more. But the words were beginning to ring hollow in his mind.

Earlier in the day he had met with the masons working on the signal tower. His thoughts would not stay focused on the task of planning exactly where the huge sheet of polished metal would be mounted.

When Benedict had tentatively approached him about running an errand to Peterburn, one of the family's smaller keeps, Tristan had leaped at the task. Benedict had seemed to note his brother's eagerness with some surprise, but made no comment on it.

Quickly Tristan had made ready for the journey. He often took over such duties for Benedict. The sheer size of the estates made it a daunting task even for one as dedicated as the Baron of Brackenmoore. Added to that, during recent years, Benedict had often been away in his efforts to support Richard's bid for the throne.

Tristan dared not allow himself to go near Lily after what had happened the previous night. He realized his reaction to her brief memory of the carriage accident had made him think, hope that... Well, he had been overcome with feelings he still could not explain.

Yet to her it had meant nothing. She could not let herself believe.

Her family and the lies on which they had built her reality meant too much to her. Her unwavering loyalty to them sickened him even as he knew a grudging envy of it. He had once been the recipient of that same loyalty and love. When Lily loved it was with her whole self, holding nothing back.

Frustration rose inside him like burning tar. The very folk who had done her the most ill were the ones she defended no matter what.

Even if she did not ever wholly regain her memory of the past, would she not be better off with him?

Immediately Tristan shook his head in horror.

He was bound to Genevieve.

What had been between him and Lily was finished. Any attraction he felt for her now was brought on by the memory of the love they had shared. No matter what came, no matter how difficult it might be between them, he would not deny the truth of what they had had together. There was no shame in that, no betrayal of his intended bride.

No one would be allowed to take the past from him. Not even Lily herself.

* * *

Lily wrapped her cloak more closely about herself and tried to ignore the chill that seeped beneath it. She had left Sabina playing not only with Genevieve, but with Marcel, who to Lily still seemed more attentive to the young woman than a mere brother by marriage. Yet as neither Genevieve nor any of the others appeared to take any note of his attention, Lily did her utmost to convince herself that it was not true. She need not suspect others of untoward behavior because her own had proved so wanton.

"Good morrow." A deep voice greeting her made her raise her head in surprise.

Her surprise only deepened when she saw Benedict standing there. Other than at mealtimes she had not seen the man since the night she'd arrived at Brackenmoore. For the first time she realized that physically he was an older and even more broad-shouldered version of Tristan. Yet in him she sensed a cynicism that was not present in Tristan, who seemed to have a great thirst for life in spite of everything. She suddenly understood that of his brothers, Marcel was the most like the baron, watchful and reserved.

Benedict's assessing gaze made her wonder if this meeting was not one of chance, as she replied, "Good morrow, my lord."

His direct words confirmed that thought. "I have been looking for you."

Lily stiffened and Benedict frowned, his black eyebrows drawing together over compelling blue eyes and a straight nose. Lord, even in displeasure these Ainsworths were a handsome lot.

He lost no time in coming to the point. "Do you

know why my brother is staying away from Bracken-moore?''

Her eyes widened. ''I did not send him away, if that is what you imply. How could I do so? This is his home to command, not mine.''

''You would not have to send him away with words, Lily.''

She raised her chin, affronted at the censure in his voice. ''I repeat, I did not send him away. It was my understanding that you had asked him to go on some errand of the estate.''

He nodded reasonably enough. ''I did, but he should not have been gone more than three days. It has been six.''

He had no need to tell Lily how many days it had been. She had counted every moment of those six days in guilt, regret and—though she wished she could deny it—longing.

He startled her from her preoccupation by adding, ''Is there any reason for me to have undue worry about my brother?''

Now Lily saw the anxiety in that blue gaze, and her stance softened. This man loved Tristan. His care was what made him broach this subject with her. Because of that and the fact that honesty was so much a part of her, Lily replied, ''He was upset with me, upset that I had had what might have been a memory of the past, but was not willing to simply accept it as fact. But I do not believe he would go away and not come back because of me. What I think matters not that greatly to him.''

Benedict grimaced, looking out over the curtain wall. ''I think you underestimate how much you affect him.''

She shook her head. "You do not know how things are between us."

His gaze raked her. "Do you?" Before she could form a reply, he went on. "The only thing that kept Tristan alive after the accident was the babe—your babe. I know you don't believe you are the child's mother—or that you ever loved my brother—but you are."

She opened her mouth to speak, and he waved her to silence. "You are free to think whatever you wish, no matter how ridiculous...."

Lily would not accept this, even from the imposing Benedict Ainsworth. "My opinions may seem ridiculous to you, my lord, but I assure you they are not. And I will not allow you to disparage me so vilely. It is completely without warrant. Perhaps if you were to put yourself in my place, at the mercy of someone else's version of what may or may not be fact, you would not be so ready to accept their truth."

Benedict's brow rose and for the first time she saw amusement on his face. "Mayhap that is so." He bowed. "Most humbly do I beg your pardon, lady."

Even as Lily doubted that this man had ever in his life done anything humbly, his expression changed again, this time to regret, as he said, "I blame myself in some ways. If I had made a more thorough effort to examine you that night... Yet the babe was crying and Tristan was bleeding from the wound to his head. There was so much blood. I simply did not see how you could be alive, and I felt no signs of life. You and Tristan would be married now, raising your daughter together as you should be. As it is, my brother is no longer a whole man."

Lily heard the pain in his voice. She understood his

sorrow at having mistakenly left the woman he had not known, his regret at the consequences of that decision. With complete conviction she found herself saying, "If by the remotest chance you are both telling the truth, I can assure you with a whole heart that I do not blame you in the least. There is no doubt in my mind that you would not leave me or anyone else, be they friend or foe, to die alone on the road."

He stood silently for a long moment, taking her measure. "I find that I begin to see why my brother came to love you, Lily Gray. There is more good in you than I would have expected, considering."

What he meant by the 'considering' part she chose not to question. Some things were best left unsaid, especially if, as she suspected, he was referring to her parentage. She said instead, "And Tristan is a fortunate man to have you to champion him."

He threw back his head and laughed, surprising her no small amount. "Mark me well here, damsel. Tristan does not require me to champion him. He is well able to stand on his own merit. It was he who had the foresight to build the signal tower on the point not far from here. His efforts will make it safe for not only the Ainsworth ships, but others. I know he has other projects in mind. Our Tristan pores over those dusty old drawings and emerges with treasure." He stepped closer, as if relating a great secret. "And that is because there is a great treasure in him, not just a brilliant mind, but something far more valuable—a loving and devoted heart. Should you never remember the past you once shared, I bid you recognize that in him."

Lily had no reply to such a directive. She said not a word as he swung around and strode away.

How could she tell him that it did not matter what she recognized? Tristan had no wish for her to strengthen any bond between them. That he had kissed her she dismissed as anger and frustration. His abrupt change of mood and subsequent abandonment had made that obvious.

Yet in spite of all that, Benedict's words had moved her. To hear of Tristan's grief from another made it all the more real and compelling. Somewhere inside her, where compassion dwelled in great abundance, Lily knew a sense of empathy for the pain he had suffered.

She would attempt to remember from whence his vexation with her came and try to remain unmoved by it. That much she could do without compromising her need to hold her attraction to him in check.

"My lord."

Tristan looked up from his work to see a serving woman standing nearby. "Yes, Maggie?"

"The maid, Lily, has sent me to ask your assent to take Sabina for a ride."

Tristan grimaced. He had not seen Lily since his return to Brackenmoore late last eve, though he had sent for Sabina directly before breakfast. He knew that it was an obvious break in their routine, but he did not wish to answer questions about his extended absense in front of the woman who so plagued his every thought. The seven days had seemed an eternity, and in the end he had resolved nothing by staying away.

Nor was he accomplishing anything by avoiding her now. If she wished to leave, she would get word to him. He must learn to face her and his feelings.

After a time he nodded thoughtfully. "You may tell the la—Lily—that she may make ready to go on this outing immediately if that is her desire."

The maid curtsied. "Yes, my lord."

He stopped her just as she was leaving. "You will come back and inform me of her plans."

"As you wish, Lord Tristan."

When Lily led Sabina out onto the steps of the keep, she spied the waiting horses with a frown of consternation. Yet it was not the fine mounts that caused her frown. Her displeasure was caused by the fact that it was Tristan Ainsworth himself, dressed for riding in a heavy cape of dark blue, who held their reins.

The fleeting hope that he was simply standing there in preparation of going on some outing of his own disappeared quickly when he said with the utmost aplomb, "It's a perfect day for a ride, is it not? I can scarce contain my anticipation."

Sabina pulled free from Lily's hand to go to her father. "You are coming with us?" There was no mistaking her happiness.

Tristan swung her up in the air. "I am coming with you. That is, if Lily doesn't mind." The poorly disguised uncertainty in his tone belied his confident manner.

Lily could only be glad that none of the other servants were present to hear him asking her permission this way. She forced away her irritation at the request and reminded herself of her decision to try to show him more compassion.

She smiled with studied politeness and went down the steps toward him. "Good morrow, my lord."

Tristan seemed slightly taken aback at her civility, as well he might be after their last meeting, but Lily did not give him the satisfaction of reacting as he expected.

Obviously relieved at her pleasant demeanor, he handed her the reins of the mare with a wide smile of his own.

In a matter of moments they were mounted and off, Sabina seated before her father on his stallion. Once outside the castle wall he set a fairly brisk pace, and Lily was grateful, for it discouraged conversation.

The snow of the previous week had melted, and though the air was cool, the sky was a deep shade of blue. *The same shade as Tristan Ainsworth's eyes,* came the unbidden thought.

Lily sighed heavily. Was she to have no peace from such thoughts? Was her own traitorous mind to always play the betrayer without pity or surcease?

Lily spurred her mare on, galloping across the field. The wind of her passage whipped the ribbon from the end of her braid, spreading her long straight hair behind her in an ebony tangle.

It was only as she came to the edge of the wood beyond the wide cleared area around the castle that she slowed, then stopped. She would not endanger the mare by racing her through the woods. Breathing deeply, she slid to the ground and turned to watch as Tristan and Sabina continued toward her. Lily could hear the child's excited chatter as they approached.

Tristan drew to a halt, and Sabina babbled happily, "Lily won, Lily won." Clearly she had thought they were having a race.

"But Lily didn't tell us there was a race, dear heart.

If she was racing, that means she was cheating,'' Tristan said, studying Lily closely.

Briefly she stiffened, not caring for his remark. But being accused of cheating was preferable to his knowing she had ridden off in a huff over her own thoughts. She cast them what she hoped was an easy smile. ''Your father is right, poppet, I cheated. It isn't winning unless both people know there is a race on. I should have declared my intentions first. I was simply overzealous. Next time I will state my challenge.''

Sabina began to fidget. ''Can we get down, too?''

''If you like.'' Tristan slid to the ground and set his daughter on her feet.

She pranced about. ''May I get a present for Lily?'' When he nodded, the child ran in among the trees and began to pick up cones.

Lily looked after her with genuine affection. ''She is such a delight.''

Tristan's reply made her turn back to him. ''I knew you would see that.'' She could not mistake the satisfaction in his tone.

Lily felt herself stiffen. ''Anyone would think the same.''

''Of course,'' he replied evenly, but she was not deaf to the underlying smugness in his manner as he moved to stand closer to her. Yet he seemed almost oblivious to her as his long, lean fingers toyed with the reins.

In spite of her resolve, she found that she could not look away from his hands, hands that had touched her own flesh so knowingly—so very adeptly. Wrenching her gaze away, Lily found it now focusing on the powerful breadth of his shoulders, mere inches from her own. She closed her eyes. She seemed to have no command of herself, at least not with him so close and large and male.

Acting on a need to put distance between herself and the man, Lily walked into the woods, leading her horse behind her. She moved to stand close to Sabina, who was now sitting beneath a tree, her cones scattered in her lap as her chubby fingers attempted to arrange them into a circle. Her voice sounding overbright, Lily said. "May I help you?"

Sabina beamed up at her. "Yes, you may help me."

Lily bent and fiddled with the cones, chagrined to see that her hands were shaking. Glancing over to where Tristan had been standing, Lily saw that he was still there. Thankfully he had not come after her, seemed in fact to be gazing off into the distance.

Following the direction of his gaze, she saw that a rider was approaching. Lily stood and watched as he came closer. Something about him—the almost arrogant set of his gray head, the square angle of his shoulders—made her frown thoughtfully. Indeed, she had seen him only once, had not spoken more than a few words to him, but...

Lily took two steps forward, squinting even as he continued toward them on the horse. She was aware the moment when Tristan's body tautened. Casting one anxious glance back over his shoulder to where Lily and Sabina had entered the shelter of the trees, he strode out to meet the new arrival.

Lily looked toward the rider again. A frown marred her brow as she became more certain as to whom the newcomer might be.

She felt a strange sinking sensation in the pit of her stomach. Without giving herself time to think, Lily swung around and lifted Sabina into her arms. Dragging the mare behind them, she smiled reassuring down into the child's inquisitive face. "Shh now. We must be quiet for a bit. We will have a quiet game."

Sabina whispered back, her voice filled with barely suppressed excitement, "Will we hide from da?"

Lily nodded. "Aye, we are going to hide from your da, while he talks to someone. Do you think you can be so very quiet that they will not know where we are?"

The child clamped her lips shut, but her eyes were gleeful. Moving quietly, Lily took Sabina farther into the forest and set her on her feet. Then, with shaking fingers, she tied the mare to a branch.

She bent over and whispered, "Will you wait here, and I will go back and see if he is behind us?"

Sabina nodded, totally caught up in the adventure, her gray eyes wide.

With even more care to remain silent, Lily crept back to the edge of the wood. Peeking out through the leaves, she saw what she had expected: it was none other than Maxim Harcourt. For the first time she noted the sharp haughtiness of his features as he looked down at Tristan.

"Why have you taken it upon yourself to trespass upon my brother's land?" Tristan asked coolly.

Maxim's brow rose. "That is a poor greeting indeed, Ainsworth. But I should expect no more from one of your family."

Tristan smiled, but it was a smile without humor. "Again I ask you, Harcourt, what has brought you here?"

Maxim leaned forward on his pommel, obviously deciding to get to the point, since his insult had scored no response. As he began, Lily shivered at the ice in his tone. "It has come to me, Ainsworth, that someone of this keep might have some notion of where my bride is. One of my men caught a glimpse of the man who launched a message from her over my castle walls on the head of an arrow. He had the distinct impression that the man might be wearing your brother's colors."

Tristan laughed as if he found this highly amusing, though Lily thought she sensed a hint of unease in it. "Is that so?" When he went on, she realized she must have been mistaken, for his tone was completely assured. "We had heard that you seemed to have misplaced your intended. I would wonder why you seem to have a difficult time keeping a woman by you."

Lily had the distinct impression that he was referring not only to herself but also to Genevieve. Maxim was not deaf to this and replied bitterly, "You may have fallen for that whelp Genevieve's lies, but that is your concern. I but tried to look after her. You may be sure that I do not begrudge you the task of keeping that damsel in line. Even at fourteen she was a deceitful and disobedient girl. My bride is another matter entirely."

Tristan's gaze narrowed, and his hand went to the hilt of his sword. "Nothing that was *yours* has been taken by me or anyone else at Brackenmoore. Now I suggest you go."

Maxim looked down at him for another long moment. Then he smiled and, as with Tristan earlier, there was no humor in it. "Mark me well, Ainsworth, should I learn that you have lied to me, I will make you pay." He pulled back on the reins of his horse, making him rear in the air, then galloped away.

Lily watched until he was well out of hearing, then sagged against the trunk of the tree. For a long time she just stood there in the shelter of the woods, her heart pounding as she realized just what she had done. Maxim, her own fiancé had been not more than twenty feet from her, obviously concerned for her safety, and she had deliberately hidden herself from him.

Dear God, had she completely lost her mind? Where was her sense of loyalty?

Gripped by a panic and confusion that terrified her, Lily ran back to where Sabina waited. The little one looked up expectantly from her newfound pile of cones. "Are we still hiding from da?"

Lily strove desperately to keep her feelings from being revealed in her tone. "No, now it is time for you to go out and surprise him. Can you do that?"

The little one jumped up enthusiastically. "I will. I will surprise him." She trotted off, and Lily watched her as she ran back toward her father, laughing as she went.

Lily then mounted her own mare and urged her in the direction of the keep. She didn't care what Tristan might make of her behavior. She could not face him now, not with her own motives and fealty so suspect in her own mind.

Tristan saw Sabina racing toward him and smiled, grateful that Lily had kept her hidden from the bastard until he was gone. It was only as he saw Lily and the mare streak from the shelter of the forest and gallop toward the keep that he realized anything was amiss.

Taking up his daughter, who was prattling on about playing a game, he jumped upon his own horse and followed close behind. Something told him Lily was not playing a game. Only his care of the tiny precious burden on his lap kept him from setting a pace that would overtake the unpredictable damsel.

He would reach her soon enough, he promised himself.

When they gained the courtyard he called to one of the serving woman working there. "Come, take Sabina into the keep." He had just seen Lily disappear around the edge of the stables.

The woman did not quite manage to hide her curiosity as she looked up at her master, but she made no comment. Tristan swung his mount in the direction he had seen Lily go.

When he reached the back of the stables, he saw her there, calling for a groom. When she spotted him, her eyes widened. Gathering her gray skirt in her hands, she swung her legs over the pommel, clearly meaning to bolt. Before she could get down from the horse, Tristan was upon her, nearly dragging her from the mare.

She began to struggle, but when her gaze came to rest on the man who had come to the door of the stables to gape at them, she blushed scarlet and grew still. It was without contest that she allowed Tristan to take her into the small wooden structure at the side of the stable.

Once inside, he saw that it was occupied by one of the stable boys, who was vigorously cleaning a saddle. Tristan ordered, "Go!" and the young man jumped to obey.

The second they were alone, Lily rounded on him. "How dare you? Have you lost your wits?"

He ignored her words. "Why did you run away?"

"Why did I run away, you great madman?" Her voice was husky with frustration and anger. "I ran away because I am confused."

He frowned. "Confused?"

She went on, her gray eyes as stormy as a winter sea. "I just hid from my own fiancé, the man my parents chose for me. *He* is the one I owe allegiance to, because of their choice. How do you think that affects me, Tristan Ainsworth? Or have you thought of me in this at all?"

His frown deepened, and he felt his own anger rise. "I did not force you to hide your presence. I said nothing."

"Nay, you did not. Perchance that is the trouble. Mayhap I would be less confused if you had forced it upon me. What has happened has obscured the lines of right and wrong, loyalty and trust."

He was more than slightly shocked at the depth of her honesty, but could not fathom the cause of so much anguish. Her revelations gave him great encouragement that she might be coming to her senses. "It is only your own stubbornness that makes it confusing. You know what is true."

"That is clear only to you, Tristan. For me it is not so. You do not know what it is like for me to feel that I have betrayed my family. You do not know what my life has been like these past three years, how my parents have cared for me, loved me. It is impossible to resolve the thought that they could ever do me aught but good." Her eyes glistened with unshed tears, and she turned her back to hide them.

For a long moment, Tristan could think of nothing to say. If only she would see that it was within her own power to resolve this within herself. Reason warred with sympathy inside him, causing him to feel some of the confusion Lily had claimed.

Sympathy won. He had never meant to hurt her. Doing so would do neither him nor her any good. Without thinking he reached forward and put a gentle hand on her shoulder. An instantaneous heat flared out from that point of contact and gave Tristan a start.

Lily must have felt it, too, for she spun around, drawing away from that touch.

Tristan dropped his hand at his side with a bitter laugh. "Pardon, my lady. I had not realized my very touch was so abhorrent to you."

He was even more surprised than before when she replied with misery, "Your touch is not abhorrent to me." As quickly, she added, "You simply surprised me."

Tristan felt far more disappointment at the last words than he would ever have admitted. A new wave of frustration made him speak with unintended bitterness. "I want you to tell me, Lily, explain to me why you feel such deep loyalty that you believe in your parents no matter what evidence there is to the contrary."

Her expression grew incredulous. "What you see as clear evidence is not so very clear to me. I have explained that to you. You have no understanding of what it was like, waking to find that nothing around you was familiar." She held his gaze, willing him to try to see. "I first opened my eyes on my mother's face, though I knew not who she was at the time. You should have seen her, the joy she felt at seeing me awaken. I watched as she fell into my father's arms, weeping. Her reaction could not have been feigned."

He interrupted her in a tone of calm reason. "I do

not doubt but that it was quite a touching moment. Yet you did not know them any more than you do anyone here at Brackenmoore. What did they do to gain your abject and unquestioning allegiance?''

She faced him squarely. ''They cared for me, cared with a tenderness and love that could not be mistaken.''

Tristan realized that this devotion could very well have been brought on by guilt at what they had done, but he refrained from saying so as Lily continued. ''I was so weak and helpless. My mother bathed me, helped me to feed myself. My father read to me, carried me to the gardens and sat with me for hours, telling me of the years I had lost. From his stories, I began to piece together the events of my life. And when I was strong enough, he took me before him on his horse, showed me our lands, introduced me to the folk who lived on them. They knew me, Tristan, each and every one of them. I was surrounded by people who said I was Lillian Gray, that Lord Robert Gray was my father, Lady Elaine my mother. It was impossible to doubt the certainty of so many. No one, not one soul, said a word to me of a babe or you. It is the memory of these past three years in such tender care that leaves me reluctant to set aside all I do know to believe the words of a man who...''

Lily glanced down, having barely stopped herself. She had nearly admitted that he had awakened her body and mind more than all the efforts her parents had gone to over the past years. Already she had given away too much in the heat of her distress.

Tristan said nothing, his lips a grim line.

She willed him to understand. ''Can you not see

that when I hid myself from Maxim today I betrayed them and their love for me?''

He shook his head. ''You didn't betray them, Lily. Even if what you say is true. Even if they did care for you so selflessly, does it negate all the wrong they did before that?''

She sighed heavily, the admission she was about to make coming at great expense, for there was no telling how Tristan might use it against her. ''There is something I have come to realize in all of this, Tristan, and that is that you genuinely wish to help me.'' His obvious gratification soon turned to chagrin as she went on. ''Yet even if much of what you have told me is true, even if I am indeed Sabina's mother, I have only your word for how things were between you and me. Perhaps my parents have hidden the truth from me to protect me and not themselves. Perhaps, in their minds, it is not precisely as you have described.''

He grimaced at this but remained silent for long moments, studying her, then shook his head. ''I could accept what you say, believe that you actually believed your father and mother were worthy of such blind faith, if it were not for the fact that they have given you to Maxim Harcourt, of all men.''

She frowned and he added, ''You have heard what Genevieve said? Think you she would lie? She knows nothing of your circumstances, has no reason to try to fool you.''

Lily bit her lip. ''That I do not understand. It is one of the things that confuses me most. There can be no mistaking the gentle nature of your betrothed. It may be possible that Genevieve has somehow misunderstood Maxim's intent, misjudged him. She was quite young."

"Misjudged—!" he spat.

Quickly she interrupted. "You heard what Maxim said of that event today."

His blue eyes darkened until the pupils were barely visible at the center. "And what of the way he behaved this day? The threats he made, his belligerent attitude?"

She glared back at him. "How would you have him treat you, Tristan Ainsworth? How would you behave had he stolen the woman you intended to wed?"

The coldness of his tone made her shiver. "No man of character such as his would lay a finger to what I held dear and live to tell the tale. I would kill him, slowly and with great relish."

Lily fought the urge to take a step backward, feeling it best not to argue Maxim's position in the face of such obvious hatred as Tristan held toward him. Clearly, it was getting her nowhere.

She decided on another tack. "Even if what you say of Maxim is true, why should that make me mistrust my father? I am sure he does not know him fully, if what you have related is true."

Tristan's eyes narrowed. "Your father knows him well enough, Lily. I do not see how he could be ignorant of the man's character. The only reason Harcourt is not swinging from a rope now is that he kept both feet in Richard's camp, while spying for Henry. Your father must know this. How else do you think he could become close enough allies with a supporter of the house of York to give him his only daughter? That the Ainsworths backed Richard was his objection to our own marriage. He would rather a mad king than a York. Maxim will gain your inheritance and your father secures his position, even possibly his head, by making an allegiance with one who was his ally in loyalty to Henry, while now retaining favor at the court of Richard's son.''

She wanted to decry what Tristan said, but the explanation rang true. Her father had been a strong supporter of Henry, bemoaned his banishment even now. She shook her head desperately. ''I will not believe this. You ask too much. In my memory you were a stranger to me until mere days ago.''

Before she knew what he was about, Tristan had dragged her into his arms, his mouth assaulting hers.

Lily struggled for a moment, tried to keep herself from responding, but she could not. Her lips seemed to have a life of their own as they softened, then awakened under his. Her arms crept up to twine about his neck.

Tristan growled deep in his throat, his arms tightening around her as he molded her to the hard length of his body. When he brought one hand around to cover her breast, she felt it swell, becoming tender and aching with longing.

She shifted her body to give him better access to the rigid tip, and Tristan obliged her by plying it with his thumb. His mouth left hers to scatter fervent kisses over her face and the long line of her throat. His breath was hot against her ear as he whispered, ''You know me, Lily. There is no use denying it.''

The words penetrated her passion-fogged mind with a painful intensity. She opened her eyes with a gasp of outrage. He had kissed her, touched her in order to prove that he was right.

Desperately Lily pushed away from him, her heart

hammering against her chest in wave after wave of agony. It was only with the greatest effort that she was able to sputter, "Take your hands from me, you knave."

Tristan fell back, his black-lashed eyes dark, his lean jaw hard. To her horror she realized that even now, after what he had just done, she still found him the most beautiful man she had ever seen. She still wanted him. She wanted to cry aloud in misery, but clamped her lips shut instead.

He wiped at his own passion-swollen lips with the back of his hand, his voice harsh. "Well, can you still deny that there was love between us, Lily? How can you when every time we touch you come alive?"

Lily raised her hands to cover her ears, knowing she could hear no more. Her throat swelled with misery. Why had she even attempted to explain things to Tristan? He had only managed to turn the situation around and make her more uncertain, then had used his knowledge of her physical reactions to him against her.

Surely he must be wrong about her father. In spite of her reactions, it was Tristan who was wrong. Lily was the one who betrayed her family through some wanton fault in herself that made her susceptible to Tristan's touch. Her father would not hide the past from her lest he thought it for her own good, would not give her to a man of poor character simply to satisfy his own political ends.

"Lily," Tristan said urgently. "You must begin to see the truth."

She had had enough of this assault on her senses and her allegiance to her family. Not caring now what commotion Tristan Ainsworth might choose to display, Lily ran from the shed.

Thankfully, she reached Sabina's chambers without speaking to anyone. Yet the slamming of the door behind her did not block out the endless repetition in her mind of all he had said.

Lily knew she should leave Brackenmoore, but could not do so even now, for the same reason that she had hidden from Maxim. Her parents had protected her too closely, kept her from having to face anything painful, and Lily could no longer allow that.

Something inside bade her to discover exactly what had occurred before that accident three years ago. That same inner knowing told her that it could only be found here at Brackenmoore, no matter what it might cost her to remain so near Tristan.

Chapter Seven

Tristan left the keep before the morning meal and went out to where the final construction was underway on the new signal tower. Immediately he threw himself into the physical work with more than his usual enthusiasm.

He worked until his clothes were soaked with perspiration in spite of the chill winter air.

But damn him, he still could not erase the last encounter with Lily from his mind. She had admitted that she knew he meant her no ill, but she was not ready to see that all he told her was indeed fact.

It was no use telling himself that he did not care, for Tristan was not such a fool as to be able to lie to himself in the face of his own maddening emotions. That his agitation was surely caused by the fact that Lily did not seem to care about her parents' disloyalty was of no comfort whatsoever.

After what she had revealed to him about her illness and recovery, he did have a better understanding of her feelings. He could see that realizing the truth would be incredibly painful, but he did not see how she could continue to deny reality.

Yet he saw that he had pushed her too far. It was clear that the discovery of the truth was going to bring Lily great pain, not the sense of freedom he had envisioned. Tristan now realized that the thought of causing her more hurt than she had already endured was untenable.

He would push no more. He must allow her the peace of her forgetfulness, no matter how many sleepless nights that decision brought him.

At table the next morning Lily could hardly bear to face Genevieve. After what had happened between herself and Tristan in the stables, it was just too difficult to meet those green eyes. Lily was also not ignorant of the fact that they seemed to focus upon herself for far too long when Marcel commented on how it was unlike Tristan to forgo eating with the family as he had done of late.

Lily was relieved at Tristan's lack of attendance, but not surprised that his family felt differently.

Sabina pouted her pretty lips, and even her guileless eyes seemed to question only Lily. "Where is Da?"

Benedict was the one who informed her that Tristan was quite busy working.

Again Lily felt Genevieve's gaze, and forced herself to stay still under her scrutiny. Genevieve had no reason to think that she had anything to do with his absence. In truth she did not. Tristan's actions were not governed by herself in any way.

As soon as they finished breaking their fast, she begged leave to take Sabina for a walk. Genevieve gave permission with a look that told Lily very little of her thoughts.

Lily hurriedly readied them to go out, glad to have escaped seeing Tristan this morn. *Perhaps,* she thought hopefully, *he has gone away again.* Benedict had said only that he was working.

The thought was so encouraging that it was with a light step that she led Sabina through the castle gates and out into the wide cleared fields that ringed the castle. She did not even allow the too familiar smile of the guard posted there to bother her. He did, after all, believe she was a servant girl.

If things were as they seemed, she might indeed have been flattered by the attention of the brawny young soldier. Yet things were not as they seemed.

Not caring to allow herself to delve into such thoughts, Lily set off at a brisk pace. The air was really quite chill, but she was covered from neck to ankles in the warm cloak Tristan had given her.

Sabina was equally warmly dressed, in wool clothing, a fur-lined cloak and tiny leather boots. The child began to skip through the short grass in her own awkward way, chattering up at her. Lily smiled, her heart warming as ever at her antics as they made their way across the bare hillside.

Being conscious of Maxim's appearance in the forest, Lily turned toward the shoreline. Surely no one would have the courage to approach that area, as it was in full view of the castle lookout at all times.

She told herself that her concern was for Sabina's sake. She felt no fear of Maxim on her own behalf.

The winter-dry grass underfoot soon turned to sand. They came to a place where the path forked, one branch dipping sharply down to the shore, the other climbing upward from the ledge they stood upon.

Sabina spoke with childish wonder as she looked

down toward the shoreline, where the sea crashed against an outcropping of rock. ''The bubbles are so pretty.''

Lily could not argue that point. The tips of the gray waves did indeed leave a wildly beautiful trail of frothy foam in their wake. Her gaze swung out over the wide blue sky before them. She breathed deeply of the salty sea air. What a glorious day! She would not allow any thought of Tristan to mar this time with Sabina.

It would not last forever.

The strange wave of sadness she felt made Lily turn to Sabina and speak with more emotion in her voice than she knew. ''Which way, dear heart?''

Sabina smiled widely, her gray eyes excited as she pointed along the upper pathway. ''That way.'' Lily felt herself respond to that enthusiasm. To the child every moment was an adventure.

Lily swallowed the lump of feeling in her throat as Sabina reached for her hand once again. Slowly she took the tiny fingers in her own. She carefully checked her speed as the wee one trotted up the incline.

Sabina seemed content to go on in silence now, appearing to require all her concentration to negotiate the narrow path. Lily felt her heart swell anew as she noted the frown of perseverance that creased that smooth ivory brow.

Once again she found herself wishing...

But down that road was only sorrow. There was no way this tale could have a happy ending, no matter what the truth might be.

So occupied was she with her own confused feelings that she did not take note of the fact that they were no longer moving uphill until Sabina actually came to a halt at the edge of a wide flat plateau. Lily frowned in consternation at what she saw.

It was not a geographical detail that caused her expression, nor even the enormous stone structure rising up ahead of them. Though the tall circular building must be near completion, the fact that it was not yet finished was evidenced by the scaffolding that ringed it and the men who moved busily about the base. This was obviously the signal tower Tristan had designed. The reason Lily had not seen it before was that she had never had an opportunity to visit this plateau, clearly the highest point along this stretch of seacoast.

Never having glimpsed the structure, Lily had assumed that it would be farther from the castle. Benedict had said only that Tristan was working. Could he be here rather than away, as she had so childishly hoped?

Lily knew she did not want to take the risk. She wished above all else to avoid contact with that man. She looked back the way they had come, saying, "Come, Sabina, we—"

Yet before she could finish, the little one had slipped her tiny hand free. She trotted across the short coarse grass, calling gaily, "Da!"

Lily's frown deepened. Obviously the child believed her father was here.

"Da! Da!" Sabina continued to call, making their slipping away unobserved highly unlikely.

Slowly Lily followed after her, trying desperately to think of some way to avoid seeing the man who so plagued her. Perhaps, she told herself hopefully, Tristan was not even here.

She quickened her steps and caught up with the little one. This was a construction site, and there might be any number of hazards that could cause the child hurt. As she and Sabina came around the edge of the structure, she saw that she had been wise to think thusly.

A wagon stood off to the side and three men were busy unloading what appeared to be very heavy stones. Not far from them, another man was mixing what looked like mortar in a hollowed out place in the ground. More men were taking the stones and tying heavy ropes around them, while still others then pulled them to the top of the tower.

It was a scene of intense activity. All the workers seemed far too busy to attend a very curious and precocious three year old. Indeed, it appeared that no one had even taken note of her and Lily's arrival.

Hurriedly, Lily reached down and took Sabina into her arms. She had not seen any sign of Tristan, but that was the least of her concerns now. This was no place for a small child.

Sabina squirmed. ''I want Da.''

Lily spoke gently. ''We will see him back at the keep, sweeting. We should not be here.''

It was then that Lily saw a man appear from around the edge of the stone structure. There was no mistaking Tristan's tall, wide-shouldered frame and tousled dark hair. His hands rode his lean hips and he moved with purpose, his face a study of concentration. As he looked up and saw them, he stopped still, a scowl marring his brow.

Sabina cried out loudly with glee, making several heads turn in their direction. ''Da!''

Tristan focused all his attention upon his daughter,

smiling with warm affection as he came toward them.
Realizing that she did not wish to be holding the child
while Tristan spoke to her, Lily gently set her on her
feet.

As Sabina trotted toward him, Tristan stretched his
own arms wide. She ran to him, and he scooped her
up into the air, swinging her about. Lily moved forward slowly as Sabina squealed wildly with delight,
and even more loudly when Tristan pulled her close
to hug her tightly.

Lily felt her own heart flutter then as he looked up,
his still-warm gaze coming to rest on her face. That
happy expression disappeared immediately, replaced
by a look of wariness that made her falter.

Whatever was the matter with him? It was *she* who
had been insulted and hurt by him.

Regret made her chest ache for a brief moment before she forced herself to go on. She would not allow
herself to react to Tristan. For the thousandth time
she told herself that she was indifferent to him and
his opinion of her.

Nothing short of complete acceptance of all the
things he had told her about herself, and a subsequent
condemnation of her father and mother, would please
him. She could not afford him that.

Lily stopped a few feet from the two of them. Tristan nodded stiffly, and she bobbed her head in return.

He spoke abruptly. "I had not expected you here."

Lily stiffened even more. "I assure you, my lord,
I had no intention of troubling you. Sabina and I were
simply taking a walk. When the path forked, she
chose the one that led here. I can only assume that
she has been to this spot previously and hoped you
would be here."

He nodded. "She has come here before with Genevieve." His tone did not indicate that he was any more pleased with Lily's presence than he had been before her explanation. There was no mistaking the reference to his betrothed state.

What was she to say to that? Folding her arms tightly across her abdomen beneath the enveloping cloak, Lily looked at the ground. It was true she had once again lost all sense of propriety the moment he touched her last eve, but it was Tristan who had initiated the contact.

Tristan looked at Lily's bent head with regret, seeing her upset once again, though he had not meant to displease her. If only they were not so at odds. He had not imagined this would happen when he had brought her to Brackenmoore.

What had he thought it would be like? He could not answer his own query.

All he wanted now was to have peace with her. Yet how could he do that with a clear conscience when he could not stop himself from noticing the way the December sun shone on the midnight silk of her hair? Could not help seeing how the breeze shaped her cloak along the length of her slender body? Or how this made him recall just how lovely she was without benefit of any covering at all?

Sabina's childish voice interrupted the path of his thoughts. "Can we go to the top?" She pointed upward to the top of the tower.

He nodded, grateful for the opportunity to think of something beside his unwanted and unwarranted, yet completely overwhelming, attraction to Lily.

He moved toward the structure. As he did so, Sabina, who had been looking backward over his shoulder, cried out, "Lily, too."

Tristan stopped and turned. Lily stood where she had been before, her expression at once desolate and defiant. Did she perhaps feel that he would not want her to come? The wave of compassion this thought brought was surprising. He found himself saying softly, "Lily, too. If she would care to come."

"Oh yes!" Sabina jerked her head with enthusiasm. "It is so high. She will like it."

Tristan looked into Lily's eyes, his tone gently teasing as he said, "What say you, fair damsel? Will you go up on high with us?"

She stared at him for a long moment, her gaze uncertain.

Almost without knowing he was going to say the words, Tristan urged, "Come, Lily, join us."

Sabina added her own encouragement. "Yes, come with us, Lily."

Again, she watched only him, and Tristan felt she would decline. Then something seemed to snap inside her, for she moved toward them. Keeping her attention centered on Sabina, she said, "I thank you for inviting me."

Tristan could not stop a rush of consternation. Her words made it clear that she was only humoring Sabina. He pushed it aside with a shrug. "Shall we go on then?" No more was said as he moved to enter the opening that would soon be covered by a heavy wooden door. He tried to concentrate on climbing the wooden steps that ran around the inside of the wall, but he was completely aware of her presence behind him.

There was really no danger even though the steps

were fairly narrow. Yet he was careful of where he placed his feet, ever mindful of the precious burden in his arms, and his own preoccupation with the woman behind them.

Lily focused her attention on the rows of stones that made up the wall. Anything was safer than thinking about the way Tristan's thighs flexed as he moved before her, safer than thinking about how they had felt sliding along her own. Surely anything was safer than thinking about what it would be like if she and Tristan were together, if Sabina were theirs.

Desperately she closed her eyes. Even the possibility of plunging to the bottom of the tower was preferable to contemplating her tumultuous feelings about this man and his child.

When they came to the top of the edifice, the men who were working there stopped what they were doing, casting self-conscious glances toward Lily. Tristan spoke easily. "You may all go down and have a rest for a time. Sabina will only get in your way for now, at any rate."

When the laborers had left them, Lily felt even more uneasy. Now she was alone with Tristan and Sabina, at the top of the world.

For that was the way it seemed as she gazed off over the landscape laid out before them. On one side was the sea, dark, frothy and mysterious. On the other was the land, the castle and the grounds surrounding it appearing as vast and unchangeable as the sea.

Lily could not help acknowledging that were the circumstances different, she might have taken pride and comfort in the awesome and mighty sight of Brackenmoore. As it was, she could only struggle against an unaccustomed sense of intimidation and bondage. Why, why did she feel that way? Tristan was not trying to hold her here.

Perhaps, whispered a soft voice inside her, *it is your own reactions that make you feel thusly. Perhaps you only wish you could stay. Perhaps you only wish the strength and permanence of Brackenmoore were yours, along with the loyalty and fellowship of the folk who dwell there.*

Immediate horror made her take in a sharp breath. She had no such wish.

Glancing over at Tristan she found him watching her with an assessing expression that was becoming all too familiar. She lifted her head. Watch her he might, but he could not read her mind, no matter that it might feel as though he could.

Lily pretended her reaction had been to the view, sweeping her hands wide. "It is wondrous, is it not?"

Tristan nodded, his own gaze now turning to the landscape. "Aye, it is. As a child I used to come to this point and think that I would build something here one day, something so tall that it would reach all the way to heaven." He laughed. "At the time I had no idea that I would think of anything so useful and needed as a signal tower. That idea came to me after my parents were killed along this stretch of coast in a winter storm. They were coming back from a visit to my mother's aunt Finella in Scotland."

Lily heard the pain in his voice, though she knew the incident had happened many years ago. "You must have loved them so very much."

He swallowed, not meeting her gaze for a long moment. "I did love them. They were the center of our world, taught us that family was everything."

She looked out over the vast sea, which seemed so harmless now. Yet obviously that could change at any moment. "It explains why you are so close to your brothers. And why you are so bent on seeing the tower completed."

He looked at her, his eyes holding wry amusement, along with lingering traces of grief. "Do not be sure that I would not have done so if they had not died. Such an attitude is not very flattering. I am not completely without talents, though I am a younger son."

"I did not…" She halted, biting her tongue in consternation. She had not meant to imply any such thing. But to try to explain without giving away her true feelings would be far too difficult.

He shrugged again, his tone indifferent. "It matters not either way."

Lily was not unaware of the way the muscles worked in his lean jaw. It seemed a contradiction to his words, but that could not be. She knew he had no care as to what she thought of him.

It was only as Sabina chose that moment to begin squirming to get down that Lily even recalled that the little one was present.

Tristan held her tightly. "No, minx. You may not get down. Not until the upper wall is complete."

Lily was grateful for the interruption and for the fact that Tristan intended to keep a tight hold on his daughter. There was still a large gap in the low wall that surrounded the top section of the tower, though the domed crown above it had been completed. It looked as though some sort of wide platform was being built into the wall of the unfinished section.

Before Lily could form a question as to its purpose, Sabina made a noise of irritation, even as a wide yawn escaped those pert little lips. Instantly Lily spoke up. "The child is tired. I should take her back to the keep for a nap."

Tristan looked down at his daughter, clearly noting the heaviness of her lids. "Yes, I can see that she is. Very well then, we'll go down. It is time the men started back to work at any rate. We are attempting to finish before any really severe winter storms are upon us."

His relief at the notion of being rid of them—her—seemed almost palpable. Yet she refused to think of that. She simply wanted to be on her way.

They had just started down when there was a sharp cry from one of the workers below. Other excited voices called out immediately.

Quickly Tristan moved to look out over the unfinished wall. "What is it?"

A faint reply came to Lily's ears. "'Tis master mason Jack, my lord. The donkey slipped on the wet ground, and he was standing behind the cart, talking with one of the workers. His leg seems to have got caught when it happened. The cart's run over him, my lord."

Even from here, Lily could not mistake the anxiety in the man's voice. Neither, it seemed, could Tristan, for he hurried to make his way down, anxiety marking his handsome features.

She followed closely behind him.

When they had reached the ground, Tristan looked down at Sabina and paused. He frowned, then turned to Lily, speaking softly but distractedly. "She has fallen asleep."

Peering at the child in his arms, Lily saw that it

was true. She moved toward him briskly, holding out her arms. "I will take her back to the keep."

Tristan shook his head. "Nay, 'tis too far for you to carry her."

Lily shook her own head emphatically. "It is not. I can manage quite well. You are needed here."

He frowned, but made no reply to that. Swinging around to look into the grim faces of the men gathered around the donkey cart, he said with barely held patience, "Randel, you will take Sabina."

When a tall slender man with gentle eyes stepped forward, Tristan handed the child to him carefully. "Have a care and take her back to the keep while I see to Jack."

The man bowed, settling the babe in his arms in a way that told Lily he was no stranger to children. Though she was irritated with Tristan for his autocratic disregard of her own assurances that she could manage the task, Lily felt the child was in safe hands.

She turned to go after Randel as he started for the keep, but something made her pause. She swung around, biting her lower lip as she took in the grim expressions of the men. She wondered if perhaps she could be of more help here.

What if Tristan did not want her aid? Another glance at the men's faces decided her. The devil take Tristan Ainsworth. Her own sense of compassion bade her try.

She joined Tristan behind the cart. He was kneeling beside the man they had called Jack. Lily could see the blood beginning to pool on the ground near his legs. The fellow's expression was twisted with pain, though he tried to put on a brave face as his master felt his wounded leg.

Tristan's own face was now as grim as that of the other men.

Lily crouched beside him and saw what had caused his apprehension. The man's leg was twisted badly, a sharp shaft of white bone poking through the flesh.

She felt her stomach writhe with both reaction to the rawness of the wound and also sympathy for the hurt man. Few ever walked again after sustaining such an injury.

Tristan spoke to Jack. "I will tell no falsehood, Jack. 'Tis not good."

Jack, whose fleshy face was the color of fresh whey, nodded, his voice rough with pain as he replied, "I thought as much, my lord."

Hurriedly Tristan said, "Save your strength for now, Jack. The bone will need to be set." He then glanced up at Lily, displaying no surprise at seeing her there. "We need to stop the bleeding."

Ignoring her own surprise that he would ask for her aid, Lily stood and raised the hem of her gown. She then made quick work of tearing a wide strip from the bottom of her shift.

Tristan took it and wound it around the wound, keeping the leg as straight as he could. When he was finished, his troubled gaze met Lily's. "Will you stay by him for the moment?"

She nodded eagerly. In spite of her worry and fear for the injured man, she felt a warm sense of happiness sweep over her. "Of course."

Tristan was already moving away, completely unaware of her unprecedented reaction to his acceptance. He spoke calmly but with absolute command to the men. "We need get the rest of the stones from the cart. I will use it to take him to his home."

As they sprang into action, he warned, "Have a care with removing the stones. Jack lies close to the wheels, yet I do not wish to move him more than is necessary. His pain is great."

The men were both swift and careful. Lily was amazed at how quickly they were able to remove the stones from the wagon while leaving the cart still. One man had gone to hold the head of the donkey, but that creature had not moved except to shift its head around to look at them all with a decided lack of interest.

When the cart was empty, Tristan and another man came back to where Lily knelt beside Jack. They were carrying a hastily built litter. She backed away as they crouched beside the prone man. Tristan spoke with the same grave composure he had shown throughout. "We must move you now, Jack. We'll do our best to make it swift and with as little discomfort as possible."

The man nodded. "I know you will, my lord."

Briefly Tristan reached out and put a hand upon the master mason's arm before motioning to the men who held the litter. Without preamble they got to the task of getting Jack on it and loaded into the cart.

Lily knew the poor man tried not to make a sound, but when they actually lifted the injured leg onto the litter, he could not withhold a sharp cry of agony. Then his head rolled to the side, and she was certain that he had lost consciousness.

When they had him settled in the vehicle, Lily said softly, "The bandage is already soaked with blood from moving him. I will ride with him and change it while you drive. That way we will waste no more precious time."

Tristan nodded, and she climbed into the cart. Seating herself on the floor, Lily looked up from her position next to the injured man.

Tristan was watching her with some emotion she could not name. She only knew that it made her feel again that rush of warmth and acceptance, a part of something outside herself. But all he said was "Thank you," before he leaped up into the driver's seat and flicked the whip against the donkey's rump.

The animal brayed loudly, and they started off with a jolt. Quickly Lily tore another strip from her shift and rebandaged the wound. When it continued to bleed far too profusely, she did the only thing she could think of and placed her hand firmly against it, as if doing so would somehow stem the flow of life from the unconscious man's body. To her surprise, the bleeding did slow.

The ride seemed to take a long time, though Lily was fairly certain they did not travel far. She knew the village was only a short distance from the back wall of the castle, across the cleared area and through a narrow stand of forest.

The cottage they approached at the edge of the prosperous village was neat, with fresh whitewash and a tidy plot of ground with animal shelters in good repair. As they rattled up to the house, a woman came to the door, wiping her hands upon the kerchief tied about her waist. When she saw who was driving the cart, she rushed out to meet them.

Tristan's austere expression as he drew the donkey to a halt must have alerted her to the fact that something was dreadfully amiss. "What is it, Lord Tristan?"

He looped the reins around the pole at the side of

the cart as he told her, "It's your husband, Leena. There has been an accident." Even as she gasped with shock, Tristan leaped to the ground and took her arm to lead her around the back of the cart.

When she saw her husband there, she put a hand over her mouth. "Dear heaven, Jack."

The woman, seeming oblivious to Lily, had recovered herself enough to call out, "Wallace, come out. We will need your help."

A young lad of perhaps thirteen years poked his tousled blond head from the door, then came toward them. Lily watched as several other youngsters followed him out, their gazes wide as they took in the scene. She counted seven in all, ranging from a golden-haired toddler to a girl who appeared to be slightly older than the boy named Wallace. He rushed to obey his mother, even as he asked, "What...?"

The woman shook her head sharply, clearly barely able to contain her own queries and fears. "No questions now. I do not even know the details myself. First we must get him in and see how badly he is hurt. The rest of you stay back," Leena continued distractedly. "Perhaps you should go to Gran."

Lily realized that here was something she could do to help. "I will look after the children."

Leena looked at her speculatively. Tristan spoke up. "Lily is Sabina's maid. She will do well with the children."

Leena nodded, taking Tristan's word without question. She turned her attention to Wallace. "Come, we must take your father into the cottage." She then paused, looking at Tristan as if suddenly remembering something important. "We must send for the doctor."

Tristan shook his head. "There is no need for concern on that count. I have already done so before we left the tower site. He should be arriving soon enough.''

Then there was no more conversation as Lily watched them take the injured man into the cottage. Tristan came back to the doorway only a heartbeat later, to say, ''When the doctor arrives, ask him to come right in, will you, Lily?''

She nodded and was rewarded by a brief but warm smile. She felt a rush of heat and yearning that made her heart flutter in her breast.

Then he was gone.

With a deep indrawn breath, she willed herself to constraint. There was no good in allowing herself to react to a smile. There could be nothing between them. Not even friendship, considering their opposing attitudes about her family.

She took another deep breath, forcing the feelings away.

With her wayward reactions to Tristan nearly under control, Lily turned to survey the fearful-eyed children with a look of encouragement. There was more of import than Tristan Ainsworth and his smiles to occupy her here. She knew that it would be no small task to keep them distracted from what was going on inside the dwelling.

Taking yet another deep breath, she moved toward the group of children. Surely she could recall some of the games that were played about the keep at Lakeland Park.

Chapter Eight

It was some time later that Tristan emerged from Jack's cottage. Lily had done what she could to entertain the children. They had been quite engrossed in the games she taught them, other than for a few distracted moments after the doctor arrived, and again when he had left a long while later.

Tristan nodded to the children, who had ceased their play the moment he opened the door. "Your mother says you may go in now, but you must be quiet. Your father is very ill."

The children moved to stand before him in an orderly row. The oldest of the girls, whom Lily now knew as Kyla, curtsied and said, "Thank you, Lord Tristan."

He waved her formality away with an unconcerned hand. "There is no need for that this day. Go on in and see your father. Only mind you, remember, you must go quietly. Jack has been through a great deal." He stepped aside then and allowed them in, only reaching out to ruffle the hair of the last as he swept by.

Lily found herself liking Tristan's easy manner

with the children. She also found herself responding to his concern for the man who had been hurt, his compassion. She, in fact, found herself thinking about Tristan in a way that was quite removed from the physical attraction she had been aware of since meeting him in the inn.

And far more disturbing.

When he came toward her, Lily avoided meeting those all too compelling blue eyes. She spoke with studied civility. ''The man, Jack, is he going to be all right?''

Tristan replied tightly, the strain in his voice evident. ''Yes, I believe so, though it is not likely that he will walk again. The doctor says he will not know until morning if he must remove the leg.''

Lily had feared as much. She was aware of an overwhelming sense of sympathy for Tristan, who obviously felt accountable for the accident. Without even knowing that she was going to do so before the words were out, she said, ''None of this was your fault, Tristan. It was nothing but an unforeseeable accident. You must not blame yourself.''

Tristan shook his head. ''The ground was very slippery around the building site. I should have considered that. It will often be thus during the winter months, even when the ground is not trampled and muddy from construction.''

Lily wanted to reach out to him, to smooth that line of worry from his handsome brow. Again she felt herself drawn to him, to his sense of responsibility for the men working under him.

Yet she clenched her hands into fists to keep them at her sides, for in some part of herself she knew that she must not allow herself to feel this way.

Taking a deep breath, she said, "I must return to the castle now. I have left my duties for too long already. I would not wish to raise comment among your family at any lack of responsibility on my part."

His ensuing silence made her glance at Tristan. A brief look was enough to show her that he was gazing at her very oddly, almost—she dared not think it—regretfully. Lily started off toward the castle.

She had not gone three steps when she realized that Tristan was behind her. She turned with a smile that she feared betrayed more than hid her agitation. "There is no need for you to accompany me, my lord. I know the way."

Tristan only shrugged. "It is no trouble to me."

She frowned. "But you need not. I am sure you have something of more import to occupy you."

"Nay, I do not." He met her gaze directly, and again she felt that there was more here than was being said. Turning, she started off again.

Tristan followed her, keeping step with her easily. Though her displeasure with his presence was obvious, he felt the need to be with her. In the midst of their concern over the injury to Jack, the tension that had been so evident between them from the moment they met at the inn had virtually disappeared.

During the whole episode with Jack, and even for a brief time afterward, when Lily had told him that the accident was not his fault, Tristan had felt as if they had connected again on some deeper level.

He had felt the softness in Lily when they first began to talk after he emerged from the mason's house. There were many things he had wanted to say to her. The first of which had been that he had been moved by her offer to help Jack, even though it was obvious she had little experience with such things.

Thinking on it now, he remembered that was the way *his* Lily had been—kind and concerned for others. They had once spent a whole afternoon helping an old woman they'd met in the forest to gather firewood. The two of them had gone to great lengths to plan an afternoon alone together but Lily had seemed to begrudge the elderly woman not one moment of their precious time.

Tristan wiped a weary hand over his face as he looked at the rigid line of Lily's back. Even in his state of regret he could not help seeing the way the breeze caught at the soft black tendrils that escaped the braids she had wound around her head. They fluttered about her nape, seeming to beckon his lips with every motion.

Roughly he forced his gaze away. Down that road was sheer madness.

He had Genevieve, Sabina, his whole future at stake here. He could not destroy the new life he had made for a past that was long dead.

Gladly he allowed Lily to maintain the distance she had forged ahead of him. It seemed to take far longer than usual to reach the castle.

When they entered the castle grounds, Lily slowed, seeming to become aware that she might draw attention to them by her demeanor. The space between them closed, until they entered the great hall side by side. And still she did not look at him or acknowledge him in any way, but went directly to the steps that led to the upper floors.

Tristan continued on up the first few steps with her, then paused, not knowing why he was doing this other than that he felt that there was something unfinished between them. Despite her attitude toward him, there was something he did want to say, felt he had to say. He spoke abruptly. "Lily."

She stopped and turned to him, her eyebrows raised in question. "Yes, my lord." Her expression was cool, remote, and his throat tightened in spite of his resolve to keep from reacting to her opinion of him.

Without realizing that he was doing so, Tristan reached toward her. As his hand touched hers, he felt a rush of unexpected but overwhelming heat race through him.

As if she, too, had felt it, Lily started backward. Her wide gray eyes met his with unconcealed despair. "Please, Tristan, do not touch me. I cannot bear…"

She halted then as something, perhaps a slight sound, made Tristan looked upward over her head. Genevieve and Marcel stood there on the stairs a few feet above them. Genevieve's expression registered compassion and distress, Marcel's displeasure.

Following the direction of Tristan's gaze, Lily backed away from him slowly. Then, without another word, she spun around and hurried past Marcel and Genevieve, who made no effort to halt her.

Tristan met Genevieve's compassionate and troubled eyes with regret. He did not know what to say. At the same time he understood that she would not want to hear what he might say if he did.

With a groan of frustration, he went back down the stairs, taking the steps two at a time in his haste to remove himself from the keep. It was not until he was halfway across the courtyard that Tristan was halted abruptly by a restraining hand upon his arm. He spun around to see his brother Marcel standing there, his expression openly outraged.

The younger man wasted no time in getting to the point. "Tristan, what are you about? I thought it was only jesting, those remarks about you and Lily the day she arrived at Brackenmoore, but I am now beginning to wonder if there might indeed be truth in what the words implied."

Jerking away from him, Tristan met that angry gaze with strained patience. "You do not understand, Marcel. And I am not at liberty to explain."

Marcel's blue gaze hardened even further. "Not at liberty to explain? What could you say that would make any difference, that would make things aright, other than to assure me that Lily is not your leman? Surely you would not so dishonor Genevieve, who is your intended wife, by such behavior in her own home."

Taking a deep breath, Tristan met his brother's eyes with both anger and forbearance. "Lily is not my leman. Does that satisfy?" Without waiting for a reply, he started away again.

Again Marcel stopped him by putting an iron hand on his arm. "Nay, Brother. It does not satisfy."

Tristan did not waver as he met that gaze directly. "It is all that you will get, little brother. Now leave me be."

Marcel's jaw flexed but he said no more, simply releasing his older brother's arm. His stormy expression made it clear that he was not satisfied. Not in the least.

Tristan did not remain to encourage further debate, but strode away with purpose. Even as he made his way through the castle gates, he felt a sense of sorrow. He had never intended to cause a rift in his family. It was more painful than he would have imagined, realizing that he had done just that.

At this point the right thing to do would be to ask Lily to leave Brackenmoore before any more harm was done. Tristan knew in his heart he could not bring himself to do so.

His family would simply have to believe him. Lily was not his mistress and that was the way things would remain.

It was the way it had to be, no matter what their reactions to one another.

Lily awakened early the next morning as usual, though the memory of what had occurred the previous day came rushing in to leave her feeling anything but usual. She had managed to avoid seeing Genevieve since then, but she knew she could not do so indefinitely.

How would the young woman react to her when they did meet? Lily knew she would simply have to find out.

She readied Sabina for the day and took her down to the hall to break her fast. The little girl seemed to sense Lily's agitation, for she was far quieter and more subdued than was her wont.

As on the previous morning, Tristan was not present. Neither was Marcel. Quickly Lily tried to still the rush of relief she felt at not having them there. Their absence meant that she had only Genevieve to face with her guilt over what had occurred on the stairs.

Yet Lily soon realized that of the three, Genevieve would be the most difficult to face. It was she who had the most justification for anger toward her. Genevieve made it only more difficult when she met Lily's questioning gaze with a pitying one of her own as they arrived at the table.

Lily was shocked by this and even more perturbed with herself and Tristan. Yet she knew she was likely overreacting. Genevieve and Marcel had seen nothing more than a touch, overheard only a few hoarsely murmured words. Neither of them could possibly imagine the degree of sensation generated by the slight collision of flesh.

Given her attitude now, it was perhaps possible that Genevieve thought Tristan had been offering her comfort for some matter. Clearly Lily had fretted those long hours away for naught. She had been a fool to imagine the other woman's reaction would be all out of proportion to what had actually occurred.

With as much aplomb as possible, Lily seated herself at the table and carried on with the task of looking after her charge.

Benedict was the one to bring up the incident at the tower. He turned to Lily with a thoughtful expression. "My brother tells me that you helped him to care for Jack yesterday, that you may very well have helped to save his leg."

Lily blushed, looking down at her hands. "I do not think I can take so much credit. I did very little."

"Nonsense, you curbed the flow of blood from the wound. The doctor has stated that this was of great importance in a possible saving of the limb."

Lily felt her cheeks heat even more. "You need not thank me for doing what any decent person would do. How could I behave otherwise after your kindness to me?" As she finished speaking Lily realized just how true her own statement was. They had been kind to her—even Benedict, who knew of her real identity.

Genevieve spoke, drawing all eyes to her as she echoed Lily's own sentiment back to her. "We have done nothing beyond what any decent folk would." Her gaze held Lily's. "You have done us no harm and have a right to be treated fairly. You have, in fact, earned our respect in your conscientious care of little Sabina."

The child looked up upon hearing her name, and smiled around the piece of fresh white bread she was attempting to stuff into her mouth with a pudgy hand. Hearty laughter escaped the adults gathered at the table—all but Lily, though the others did not seem to note her failure to join in their mirth. She did her best to smile, while trying to still the throb of guilt she felt in her heart at Genevieve's praise.

When the conversation resumed there was no more talk of thanks, though they did go on to discuss the accident at the tower. Lily found herself answering in a subdued voice the questions posed to her. Although Benedict had said that Tristan had already related the tale to him, Genevieve and Kendran were curious to hear the story from someone who had actually been there.

Not for the first time, Lily found herself surprised at the way they listened to her, a mere servant. Even Benedict asked her opinion of the events as if it mattered, as if she was accepted into their circle.

The sensation was oddly welcome. Her own parents would be far more apt to ask any of the servants at Lakeland for confirmation on any matter than Lily. They treated her as a young child, seeming to feel that because she had lost her memory she had also lost her ability to reason.

Immediate horror followed the thought. Her parents were simply overprotective. Never would they deliberately slight her.

Having her own loving family, she had no need to be accepted by those at Brackenmoore.

If the others noticed that she was more reticent about adding to the conversation, they gave no opinion on it. As quickly as she could do so, Lily helped Sabina to finish her meal, leaving nearly all her own untouched.

It was as Lily stood, preparing to lead the girl away, that Genevieve halted her by saying, "I mean to take charge of Sabina this morn. I wish to take the child to my own chambers to have new garments fitted, as her rapid growth requires. You are therefore free to do as you will during the morning hours, Lily."

Lily bowed her head. "Yes, my lady." Doing her best to keep from feeling that she had been left out in some way, she made her way from the hall. She told herself that Genevieve was simply attempting to be considerate and give her some time to herself, something she'd had precious little of since arriving at Brackenmoore.

When she returned to Sabina's chambers, Lily realized that she did not wish to spend her free moments in the keep. Would it not suit her to be out on her own for a time, away from where she might have fear of meeting Tristan? Surely it might help to settle some of her constant confusion.

But where could she go? She knew no one. Walking anywhere about the castle grounds, Lily ran the risk of seeing Tristan even more than in the keep.

Perhaps she would take this opportunity to see how Jack, the master mason, was faring. She doubted that he would be well enough to see her himself, but she could at least ask after him. It would give her some purpose, and she was genuinely concerned for him, especially after spending time with his children.

Quickly Lily fetched her cloak and set off toward the village. She was approaching from a different direction than that of the previous day and thus must go through the town to get to Jack and Leena's home.

Because of her common garb little attention was paid her as she walked through the narrow streets of the village, which varied greatly from her experience at Lakeland. All there knew her as their overlord's daughter. There was something almost comforting in this new anonymity. At her home she had always felt lacking because of the fact that everyone knew she had lost her memory—that her mind was no longer whole.

Here Lily was able to look about freely as she passed neatly kept shops and residences. The folk she met along the way seemed content and prosperous, some of them nodding politely as she went by.

From the looks of things, Lily would imagine that Benedict was a kind and fair overlord. She could not help wondering what manner of overlord Tristan would be.

Lily had noted the way he had behaved yesterday. He had shown great care by seeing to the injured Jack himself, rather than delegating the responsibility to others. She felt he, too, would prove commendable in the position of master.

The man she married would have to conduct himself with just such wisdom and care. Lily was her father's only child, his heir. That was why he had chosen Maxim, who he had assured Lily was strong and dependable, to oversee his own lands. Her father was sure Maxim would manage Lily's inheritance well, with a competent hand.

Yet she felt that Maxim would also rule with a rigid grip. Her brief encounters with him had shown her that quality in the way he treated his retainers, seeming to prefer they adhere to a very strict code of behavior. She couldn't imagine Maxim telling a group of village children that they had no need to stand on ceremony with him. Or even his own children, for that matter.

She knew his would be quite unlike Tristan's more relaxed manner with Jack's offspring, or his open warmth and affection toward Sabina.

Determinedly she quickened her step, now looking neither right nor left as she went on, since everything she noticed seemed to bring thoughts of the man she least wished to think about. It was with some surprise that she glanced up only a short time later to see that she had reached her destination.

Her resolve to get to the cottage was what gave her the courage to walk right up to the door without hesitation. Her soft knock was rewarded a moment later.

One of the children, the girl of fifteen whom she had met yesterday, opened the narrow wooden door. "Good morning, Kyla," Lily said immediately.

The pretty blond girl was clearly surprised, but she smiled hesitantly. "Lily."

Lily felt suddenly shy. "I do not mean to disturb

you. I was simply wondering how your father is today. If you could just…?''

Before she could say another word, Leena appeared beside her daughter. ''Lily, how good you are to visit. Please, come in.'' She pulled the door open wider in welcome as she said, ''Lord Tristan is come as well.''

Lily froze as her gaze swung to Tristan, who sat on a chair next to the wooden table. Shock rippled through her in a wave that was equal parts apprehension and unexpected yearning. She had not thought to see him here, and her defenses were down.

Lily fought an overwhelming urge to run away from him and her own reactions to him. What would he think if she did that?

Besides, both Leena and her daughter were standing there beaming at her. Which, in other circumstances, might actually have been very gratifying. They thought of her as nothing more than a castle servant, who had rendered them a slight service the day before. In spite of her consternation at seeing Tristan, she could not help being moved by such a welcome.

Even as these thoughts passed through her mind, Tristan got to his feet. ''Good morrow, Lily.'' His voice betrayed nothing of his own feelings.

Lily nodded stiffly. ''Good morrow, my lord.''

Leena urged, ''Please, come in. You are most welcome in our home.''

There was nothing Lily could do but enter. As she did so she could feel the intensity of Tristan's gaze upon her.

Glancing about—anything was preferable to meeting Tristan Ainsworth's compelling blue eyes—Lily saw that the interior was as tidy as the outside of the

home. The main chamber contained the fire and the
eating area. Numerous chests and benches rimmed the
outer wall. Lily knew these had been built for the
family to store their belongings, as well as for seating.

A curtain at the far end of the room had been drawn
back to reveal a bed. Lily could see Jack lying beneath the coverlet. He seemed quiet enough, and she
sent up a quick prayer of thanks that he was not suffering too greatly.

With barely suppressed energy Leena moved toward the table, drawing Lily's attention as she said,
"I have warm mead if you have thirst, my…" She
laughed as she halted herself in the act of speaking.
"I nearly called you 'my lady.' Is that not whimsical?" She shrugged. "You just seem so ladylike for
a maid, Lily."

Of its own accord, Lily's gaze flew to Tristan. He
spoke easily, even as he glanced at Lily with silent
warning. "Lily spent some of her childhood in a noble household."

Leena seemed to accept this without question.
"That would explain it." She turned to Lily, holding
up an earthenware jug. "The mead?"

Lily nodded as she moved to the table. She needed
something to do with her trembling hands. She had
thought herself so adept at playing her part. Was their
ruse so transparent that this woman could notice so
quickly that something was amiss? Lily did not know
what she would do if they were found out. The more
people who knew, the more likely that Maxim would
eventually learn that she had been here. Casting a
surreptitious glance toward Tristan, she saw that he
was seated again and looking very relaxed and sure
of himself.

In that moment Lily resented him for being so cool, especially when she was the precise opposite.

"A cup, please, daughter," Leena directed, and Kyla hurried to the shelf. She quickly brought a cup, which her mother filled and put on the table across from Tristan. Lily perched on the edge of the bench and placed her hands around the cup. Its warmth did little to relieve the chill in her icy fingers.

Leena seemed not to notice her unease as she spoke. "The doctor has come and gone this morn. He gave Jack something to help him to sleep." Lily could sense the concern for her husband behind the woman's hospitable demeanor. "He said it would be best that he sleep as much as possible until the worst of the pain has passed."

That explained why he appeared so quiet. Lily asked softly, "Has he been in a great deal of pain?"

Leena nodded, her face growing solemn. "He was in a bad state last night after the setting of that leg. If the doctor hadn't left some of that sleeping potion I don't know what I would have done. I sent the other children off to my brother this morning so it would be quiet in the cottage. I kept only Kyla at home in case I had need to send for…someone." She stopped abruptly, obviously not liking the implication of what having to send for someone might mean.

Leena looked up at Tristan then, smiling too brightly. "I never expected Lord Tristan to turn up again after all his kindness of yesterday. And the news he's brought! What a relief to know we need have no worry about the future." She blinked back grateful tears as she gazed at Tristan.

Kyla put a comforting hand on her mother's shoulder. "His lordship has brought Mother the deed to a small farm near the village. The doctor says Father will not lose his leg, but he will not be able to walk again. With land of our own to grow a crop we will do very well.''

Lily turned to study Tristan, surprised to see just how uncomfortable he appeared at their praise. He practically squirmed in his seat.

Lily realized that Tristan had acted quickly indeed if he had already been to his brother and arranged to have this done. Again, though she did not wish for it to happen, she felt a warm softness in her breast at his kindness.

But she did not want him to know this. She looked at Leena. ''I am very happy for you all.''

Leena was still smiling at Tristan. ''The Ainsworths have ever been ones to act with fairness toward the village folk. My lord Tristan, and Lord Benedict, of course, have continued in that order.''

Tristan spoke up. ''There is no need to be so grateful, Leena. The accident was no fault of Jack's. How could I do other than feel responsible for his wellbeing? As overlord, Benedict was in complete agreement with my suggestion. He also agreed that we must try to prevent such a thing from occurring in future.'' He shook his head thoughtfully. ''The ground was very slippery and may continue to be a problem at the signal tower, especially when the weather worsens.''

Lily frowned, his words making her think of something that hadn't occurred to her yesterday because of her distress over the accident. Hesitantly, not knowing how her opinion would be taken, she said, ''I do not wish to offer aid where none is needed or welcome, but I just recalled something.''

There was no hint of censure in Tristan's tone as he replied, "Feel free to speak your mind, Lily."

She shifted in her seat, uncomfortable with offering her suggestion in spite of his invitation. When his blue eyes seemed to do nothing but encourage her, she knew she must go on. "I was thinking that at home in my father's gardens, the walkways can be very slippery when it is quite cold. But the ones made from small pebbles do not seem to become so as quickly. I was wondering, would it be possible to cover the ground at the base of the signal tower with pebbles?" She halted abruptly, feeling no less unsure of herself now that the words were said.

As she spoke, a pensive frown had creased Tristan's brow, and now he said, "Very interesting." He fell into a thoughtful silence.

Lily continued to feel unsure of herself as she studied him. Finally he nodded. "That might very well help, Lily. The stones that are left over from the actual building of the signal tower could be broken up into smaller pieces and spread around the area. Even if they settled into the ground after a time they would help." He smiled at her then. "What a fine idea you have had."

Lily could not stop the rush of satisfaction and happiness his praise brought. She looked down at her hands to hide the heat of exhilaration that rose in her cheeks.

Something, some inner sense, made her look up into the eyes of Leena. The woman was studying her with no small amount of interest.

Hurriedly, Lily tried to think of what she might have done to bring about such inquisitiveness. Could it be her reaction to Tristan's praise? She thought not, for the woman was not looking at him. Lily reconsidered all she had said, and as she did so knew a sinking sensation in the pit of her stomach.

She had spoken of gardens—her father's gardens. It was unlikely that the father of a servant, as Lily professed to be, would refer to the gardens as his own. Lily realized that she had made a terrible error in speaking that way. Yet she was saved from having to think of how to explain the slip when a soft moan came from the direction of the bed.

Immediately Leena rose and went to her husband's aid. Tristan followed her.

Lily took the opportunity to stand and say, "I really must be getting back to the keep now." All she wanted was to be away. Even though she knew it was not meant in malice, she could not escape the presence of all-hearing ears and all-seeing eyes, even here.

Kyla stood, too. "You need not go."

Lily did not meet that artless gaze. "Oh, really, I must. Your mother is very occupied with your father and I am expected back at the castle," she assured Kyla earnestly.

Kyla nodded. "You have our thanks for coming."

"And you mine for your hospitality," Lily answered. She held her breath as she followed Kyla to the door and made her exit.

Lily was nearly to the roadway when she heard Tristan call her name. She paused, biting her lip, not wanting to talk to him, to see him, to feel the way she did when he looked into her eyes.

Yet as she listened to his approach, Lily knew she could not remain standing here with her back to him. What would he think of such a thing? Slowly she swung around, focusing her attention on the silver chain that fastened his dark blue, fur-lined cloak. "My lord."

He replied with gentle admonition. "There is no need to stand on ceremony, Lily. We are alone."

She glanced at his face and away, but not before she saw the uncertainty in those handsome features. She wondered at it even as she answered, "I do not wish to forget again, my lord Tristan. It is best to remember my professed position at all times. You heard what just happened inside. Leena will be wondering about me now. I would think that you would not want to draw attention to us—me—especially after what happened yesterday."

For a moment there seemed a hint of bitterness in his tone as he said, "I do not believe you will ever allow yourself to forget your assumed position here, Lily. And as far as what happened yesterday, what has it to do with anything?"

She could hardly believe her ears. "What has it to do with anything? Why, you were caught attempting to force yourself upon me by your very own intended bride."

His eyes narrowed to mere slits. "Force myself upon you, Lily? Both of us know that was not what happened. Not once have I had to force myself upon you. You have come to me each and every time by your own will. And if you permit me to say it, quite enthusiastically."

He caught the blow she aimed at him before it landed, his large fist engulfing hers. Her eyes burned with outrage, which was even hotter at the knowledge that he spoke the truth. Yet she could not admit that. "It was not I who laid hands upon you. It is only because of her own generous nature that Genevieve does not guess at the extent of what she saw."

Tristan dropped her hand and his gaze. "Dear God, you speak truly of Genevieve." He looked at her then, his eyes dark with sadness. "You must realize that I intended no wrong. I but wished to speak of my gratitude for what you did for Jack." He took a deep breath and let it out slowly before adding, "Why can we not find a moment of peace between us, Lily?"

She looked at him for a long heartbeat, her own chest aching at the painful reality of their circumstances. "Perhaps our...association would have turned out this way in the end anyway, Tristan. Perhaps fate stepped in to favor us in tearing us apart."

The degree of shock that registered on his strong features rocked her to the very core. When he spoke she had to strain to hear the words. "You may tell yourself that, Lily. The fact that you would even utter such a lie is proof to me of how greatly you have changed." His gaze burned into her, scorching her. "Yet neither you nor anyone else will rob me of the love that we once shared. That you do not remember it is a thought so indescribably shattering to me that I ache with pity for you. My hope of your eventually recalling even the memory of it, for your own sake, is all that keeps me from sending you away."

Lily stood then, struck silent as he stalked off. Even if she could risk creating a scene by calling him back, she would not have done so.

The degree of his fury showed that she had gone too far already. And all in aid of doing nothing more than protecting her own battered feelings from possible hurt by him.

Chapter Nine

Lily spent a long and sleepless night.

On one hand she did not care if she never saw Tristan again. On the other hand she knew that she was as much to blame as he for the things that had been said between them the previous day.

It was not surprising that Tristan had become so very angry over her accusing him of forcing his attention on her. Her insecurity had made her say such a thing. Tristan had done many things to enrage her, not the least of which was kidnap her, but he had never actually forced himself upon her.

She had been an all-too-willing participant in each incident. Perhaps for that very reason she should go from Brackenmoore. She kept telling herself that she was not yet ready, but was she perhaps only delaying the inevitable? And for what purpose?

All along she had thought she could somehow make sense of her feelings. She had gained nothing, felt further from understanding than she had ever been. The question was, could she bring herself to leave now, ignore the still-compelling need to stay?

Morning found her no closer to making a decision. She told herself that she was simply too tired.

After the meal she took Sabina out for a walk, but not for long. The child seemed listless, and there was a sharp chill in the air.

They spent the rest of the morning in her chambers, where Sabina played beside the hearth with her toys, though even they did not hold her attention as usual. Not long before the noon meal she curled up on Lily's lap and fell asleep.

Not wanting to wake her when she seemed so tired, Lily did not go down to the hall as the appointed hour came. When Genevieve, as beautifully garbed as ever in rich satin, opened the chamber door a short time later, Lily looked up from stroking the child's head and gave a hesitant nod. "My lady."

Genevieve's gaze was fixed on her hand as it stroked that dark head. There was an expression of resignation in her green eyes, tinged with something that Lily could only call sadness. Genevieve took in a deep breath as she looked up and met Lily's gaze. "Is there aught the matter with Sabina?"

Lily shook her head, speaking softly. "I do not know. She just seems a bit tired this day. I did not wish to waken her until she had rested. I realize I should have sent someone to beg your leave to allow her to sleep through the meal."

Genevieve shook her own head. When she spoke there was no hint in her voice that she held any resentment toward Lily for not gaining her permission. "Do not worry on that score. You are in charge of her care. I simply came to see if all was well. Tristan has gone away from Brackenmoore for the day or he would have come himself. He is ever the one to see to the child's welfare. He has only been less occupied with her since your arrival. No doubt it is because he is very busy with completing the tower. I am certain you will have more direct contact with him when that is done.''

Lily felt herself cringe inside. She had no need to see more of Tristan. She replied in that vein. ''I am content with things as they are, my lady. I but wish to care for the child in the best way I can.''

Genevieve simply looked at Lily and Sabina for a long moment. ''You have the child's best wishes at heart, of that I am certain.''

Again Lily was assaulted by guilt at the way she had betrayed this woman with Tristan. What would Genevieve say if she knew all that had happened between them? Lily could not imagine the degree of hurt she would feel if Tristan were her intended husband.

Lily looked directly into those searching green eyes. ''I mean no harm to anyone here, my lady.''

Genevieve returned the look. ''I know that, Lily. Things would be completely different were it otherwise, wouldn't they?''

The woman's directness shocked Lily into silence, and she glanced down to collect her thoughts. The statement seemed to imply that Genevieve knew Lily was here for some reason other than what had been stated, but that she understood Lily was only doing what she must.

Lily took a deep breath. Surely Tristan's fiancée did not mean all that Lily had read into her words. She could not, else why would she allow Lily to remain at Brackenmoore?

Taking another breath to gather her courage, Lily raised her head. Genevieve was already gone.

Lily was not sure if her leaving without explaining herself further was a blessing or a curse. The questions boiling inside her had not been answered.

Yet perhaps they should not be.

Sabina continued to be listless throughout the day. Someone, obviously Genevieve, had had a tray sent to Sabina's chambers not long after she had visited. It held more than enough for two, but neither Lily nor the child had eaten more than a few bites.

At the dinner hour there was no change in Sabina's condition. Genevieve came to the room again and asked after the young one, who was this time awake, precluding any but polite conversation. When Sabina asked for her father she was told that Tristan had not yet returned to the castle, but that he was due home that very night.

When the child fretted about this Genevieve seemed to grow slightly more concerned, for it was unlike Sabina to do so. She held the little one for a time, but like Lily, she could find no clue as to the problem. In the end they decided that Sabina must just be overtired. She had stood for some time having her new gowns made the previous day.

That night Lily woke to the sound of deep ragged breathing coming from the child's bed.

She ran over to check on her charge. The fire had died down in the grate and the room was only dimly lit, so Lily had to strain to make out Sabina's face. She appeared flushed in the gloom. Even as Lily watched, the child tossed restlessly beneath the covers.

Lily reached out to smooth the hair back from the little one's brow and realized that her face felt unusually hot. Whatever malady had been lingering in her the whole day had finally come to the fore.

Now what was she to do? Lily had no experience with illness in children. She was not sure what action to take. She had no notion how serious this illness might be, thus making the idea of waiting until morning unthinkable.

Yet whom should she call for aid? Not Genevieve—not after what she had said that morning. It would be too difficult to face her alone with the intimacy of night pressing around them.

Sabina tossed restlessly, murmuring, "Da."

Lily knew what she had to do. The child wanted her father. No matter how difficult it might be to face him, Lily had to fetch Tristan. He would know what to do, of that she was certain.

Though she had never been there, Lily knew that Tristan's chamber was at the far end of the hall. Sabina had pointed it out to her nearly every time they passed by.

Without giving herself time to consider her actions, Lily went to the chest and pulled on her cape over the sheer nightdress she had worn the night Tristan abducted her. She had no other bed robe. Quickly she lit a candle and hurried from the bedchamber.

The candle cast little illumination in the darkened hallway, but Lily knew where she was going. She had found herself more aware of the door to Tristan's chamber than any other in the castle.

Yet when she arrived before that well-known oaken

panel, Lily hesitated. Should she knock upon it? Should she simply go in?

She scowled in indecision.

She glanced about the hall, as if doing so would somehow help her solve her dilemma. The castle was still as a midnight sky.

Surely if she knocked loudly enough to wake a sleeping man, Lily risked waking not only Tristan but the whole household. She could not face the thought of what she would see in Genevieve's eyes if she were discovered standing here outside the door to Tristan's chamber in the dead of night.

It would be especially uncomfortable after their strange exchange of the morning. The fact that her presence could quickly and reasonably be explained would not prevent those initial moments from being too incredibly painful for them both.

With the thought of that impossible scenario riding hard on her heels, Lily turned the handle and held her breath as the door swung open. Quickly she stepped inside and closed it after herself.

She hesitated, her heart pounding as she pressed her back against the solid surface of the door. The room was very dark, the furnishings no more than hulking shadows in the gloom, as the coals had nearly died out in the hearth. The thought of waking Tristan made her swallow around the dryness in her throat.

That was why she had come here and that was what she had to do. Keeping in mind the fact that Sabina needed him, Lily moved toward the bed. The candle-light fell in a golden circle around her, shedding its glow upon first the edge of a thick carpet, then a table piled with books and scrolls, then an open chest. And finally a bed. It was a huge piece of furniture, with heavy hangings pulled shut against the chill of night.

Taking a deep breath, Lily moved forward and put her hand upon the heavy brocade hanging. Taking another deep breath, she closed her fingers around the edge and jerked it back before her courage could completely fail her.

Before she could even say a word, Tristan rolled toward her, his blue eyes alert in the darkness.

Lily dared not even attempt to read the array of emotions that raced across his expressive face as he saw her there. Quickly she blurted, "It is Sabina. She has fallen ill."

"Sabina!" Shock showed in both his face and tone. He had thrown back the covers and reached for his clothing from the chest at the foot of the bed before she could say another word.

Lily did all she could to ignore the way the light of the candle shone on the smooth skin of his lean flanks as he pulled on his leggings. She wanted to turn away when he reached up to drag his tunic over his head and the light danced on the hard muscles of his chest and arms.

When he swung around to face her, fully dressed, it was some seconds before Lily was able to find her tongue. It was Tristan who spoke. "Have you sent for Genevieve?"

She shook her head to clear it of the images that made her breath quicken, as well as in denial. "I have not. Sabina asked for you and it was to you I came. I did not know what else to do."

He strode toward the door, forcing her to run after him. "We must go to her."

She hurried along behind him. Tristan appeared not

to need the light from the candle to find his way. His path was lit by worry and love for his daughter.

When they reached Sabina's chambers, Tristan went to the bed and bent over her, his eyes shadowed with concern. Lily moved to stand beside him, watching as he smoothed her brow in the same manner that she had done earlier. His large hands were so strong yet gentle.

As he touched her, Sabina opened her eyes. "Da."

He leaned over her, kissing her forehead. "Sweetness."

She looked around them, saying petulantly, "Why are you here in the night?" Obviously she had been only partially aroused from her sleep earlier and remembered nothing of asking for him.

He smiled tenderly. "I am here because Lily came to tell me that you are not well. You do feel warm to the touch, love. Do you have any pain?"

Sabina looked to where Lily stood beside her father. "My throat feels bad and my nose is closed." She rubbed a chubby hand over her throat.

Tristan reached out and lifted her into his arms. He then went to the chair where Lily had sat with her earlier in the day. "Nothing else, sweeting? You are sure there is no other pain?"

She shook her head. "No. I not hurt anywhere else." From where she leaned against her father's chest, she looked over at Lily. "You and Lily not worry."

"We aren't going to worry, moppet. You just rest here and Lily and I will make you feel better, all right?"

Sabina nodded.

Tristan looked at Lily and found her eyes round

and silver as twin moons in the candlelight. Comprehending how distressed she was, he spoke evenly and gently. "It seems the child has caught a chill. I do not believe there is any real threat. We need only nurse her through it."

She rubbed her hand over the edge of her cape nervously. "What shall we do then?"

He indicated the candle she still held in her hand. "You may light more candles." She moved to do so even as he added, "Then I would like for you to get a clean cloth and a bowl of water."

She turned from lighting the candles. "Should I awaken someone else?"

Tristan shook his head. "There is no point at the moment. They can do no more than we two."

Lily nodded determinedly. Now that he had given her something to do she seemed less frightened, and moved of her own accord to put more wood on the fire.

Tristan had not requested this, and he was grateful to see it. It meant that Lily was beginning to think more clearly again. The child must certainly be kept warm.

He smiled, albeit stiffly due to his concern for Sabina. Together they would do very well here.

Tristan continued to watch Lily as she scurried to fulfill his other requests. He realized that she must have had little experience with childhood illnesses. The last three years had taught him much about such things. Seeing Sabina and talking with her had allayed much of his own fear, although he was willing to admit that his apprehension was not completely gone. He realized that children simply fell prey to these sorts of ailments and could as quickly recover from them with no lasting harm.

In deference to the fact that Lily very likely did not know this, he said, ''Sabina has had such illnesses before and recovered quite well, sometimes by the next morn. It is thus with children.''

She turned to him, smiling hopefully, and he felt his heart swell with reaction to her vulnerability and anxiety for his—their child. ''Truly?''

Inexplicably, he felt an overwhelming desire to reach out and comfort her, but Sabina's soft weight in his lap reminded him that this would be a mistake. Had he not already risked his daughter's future enough because he could not keep his hands from Lily?

All the day long her words had haunted him. He had thought of nothing else as he had ridden out to help repair the wagon that was bringing the polished metal shield for the signal tower. He had thought of nothing else as he sweated to help lift the wagon for its new wheel. He had thought of nothing else as they made the journey to Brackenmoore, even though the arrival of the shield meant that the project he had worked so diligently to complete would soon be finished.

All that mattered was that he had told Lily he wished he could send her away. In the deepest, darkest part of his soul, Tristan knew that this could not be further from the truth.

He told himself it was because he was certain she was close to the truth, that it was only her own fear that kept her from remembering all now. Kept her from recovering her past and thus herself. He suspected that she had accused him of force because she was as upset at the thought of hurting Genevieve as he was.

But to tell her he knew what she was going through would serve neither of them. The fact that their physical reaction to one another kept getting in the way of any true understanding between them was all too obvious.

Instead Tristan pulled his scattered emotions about him. He spoke with what he hoped was assurance as he watched her pour water from the pitcher on the table into the washing bowl. "Aye, truly, Lily. I know what must be done. Bring the cloth and the water, and you shall see how quickly she is made better."

Lily brought the items promptly. "The water is cool as you asked."

While she stood before him in that quietly elegant way she had, Tristan recalled how very surprised he had been to find her bent over his bed not so very many minutes gone by. He could not admit to the anticipation and gladness seeing her there had awakened in him. That those feelings had immediately been replaced by his fear and concern for Sabina did not completely erase them from his mind.

What would he have done had Lily been there for the reasons he had first supposed? Would he have found the courage to deny them both?

That was a question Tristan could not answer. He hoped not to find himself in a situation where he must do so.

He reached out and took the cloth from her hand, making sure not to touch her. It was no small irritation to him when he saw that his hand was trembling.

He concentrated on Sabina, dipping the cloth into the bowl, then wringing most of the water from it. He

could feel Lily's close attention as he smoothed the
cloth over Sabina's heated brow. The child sighed as
if the coolness was comforting to her.

All the while, Tristan's attention was on Lily and
the length of scantily clad leg exposed by the cape,
which had become parted during her activities. Tristan felt sweat break out on his upper lip and wished
that he could wipe it away with the cloth.

He could not, not without giving away far more
than he wanted to.

Irritation with himself made his voice unexpectedly
rough as he said, "Fetch the table over here to set the
bowl upon. There is no need for you to stand there
and hold it."

He felt her stiffen, but she said nothing as she went
to get the table. When she returned he could still feel
the rigidity in her body and knew that he could not
blame her for reacting thus. She had done nothing to
cause his frustration—other than be Lily.

Pausing, he looked up at her and said, "Forgive
me. I did not mean to speak so harshly."

She looked at him closely, her eyes becoming soft
with sympathy. "You are forgiven. I understand that
you are worried. The matter is already forgotten."

His gaze shied from hers. What she said erred too
kindly in his favor. Yet he could not admit the truth
of his thoughts about her. He reminded himself that
it would serve neither of them to do so.

He dipped the cloth back into the bowl, which now
rested upon the table. He continued to minister to his
daughter, hoping against all hope that concentrating
hard enough on the task would make him forget how
very much he was aware of the woman who stood by
them.

The minutes passed and the child's skin began to cool. It was not until Lily spoke up, saying, "I believe she is resting comfortably now," that he realized it was indeed true.

Sabina was breathing much more easily and seemed to have fallen into a peaceful sleep.

Tristan dropped the cloth into the bowl and sat back with a sigh of sweet relief. In spite of his preoccupation with Lily and his assurance to her that all would be well, he had been concerned for Sabina. She was the focus of his life—his very reason for living. Even her smallest discomfort was of the utmost import to him.

Lily was relieved that they had managed to get through this crisis without having to discuss that last painful scene between them, nor anything else of an uncomfortable nature. Her voice was filled with relief at this, and at the fact that Sabina's state seemed to have improved greatly. She spoke softly to Tristan, not wanting to awaken the babe. "Do you wish to put her back into bed now?"

Tristan looked up at her with his blue eyes so filled with love for his child that it made her own chest ache for something she could not dare name. She did her best to concentrate as he said, "Aye, I think she will rest better in bed."

Giving herself something to do besides stand there staring at Tristan, Lily hurriedly moved to smooth out the covers. She heard him rise and come across the floor toward her. It was impossible for her to look directly at him. All the feelings she was trying so diligently to put aside had come racing to the fore.

Tristan's tenderness toward Sabina moved Lily far

more even than the passion that erupted so easily between them. He was such a good and loving father.
He could have sent for Genevieve or any of the other
castle women. He had not done that, but had set himself the task of tending to his sick child.

Lily watched as he gently laid the babe on the bed,
his face betraying the strain he had been under. Even
though he had done his best to allay any fear that Lily
might be having, he had been very worried.

Lily knew in that moment that she had deep feelings for this man. She realized that even if she had
not cared deeply for him when they had known each
other before, living in such close proximity with him,
seeing the way he treated others had made it so now.

She blinked back tears of sadness that things could
not have been different.

At that moment Tristan turned toward her. Lily
looked down, attempting to hide her tears from him.

But he would not allow her that. He reached out,
lifting her chin with his strong but gentle fingers.
"What is it?" She shook her head, her gaze coming
to rest upon the sleeping child. He saw this, obviously
reaching the wrong conclusion, for he said, "There is
no need to be so frightened. She will be fine, of that
I can assure you. But I will say that your concern
does you credit. It tells me that you have come to
love her in spite of everything else."

Lily knew it was not right to allow him to believe
that this was the cause of her sadness. Yet it was true
that she did love the child, and that made it easy for
her to say, "Yes, I do love her, more than I ever
thought I could."

He spoke in a rush. "Lily, there is something I
have to tell you. I am so very sorry for what I said

to you yesterday. I would never ever ask you to leave Brackenmoore.''

Lily blinked back the tears that threatened to spill forth. ''I know that, Tristan. I do believe that you allowed me to come here out of nothing more than simple human kindness. Knowing you…'' She halted, averting her gaze when she realized that she had been about to say more than she wished to. ''Knowing Sabina has been worth all the possible upheaval that may arise from my coming here.''

He looked at her closely, his brow furrowed, then seemed to come to some decision inside himself. He took a deep breath and said, ''Have you thought about—considered staying on here at Brackenmoore?''

She stared at him, aghast. ''Have I thought of staying? Are you mad? How could I even contemplate such a crazed thought? What would possibly lead you to ask?''

He frowned, his eyebrows meeting over his suddenly disapproving blue eyes. ''Why is it so very crazed an idea? You love Sabina. She loves you. Even if you are not completely certain of your relationship with me, you will miss her if you leave. Do not attempt to convince me that you will not.''

''You want me to stay on here as her maid then?'' Lily could hardly credit that they were having this conversation.

Tristan's frown deepened. ''I…it is within my power to make your situation here more comfortable. Is it not true that you have already been treated well by my family and myself? I have told the story that you were raised in a noble household. I would simply make it clearer that you are the daughter of a knight or such. I could see to it that you were afforded every courtesy that position would allow.''

She looked at the floor. ''Tristan, even if I could put aside the responsibility I have toward my family, you do not realize how I feel.'' She raised her head, pleading with him to understand, to see. ''Genevieve has been nothing but good to me since my coming here. How can I continue to allow her to believe a lie?'' She blushed but made herself go on. ''Especially knowing what has passed between you and me?''

He blanched. ''But we have conquered that. It will be no more.''

Perhaps you have, Lily replied silently. Aloud she said only, ''And of my own intended husband, Maxim, and my promises to him?''

Tristan took a step closer to her, his face showing displeasure at the name. ''Promises you have made to a man who is completely undeserving of them. You know what he is.''

She took a deep breath and let it out slowly. ''We have been over this ground before. I know what I have been told. I would think that you would see that I cannot simply judge him ill in that way. I do not believe Genevieve would lie. She is a good woman, kind and generous, but she was very young. I have heard from her own lips that she wished to be here at Brackenmoore and those she felt close to. Could her desire to be here with you all not have colored her thinking about something that could have been meant in all innocence?'' Lily halted, realizing that she of all people would understand that sentiment. Did her own inner desire to stay here at Bracken-moore not cloud her thinking, make her wish for things that could not be? She could not tell Tristan just how tempting his suggestion was.

When she raised her gaze he was shaking his head, his expression cold. "You choose to see things only as they will please you, Lily."

Unable to face him for another moment, Lily turned her back on his all-too-compelling presence. He could not be further from the truth. She chose to see the situation as it must be for fear of giving in to the dishonorable desires of her own heart. She must do what was right here. She could not allow herself to ruin so many lives.

She continued to feel him there behind her, the sheer force of his will. Yet she would not turn around—could not.

Lily knew there was only one way to end all of this suffering, and she had to tell him now, before she lost the courage to do so. She swung around to face him. "Tristan, I have realized that I can no longer remain at Brackenmoore. I must return to my life. I have gained nothing for myself or anyone else by being here. With your aid I will send a message to my father at Lakeland. I will instruct him to come for me himself. By being discreet we may well salvage his plans for my wedding to Maxim."

Tristan's face mirrored shock for a long moment, then he raised those dark eyebrows, his expression sardonic. "When you have your letter ready, I will see that it is sent."

Lily nodded, staring down at her clasped hands. "You have my thanks."

She did not look up until he was gone. She could not, for fear of his seeing the tears that she could no longer hide.

Chapter Ten

"Lily."

Lily heard her own name as if coming from a very long distance.

"Lily?" The voice came again.

She struggled up from the depths of sleep, opening one eye with the greatest of efforts. And saw Sabina's tiny face bending over hers.

Sabina smiled and spoke over her shoulder excitedly. "She is awake." She turned back to Lily. "Uncle Kendran wishes to take me down to the hall." She pointed behind her.

Lily sat up, her eyes trying to track the path indicated by that chubby finger. As she did so, her gaze came to rest on the face of a widely smiling Kendran Ainsworth. Pulling the blanket up to cover herself to the chin, Lily leaped from the bed. "Forgive me, my lord, I did not mean to remain abed so long."

Kendran shrugged. "Have no care for that. I went to speak to Tristan earlier, and he told me that the two of you had been up with our girl for most of the night. I just came to see how she was. She told me that she had awakened with a desire to break her fast, but she did not want to wake the sleeping princess.''

Lily blushed. ''Sabina, I am no princess and you need have no concern about waking me. It is my duty.''

Kendran reached out and said, ''Come, sweet.'' Sabina ran to him and he scooped her up in his arms. He then looked at Lily with an expression that brooked no argument. ''Forget your duty for a few hours. You have no need to concern yourself about anything this morning, Lily. I only told the child to wake you so that you would not worry in the event of rising to find her gone.''

With that he turned and strode from the room. A speechless Lily was left with the impression that though he was young, Kendran certainly showed signs of growing to be as autocratic as his elder brothers.

She tried to be charitable by telling herself that he had meant well.

Yet his effort seemed wasted, for Lily certainly could not sleep now. She dropped the cover on the bed and went to the chest where she kept the three gowns and other items of clothing that Genevieve had given her. Quickly she dressed in the blue gown with the lighter blue underdress.

It was then that she realized she had nothing to do. She could of course write the letter to her father, but that would mean asking Tristan for writing materials. And even if she had wished to speak with him, she felt strangely reluctant to send that message.

She told herself that she could easily write it later in the day.

That decision did not solve her problem. Lily had

grown accustomed to looking after Sabina, actually enjoyed doing so. Now that she had made the decision to leave Brackenmoore, the remaining moments she had with the little one seemed all the more precious.

But she could not go down to the meal. Kendran had acted out of kindness and concern for her. That was not a gift one took for granted.

With a sigh, Lily looked about the chamber. At least she could tidy the bed and the clothing Sabina and her uncle had scattered about as they readied her for breakfast. Lily tried not to think about how foolish she felt to have slept through the whole procedure.

She was just putting away the last of the tiny garments when the door opened. It was Maeve. She held a tray in her hands. "Lord Kendran bade me bring you food. He told me you had been up in the night with the babe."

The kindness in the woman's face was moving. First Kendran and now Maeve. Lily had been quite unused to this sort of thing before coming to Brackenmoore. Her parents had looked after her, but that had been due to her own illness and subsequent helplessness. No one had ever behaved as if they owed her gratitude for her efforts. Her mother and the other serving woman took care of all that needed doing at Lakeland.

It felt good to know that she had done something that mattered. That she, Lily, had been of use.

She knew she would hold these memories close to her heart. It would not be long before she would be gone from here.

Lily tried to convince herself that she might find such acceptance at Maxim's keep. A nagging feeling of sadness told her that was not likely to be the case.

The Earl of Harcourt seemed one who might wish to receive all merit for what went on in his own holdings.

Rousing herself to smile at the head woman, who was still waiting, Lily said, "Thank you very much, Maeve. This is very kind of you."

The older woman came forward, then turned from setting the tray on the table. "Nonsense. 'Tis not so very kind, not any more than your care of the child during the night, nor your care of master mason Jack, who is a cousin to me. We all look after one another here at Brackenmoore. It has always been that way and always will be. You will soon come to understand that."

Lily only nodded; she saw no purpose in telling the woman that she had already learned that lesson but would not be here to enjoy the fruits of it. She said simply, "Nonetheless, you have my thanks and gratitude for your kindness to me."

Maeve shrugged and turned to go, then paused and looked at Lily for a long moment. Finally she said, "What's done is done. No one can change the past. It is now that matters and now that anyone should be judged by."

Lily could think of absolutely nothing to say to this odd pronouncement. She could not allow herself to grow too attached to these folk. She was going home. *Home.* The word felt strange.

Quickly she summoned up her courage and said, "Maeve, would it be possible for me to have the materials to write a letter?"

The head woman shrugged. "Of course." Her gaze was decidedly curious as it raked Lily, but she said only, "I will have them brought here to you."

Lily was saved from feeling that she must explain herself further by Maeve's unceremonious departure.

Yet when the woman was gone she could not help wondering what she could have meant by talking about living in the present. It was almost as if she suspected... But no, 'twas not possible.

First Lily had conjectured that Genevieve knew more than she could, and now Maeve. Surely Tristan and she had been very careful in keeping their secret.

Going to the table upon which the woman had placed the tray, Lily forced herself to eat some of the bread and cheese, drink some of the mead. It was the least she could do after Maeve's troubling to bring it.

Lily found she had little more appetite than in the past days. Too much had happened of late, not the least of which was her decision to leave. She had told Tristan she was ready to do so, but the notion held even less appeal than last night when she had made the pronouncement.

When a servant came to open her door some time later, writing materials in hand, Lily pushed the food aside with a heavy sigh. She knew what had to be done and would do it.

It was some time later that Genevieve herself appeared in the doorway of Sabina's chamber.

Lily was fully conscious of the completed letter to her father. It was safely tucked beneath her pillow in preparation of the time when she would see Tristan again. Seeing the other woman made her even more certain that she was doing the right thing in sending it.

Lily moved from the window, where she had been looking out on the grayness of the day without actually seeing it. "Would you like me to go to Sabina?"

Genevieve shook her head. "Nay, do not worry. You are to have the morning to yourself. Tristan has ordered it by way of Kendran. Sabina is fine. She is playing with her uncles in the hall."

Lily was still amazed by this drastic change in the child's condition. "But she was so ill last night."

Genevieve watched her closely. "And is feeling quite herself this morn. That is the way with children, Lily. They become ill quickly and recover with a speed that is shocking at times."

Lily looked at the floor. It was the same thing that Tristan had told her in the night. Genevieve must certainly wonder why she would not know this if she was accustomed to caring for children, which Tristan had certainly implied when he brought her here. It also served to illustrate the younger woman's fitness to act as Sabina's mother.

Genevieve drew Lily's attention back to her as she indicated the things she carried in her arms. "The laundress has cleaned some of Sabina's clothes. I wanted to put them away."

"I can see to that."

Genevieve shook her head, offering too bright a smile as she crossed the room to the chest at the end of the bed. "I will do so. It is only a moment's work, and you have spent a restless night with Sabina being ill." She knelt before the chest.

As she laid the tiny garments inside, Lily watched closely, agitatedly pleating the skirt of her blue gown with her fingers. Something in the other woman's manner alerted her that all was not well.

"I do appreciate the concern you have all shown me, but you need not be so careful of me. I am fine," Lily insisted.

Genevieve gave another one of those overbright smiles and continued what she was doing.

There was no mistake. She seemed quite unlike herself this day. Guilt stabbed at Lily anew. Could it be the fact that Tristan and Lily had looked after the child alone together that troubled her?

Thinking to alleviate the other woman's distress, Lily spoke up without even considering anything besides giving comfort. "Genevieve." She bit her lip, realizing that she had slipped in addressing the other woman in too familiar a manner for a servant. She recovered quickly. "My lady, there is something that you should know."

Genevieve turned to her sharply, seemingly oblivious to Lily's error. "Yes, Lily?"

She hurried on. "I want you to know I will be leaving Brackenmoore soon." Surely her father would not delay long in answering her request for him to come for her.

The young woman stared at her in amazement. "Leaving? But how can you leave? Where would you go?"

Lily shrugged. "To my own home."

Genevieve shook her head in confusion. "But I had thought that something had happened to send you from there."

"Why would you think so?"

The green-eyed beauty met her questioning gaze. "I had thought it because you came here to be with your daughter—"

"To be with my daughter?" Lily interjected in shock. She was caught so off guard that it did not occur to her attempt to deny it. "You mean you know?"

Genevieve blinked. "Of course I know. How could I not? It would surprise me not at all to learn that many people know—or suspect, at the very least. Did you think that no one would see the resemblance? Looking at you is like looking into a mirror and seeing what Sabina will be like as a woman."

Slowly Lily sank down on the end of the bed.

She put a hand up to cover her face. She and Tristan had been mad to think they could fool anyone, mad and selfish.

Raising her head, she faced Genevieve directly. All this time she had known and felt that others did, too. Yet she had held her head high, had been kind where another might have been cruel. Lily would give her no less than she had given.

"I am so very sorry," she said. "I had no wish to harm you or anyone else."

Genevieve answered, "I know that, have been certain of it from the beginning." She laughed, albeit somewhat wryly.

Lily looked down at her hands, clasped tightly together in her lap. "In spite of that, another woman would have spoken of her suspicions, would have refused to have me in her home."

"What think you—that I am some long-suffering saint? I assure you, Lily, I am no saint. I would not have gone on without protest did I think you meant any ill or that I had anything to gain in refuting you."

"But Tristan is your fiancé."

"And has treated me as well as he knew how in this. I knew he did not love me as anything but a sister when I asked him to marry me. I love this family, love these outspoken, loyal, maddening Ainsworth brothers as if they were my own. I asked Tris-

tan to be my husband because I knew that his heart
had been lost to Sabina's mother, though I thought
she had died. It was clear that he would never love
another as he had her. The others still had their hearts
to give. I knew that marriage was not something I
could ask of them. When you arrived I knew you had
not died and that Tristan still loved you, though he
does not know it."

Lily was struck dumb by the statement that Tristan
still loved her. Desired her, yes, but that was not love.
Tristan loved the girl she had been.

Not unknowing her thoughts, Genevieve moved
closer to Lily, her eyes asking for understanding.
"How could I take from Tristan anything that might
make him happy? If the two of you could come to
some terms, then that was meant to be. If you did not,
then I would still wed him, knowing as I had before
that his heart was not mine but that he would be a
good man and treat me well."

For a moment Lily still did not know how to reply.
Never had she thought that she and Genevieve would
say any of this to each other. It was just too unbelievable—too unreal. Perhaps that was why she finally
spoke with such honesty and directness. "I appreciate
your generosity more than I can say, but there is
something you must know. Although there is a certain…attraction between Tristan and myself, he does
not love me. On that you must be assured."

Genevieve looked at her with sympathy, shaking
her head. "I know not what goes on between you,
but I do know what I know. Should you choose not
to see, for some purpose of your own, then so be it.
It is not my place to convince you."

Lily had no words to say to that. She knew how it

was between herself and Tristan. Perhaps only he would be able to convince Genevieve of the truth now.

The young woman took a deep, exhausted breath. "I must go, Lily. I find I have no more heart to speak of this now."

Sorrow for her pain brought an ache to Lily's chest. "I am so very sorry." She had said the words before, but they were all she could give if Genevieve did not believe that Tristan loved her.

When she was gone, Lily stood there, not knowing what to do. Genevieve knew—possibly others knew—that she was Sabina's mother and thus that she and Tristan had been...

Dear heaven, what would he say to all this?

Without giving herself time to think, Lily turned and left the room. She went immediately down the hall to Tristan's chamber. She did not know if he was there, but it was the first place she could think of to look for him.

She must speak to him, and without delay.

All their hopes of secrecy had come to naught. How was she to face them all—the servants, Tristan's brothers? And what must they think of her?

Lily met no one as she went, a fact for which she was grateful. As during the night, she paused outside the closed bedroom door, biting her lip in indecision.

Taking a deep breath, she pushed the heavy portal open. Her eyes rounded in surprise at what met her gaze, and she halted there in the opening.

Not only was Tristan in his chamber, but he was just climbing, wet and gleaming, from a large copper tub—the same tub that was brought to Sabina's room for bathing. Lily was aghast, wanting to turn away, but completely unable to drag her eyes from the sleek line of his golden flank as he stepped from the tub.

What was he doing taking a bath? Why would he ever do so in late morning, when others were up and about for the day?

Because you and the others have the use of it in the evening, her mind replied.

That did not explain why she was simply standing here staring at him this way. *Because you can't not stand here staring at him,* that voice in her mind responded.

Tristan himself seemed shocked at seeing her there, his blue eyes, the color of sapphires, growing round. It was he who found his tongue first. "Lily?"

Only then did she spin around to leave.

He halted her with a word. "Wait."

It was the fear in his tone that made her stop. Obviously he thought something was wrong with Sabina again. Lily could hardly blame him for that, considering her temerity in coming here without warning of any kind.

She stopped, but did not look around. "I must beg your pardon, sir. I had no idea that you would be—"

He interrupted, "Have no care for that, Lily. What has happened?"

Lily spoke up quickly. "Have no fear for Sabina. Naught has happened to her. She is still with Kendran, who came and took her down to the hall this morn."

She heard the relief in his sigh. A moment later, he stated, "You may look around now, Lily. I have covered myself."

Lily blushed even as she slowly turned to face him. Tristan had put on a long, dark blue robe, which covered all of that golden skin from neck to foot. She did her best to tell herself she was thankful, but her mind produced an image of golden skin over hard muscle as if to taunt her.

Lily folded her trembling hands over her stomach as Tristan moved toward the table and poured a cup of wine. "What then can I do for you, Lily? I would have thought that you wished to remain as far from me as possible until your father came for you."

Lily blushed. "I..." She raised her head, then, using pride as her ally, said, "I...do think it best if we have as little contact as possible until I leave. You will likely agree when I tell you what has happened." She had his undivided attention now, and Lily had to force herself to go on beneath his close scrutiny. "Genevieve has just told me that she knows I am Sabina's mother. She is under the impression that others in the keep may be privy to our secret as well."

Tristan came toward her swiftly, grabbing her arm. "What are you saying?"

Lily swallowed hard, barely aware of that grip in the force of her own scattered feelings. "Genevieve knows, Tristan. She believes that others do, too."

He looked into her eyes, his own dark with a growing emotion that surprised her, an emotion she did not want to see, did not want to feel mirrored in herself. He spoke quickly. "If Genevieve knows, then we no longer have anything to hide, no more lies to tell. There is nothing to drive the guilt that accompanies nearly every thought both night and day."

She was glad that Tristan was not angry as she had expected him to be, but she did not understand his near...elation, nor the embers of—dare she think it?—barely suppressed passion she saw in his gaze.

She shook her head trying to clear it of the realization of her own inner stirrings. She reached up, tucking a loose strand of hair behind her ear.

She gave a start as she felt his hand follow hers to release the errant strand. Lily's vision blurred, and she swayed as she remembered herself tucking a strand of hair behind her ear...felt a hand, large, male and familiar, move to free that same lock...felt herself looking around to confront a pair of familiar blue eyes.

Lily came back to an awareness of the present as she heard her name. "Lily."

Her gaze focused on Tristan's worried face, then on his hand. "You have done that before, haven't you?" she asked.

He frowned. "Done what?"

"Taken my hair from behind my ear."

Realization dawned in his eyes, accompanied by a gladness she could not fail to see. "Yes, Lily. I have done it before. You used to put your hair behind your ear when you got excited or engrossed in anything." His expression grew whimsical and gently amused all at the same time as he went on. "Once I reached out and untucked it, and you tucked it back, and I untucked it and so on.... You had been talking about our future and how you were going to make your parents understand that we loved each other...and had to be together. When you finally realized what I was doing, you leaped on me and..." His eyes darkened at the memory of an event she could not recall. "Well, we..." He stopped, his gaze going to hers.

The implication of what had followed was clear in the scorching heat of his eyes.

Her breathing quickened in spite of herself. She

whispered, "I do not recall. I remember only that gesture."

His eyes continued to burn into hers, and she could not look away no matter how she tried as he said, "But you know what happened. How we—"

She put her hand up to halt him. "Do not say it, Tristan, do not, please?"

"How can I do otherwise? You do not require the wholeness of your memory to want to be with me, as I do with you. In truth, is this not why you came here to my chamber? You knew as I do that we could now be together without the shadow of our own lies to keep us apart." His breath felt hot on her face as his head came toward hers.

Was he right? Was that why she had come to him? It did seem almost preordained that she would come here and find him naked and clean from his bath, and so very beautiful that it had made her ache with longing just to look upon him.

She could not do other than raise her mouth for his kiss.

And when their lips met, she was lost, lost as she had been each and every time he touched her. She felt herself pulled close against his warm hard body. At the same time, she realized that it was smooth skin beneath her questing fingers rather than blue velvet. She knew that his robe had come open, and she reveled in the knowledge, letting her hands slide inside and down, to run over the same smooth, lean hips she had glimpsed earlier as she came into the room.

His skin felt every bit as good as she had known it would.

Tristan gasped, feeling his body harden at the touch

of Lily's fingers on his flesh. God, how he wanted her, would always want her.

His relief that Genevieve knew about Lily was palpable. Surely Lily's coming here like this meant that she now wanted to be with him. The details they could work out later—much later—after the passion that had been building in both of them over the past days had been slaked.

Lily heard his reaction to her touch with a thrill that raced through her blood to settle in her lower belly. She tilted her head back as Tristan's mouth left hers. He obliged her by pressing his hot lips to her throat, then sliding his tongue over that tender flesh. She shuddered in response, her knees buckling.

Laughing huskily, Tristan lifted her in his arms to carry her to the bed.

Once there he laid her down even as he ran a hand up under the hem of her skirt. His Lily was far too overdressed for his liking.

His Lily.

The words were like an aphrodisiac. For that was what she could be now that their secret was out. No more must he deny the desire that burned in him each time she was near. The knowledge gave his pleasure an even sharper edge as he drew her garments up and over her head. He caught his breath at the beauty of her, of her sweetly rounded breasts with their raspberry tips. He traced the slim line of her waist and gently curved hips, those long creamy legs and delicate, slender feet. Each and every curve was sheer perfection in his gaze.

Lily was aware of his eyes upon her, felt the heat of them scorching her flesh as she settled back on the bed. She shivered, experiencing her response in every tingling inch of her flesh.

Tristan watched as the tips of her breasts hardened beneath his gaze. He gave a soft groan of pleasure, reaching for her even as she raised her own arms to him. They cradled his head as he took the tip of one breast into the warmth of his mouth, his tongue circling it even as he reached to take the other between his thumb and forefinger, squeezing gently.

Lily gasped, throwing her head back. Her hips arched toward him, bringing the lower half of her body into direct contact with the lean muscled length of his thigh. Automatically her own thighs clasped him more closely to her.

Tristan slid one hand down her side, tracing the curve of her waist and hip, then pressed it between their clasped bodies to brush the tangle of curls he found. He was gratified when her belly fluttered under his fingers, and she shifted to allow him better access. As he dipped his hand lower, cupping the curve of that sweet mound, he pressed his mouth to hers.

Lily felt Tristan's hand on her and sucked in a breath at the ache of longing that touch bought. Her body arched, seeming to beckon him on. He dipped his fingers lower and she caught her breath in a gasp of pleasure. "Tristan." She did not recognize the sound of her own pleading voice.

He heard the need in her voice, knew that they could wait no longer. He raised up over her, and she opened to him. Her face was flushed and tight, and as he slipped inside her, she sighed, arching her head with a soft murmur of pleasure that drove his own passion to a sharp and piercing spike. She reached for him, ran her hands down his sides to hold his hips, her body setting a rhythm he was eager to follow.

Tristan bit his lip, trying to control the ecstasy building inside him. But the feel of her soft, cool hands gliding over his flesh made that nearly impossible. He closed his eyes, willing himself to wait. Above all things he wished to feel her reach her own fulfillment.

Lily held Tristan to her, her body acting out of need, driving her on. And so the deliciousness built and built, one wave of sensation upon another, until she lost all ability for coherent thought. Lily knew only herself and Tristan, seamlessly joined, riding together on a sea of indescribable delight. She held her breath, feeling that she would surely explode. And then the waves broke over her, crashing down in a bliss so intense that shudder upon shudder took her and she could do no more than cry out in wordless abandon, unable to give coherent voice to the rage of emotions and feelings inside her.

Only when he felt her body tighten around his in rapture did Tristan let go of the tight hold he had on his own desire, arching above her, calling out in a hoarse whisper of ecstasy, "Lily!" And then he was tumbling down into a well of sweet fulfillment, where there was nothing but rapture and the soft yielding warmth of the woman he held in his arms.

Chapter Eleven

Tristan knew not how much time had passed when he came more fully to himself and rolled to the side, pulling her into the circle of his arms. He did not care.

He held Lily close, reveling in the fact that they no longer had anything to hide. He stroked his hand over her silky, midnight hair. "How did it come about?"

Her voice was still tinged with a slight breathlessness and, though he did not wish to hear it, strain. "How did what come about?"

"Your learning that Genevieve knew? How did you explain to her about us?"

She pushed back, looking up into his face with a frown. "I did not explain anything, Tristan. I would never do so, knowing that I would jeopardize all our futures."

Tristan felt himself stiffen, though he tried to stop it. Lily could not mean what she seemed to be saying. Surely she was not still bent on leaving.

He looked at her very closely. "Surely I have misheard you just now. You cannot mean to go forward with your plans to send for your father?"

"But—but I must," she sputtered. "Genevieve did

not say that she knew of my true identity, only that she was aware that I am Sabina's mother. Although there no longer seems any point in trying to pretend to her or your brothers as far as that is concerned, we need not expose all. We may still manage to see me away from Brackenmoore without Maxim ever learning the truth of where I have been these last weeks.'' Lily pushed away from Tristan as she finished speaking, then stood, taking the coverlet with her.

Tristan viewed this renewed sense of modesty with grim irony as he rose to face her. On one level, he told himself, he was glad of her tenacity. It was a clear sign that she was gaining a clearer sense of herself.

Lily had ever been stubborn. She did her utmost to follow through with a course once she was set upon it. The problem was that being with him had once been the course she wished to follow. Being on the opposing end of her determination was not quite as gratifying.

He knew he must try to reason with her, though he was not sure why or what he hoped to gain. What could they be to one another if she did remain at Brackenmoore? There had been no words of love between them in spite of the ever-present passion. And though Genevieve knew about Sabina, she did not know about Lily and him being lovers now.

In spite of that he racked his mind for some coherent thought, some reason to keep her at Brackenmoore. ''Did you not say that Genevieve believes others know? If so it will be near impossible to keep each person who has a suspicion about your being Sabina's mother from ever speaking of it.'' He paused, then added, "Did Genevieve say anyone had actually spoken to her of this?"

Lily scowled, shaking her head. "Nay. I believe she has simply surmised that they do. It is not so farfetched that she should think it when she herself has guessed the truth. I chose not to quibble with her on that count."

"And you did openly admit that you are Sabina's mother?"

Lily stepped back from him, frustrated at his stubborn desire to try to continue their ruse. "Tristan, how could I do otherwise? I simply did not tell her anything about us."

He raked a hand through his still-wet hair. "Of course you could not do otherwise. What is truly maddening is your ability to continue to have any uncertainty about what we were to each other. I am simply overcome by your complete and utter stubbornness."

Lily glared at him. "I am not stubborn. You know what I believed and why." She looked away. "That brief flash of memory that came to me only moments ago has changed that. It has further convinced me that you and I did indeed have deep feelings for one another."

He took a step toward her. "And saying that, can you still tell me that you intend to leave?"

She rubbed a trembling hand over her troubled brow. "As long as there is any chance of salvaging my family's future, I must. You think that I am too tightly bound to my parents and without just cause. This may indeed be so, but I owe them my loyalty for all the love they have shown me. I must marry Maxim even if it is only to secure my father's position in the new court. If I had been a more dutiful daughter in the beginning, had not disobeyed them and got myself with child, none of this would have occurred.'' She forced Tristan to meet her gaze. ''Put yourself in my father's place if you can for a moment. Imagine what it would be like if someone were to take Sabina away from you.''

He exploded in outrage. ''It is not the same. I would not so attempt to control my daughter by deciding whom she could love.''

Her eyebrows arched. ''Even if that man was someone such as…say, Maxim Harcourt?''

''She would never care for one such as he!''

Lily shrugged. ''You are likely correct if all you say about him is true.'' Warmth suffused her at the thought of Sabina. ''The little one has a good sense of her own worth even now. Yet I do know that you would do what you must to protect her were it otherwise.''

Tristan did not deny this, and Lily went on. ''Can you not see that I do this of my own will, Tristan? You say that I am controlled by my father and mother, yet you wish me to allow you to control me.''

''That is not true.''

She shook her head. ''It is true.'' She looked away. ''There is one thing that I am grateful to you for. In bringing me here you have given me the opportunity to begin to think for myself. When I no longer had my parents to tell me what I was, while at the same time being forced to question all you said, I began to see who I really am.'' She turned back to him, her gaze full of entreaty. ''Can you not accept that I have made a decision that I feel is best for everyone? Even if it proves a mistake, it will be one that I have made.''

He raked a hand through his thick dark hair. "Are you willing to sacrifice yourself in the process?"

She answered simply, "Aye, if that is the price for making my own decisions."

Tristan shook his head in obvious frustration.

Lily sighed, realizing that she was getting nowhere. "I have written the letter to my father. Would you have it sent for me?"

He put his hands on his lean hips, his jaw set. "So be it then, Lily, if that is what you desire. I will send a servant to collect and take it this very afternoon."

He paused, then went on, his handsome face as hard as stone. "I also have something more to say. I am glad that Genevieve has determined the truth. I cared not for keeping it from those I love, but for your sake, I will attempt to keep others from knowing any more than they already do."

Lily cringed inside. She had known that Tristan did not love her as Genevieve suggested; yet it hurt to have him say it, especially after what they had just done together. Even if the woman he did love was the one he was going to marry.

Genevieve had told her that she and Tristan were not in love, that his heart had been given. Obviously he had found it again, and for Genevieve's sake Lily was glad.

This driving, overwhelming passion she and Tristan felt for one another was wrong and only a reflection of what they had obviously once shared. With her gone, Tristan would no longer be confused. He and Genevieve could make a future built on the love he bore her.

Lily held her head high. "I thank you for that. I understand your feelings about Genevieve—and about your brothers, having seen how close you are to them. I realize now that, with them, there is no point in keeping up the pretext that I am a servant. I would feel more the fool knowing they were aware that I played a part. I do not think I can continue to do so. I ask simply that we do not tell them who my family is. It can gain us nothing.''

He nodded. ''I agree to keep your true identity secret, if that is your wish, though we will no longer hide the fact that you are Sabina's mother from my family. Except, that is, from Sabina.''

Lily's heart twisted. Of course, it made sense that they would continue to keep the truth from the child. Lily loved her enough to want to protect her from any hint of sorrow, and learning that Lily was her natural mother could do her naught but ill.

Allowing herself to think anything else would only bring grief to them all. But Lily could not form the words to say so around the aching lump in her throat. She could do no more than nod in acquiescence.

Tristan bowed briefly in formal thanks. Then he reached down and picked up her clothing from where he had tossed it beside the bed. Lily took it in a trembling hand. When he turned his back, she was grateful for his consideration, yet she drew the garments on with difficulty.

Though neither one of them said the words, the fact that there could be no more intimacy between them was clear. She was glad that he did not look around when she was done, and she left the room without speaking another word.

They had each made themselves clear. There was nothing more to be said.

* * *

Tristan watched Genevieve as she looked up from pouring drops of sweet oil into the vat of tallow that hung over the low fire. Several other women readied the wicks and other items that would be used in making candles. As was always the case when a meal was not in process or preparation, the rest of the kitchen was in fine order. The many cooking pots and utensils hung on their hooks along the wall. The counters were scrubbed clean, the linens put away. He knew Genevieve was responsible for this.

There was a sweet compassion in her expression when she saw Tristan, which surprised and awed him, knowing as he did that she was aware of Lily being Sabina's mother. He felt his heart twist with sadness.

Why could he not have loved this woman? She was everything that a man could want in a wife.

But she could not be the one thing he seemed unable to do without: Lily.

He was called back to reality by Genevieve's voice. "Tristan, you wished to see me?"

He replied in as easy a manner as was possible considering the circumstances, considering the fact that he had just come from making love to Lily. "Yes, if you are not too busy."

She shook her head. "I am never too busy to speak to you." She handed the tiny flask of fragrant oil to one of the other women.

She smiled again as she came toward him. "Shall I have one of the servants fetch my cloak? We can go for a walk. I would love to get some fresh air."

Tristan nodded. "Yes, that would be fine."

Only a short time later they were walking along the battlements of the castle wall.

As soon as they had fallen into a comfortable

rhythm, Genevieve turned to him. "Am I presuming too much to think that you wish to talk to me about Lily?"

Tristan halted. "Genevieve—"

She interrupted him. "I am all right, Tristan. There is no need to make long explanations and apologies."

"But I want—need—to ask your forgiveness."

She looked at him with sympathy in her lovely green eyes. "For what? I knew that Lily was Sabina's mother from that first day. I told you then that you had no need to reveal all to me."

"But you do not understand why and how it happened that she came here."

"That is true. Seeing her at Brackenmoore did surprise me no small amount, I can assure you. Before that I had simply assumed that the babe's mother had died, as you had told us all. I was forced to realize that she was indeed very much alive and therefore had been at some other location. That made me think that the two of you must have had some kind of falling out. I further assumed that Lily's circumstances had changed, that she had need of a home and you had offered one to her. She spoke of a fire...."

He scowled. "That is not entirely the case. It is true that Lily and I had not seen one another for some time. But it was not because we had a falling out, nor was there a fire." He paused before going on. "I truly thought that Lily was dead, as I had told you all."

Genevieve's gaze became disbelieving and incredulous for the first time. "But how could that be, Tristan?"

Quickly he told her of the accident and Benedict's rescue of himself and Sabina, his belief that Lily was dead. Tristan ended by adding, "I did not reveal her identity, as I did not wish for her family to learn of the babe's survival, and attempt to take her from me.'' He could feel the tension in himself at the very thought.

Genevieve's horror mirrored his own. ''Would they do such a thing? And why did she not come to you when she recovered from the accident, which she obviously has done?''

Tristan took a deep breath. ''Lily awoke with no memory of what happened before the accident. She did not know me nor remember that she had a child.''

''But her family, how could they keep such a thing from her? Who are they, Tristan?''

He shook his head. ''Lily has asked that I not reveal their identity, and I have said that I would not. At any rate, I am forced to agree that she is right to keep it secret.'' He could hear the pain in his own voice and was not pleased.

Obviously, Genevieve had heard it, too. ''I do not understand the need to keep this hidden, but I will try to do so. Yet there is another matter that I cannot ignore.'' She held his gaze, her own searching. ''Your relationship with Lily has not run its course. You still have feelings for her?''

Tristan looked away, but he would not lie to her. There had been far too much of that already. ''Nothing that cannot be conquered.''

''I see.''

He faced her then, directly. ''You must believe me, Genevieve. What was between us is done. Lily must return to her own home, her own...'' He straightened. ''There are those whom she does not want to know that she has ever been to Brackenmoore.''

Genevieve took a deep breath. "Is it possible for her to hide it?"

Tristan took her icy hands in his. "It is not only possible, it is imperative. Lily is the daughter of a nobleman, Genevieve."

"Lily, a noblewoman." She shook her head thoughtfully. "I should not be surprised by this news. She has such delicacy and refinement about her. I allowed myself to believe that she was very likely the daughter of some lesser knight or some such thing. You said yourself that she was gently reared. Then when Leena told Maeve that Lily had nearly said as much to her, I simply accepted it as truth." She looked at him. "I see now that this was only wistfulness on my part."

Her eyes opened wider then. "How can you let her go, knowing this? She is the mother of your child."

He refused to acknowledge the hurt he felt at his next admission. "It is her own wish. Her father has arranged a marriage for her, and she is determined to go through with it in some misguided notion that she must do so in order to save her family from possible retribution from the crown."

"But how?"

"Her father was an open supporter of King Henry. The man her father has chosen for her managed to keep his own support of Henry secret from Richard. He did this by way of acting the spy for Richard, thus having his own political position assured. The marriage is meant to show King Edward that her father's loyalties have now changed."

"How can she wish to marry this man? He sounds far too like Maxim Harcourt for my taste." Her expression was openly disgusted.

Tristan's lips tightened as he replied, "Does he not?"

At that moment Genevieve's eyes widened, and she gasped. "Harcourt! Benedict said that he has been scouring the countryside searching for his bride. Dear God, Lily is that bride. She is to marry Maxim Harcourt?"

He nodded grimly at her too perceptive conclusion. What could he do now but ask her to keep this knowledge to herself? "I beg you, Genevieve, do not discuss this with anyone. I have given my pledge."

Her eyes and voice were filled with anxiety as she answered, "I will not tell, but it is so wrong. Though she appears strong, Lily is also kind and gentle. Marriage to that man will likely destroy her."

There was nothing he could say except, "It is by her own choice, Genevieve. She will not heed me in this. She would be married to him now if I had not seen her in an inn that night on my way to Molson. I…" He halted, but made himself go on, to tell the truth of what he had done no matter how difficult. "I saw her there with his men. Thinking that she had betrayed me not only by not telling me she lived but also by marrying another man, I went to her room that night and took her by force with me to Molson. When I realized that she did not in truth know me, that she had been told nothing but lies about her past, I realized that she had been robbed of all that had mattered to her. I knew it was wrong, but I told her she could come here, see if being with Sabina would help her to remember."

His brow knit. "She has remembered precious little, though even that small amount has convinced her that I speak the truth. Yet it has changed nothing. She is willing to give up all to help her family, to whom she believes she owes a great debt for their care of her when she was ill. She somehow thinks that she was not a proper daughter to them before or she would never have disobeyed them to be with me." He had to stop for a moment as emotion rose up to block his throat. When he went on, he heard the tightness in his voice, the note of despair. "She feels that she must help them in order to make up for all the trouble she has wrought in seeing me against their will. Even if it means marrying Maxim Harcourt, whom she has managed to convince herself is merely misunderstood."

Tristan faced Genevieve, knowing he had given away more than he had ever meant to. Even hearing all this, it was clear that she was attempting to give him the benefit of the doubt when she said, "Dear heaven, Tristan, you must have been beside yourself all this time, keeping so much inside."

He could stand it no more, knowing that there was so much more that he had not said. "How can you be so kind? Have you no anger, no resentment for what I have done to you?"

She looked at him directly. "How can I judge you? You are as my brother. Your pain in this matter is so real it can almost be touched. I know you did not want to hurt me. You loved Lily before I asked you to wed me." She glanced away, then took a deep breath before meeting his gaze once more, her green eyes filled with determination. "When I asked you to marry me, I did not believe that our union would cost either of us. Now I know that it would."

He stared at her, aghast, her words seeming to suggest something that he did not want them to. "You cannot mean that you wish to release me from my promise. Have you not heard me? Lily is going away. I do not wish for this situation, my own foolish mistakes to destroy your life.''

She smiled. ''You have not destroyed my life. I am making a choice for my own sake. I could accept a man who loved a dead woman. I do not wish to take second place to one who is very much alive and loved no matter how unavailable.''

Tristan felt as if he had been hit in the chest. Not only had he devastated his own life, he knew in spite of what she said to reassure him that he had ruined her plans for the future.

Yet on another level, he was aware that she was right about one thing. He now realized, after talking to Genevieve like this, that his feelings for Lily went far deeper than he had even imagined. He could no longer deny it. He loved her with an intensity that was frightening. The thought of not seeing her, not hearing her voice, knowing that Sabina would never know her, left him empty and cold. He held out his hands in supplication. ''Forgive me. I never meant to cause anyone hurt, least of all you, Genevieve.''

She took his hands in hers. ''Tristan, you have not hurt me. You have more likely helped me to find my senses. You owe me nothing, and I need not settle for one who cannot love me truly.''

She paused, then went on. ''There is just one thing I would ask of you, Tristan.''

He shrugged. ''Anything that is within my power to grant. I owe you that.''

She shook her head, but said only, ''I would ask that you do not tell anyone of our canceled engagement until Lily has left Brackenmoore. She is a good woman, Tristan, has tried only to find herself in all of this. I would not have her take all the guilt of our parting with her as well as the other pain she will carry."

Again, Tristan found himself wishing he could love Genevieve. She was too generous, even now. He spoke harshly, disgusted with himself. "I will keep my own counsel on this until you give me leave to do otherwise. And should you change your mind, I will marry you and gladly."

She smiled sadly. "I will not change my mind."

Tristan nodded. "So be it then. I will never again ask for your forgiveness in any of this, Genevieve, for I do not deserve it."

She squeezed his hands. "In time, Tristan…"

He wrenched his hands from hers and strode away from her sympathy. There was no repairing what he had done.

Madly, foolishly, unthinkingly, he had allowed himself to love Lily—all over again. And not just for the girl she had been, but for the honorable, brave woman she was now, the woman who would toss away her own life to care for others.

Later that afternoon Lily took Sabina out into the courtyard to play, even though the child had wanted to venture farther afield. There was a very sharp chill in the air, and Lily had not forgotten the little one's recent illness.

Sabina ran ahead, laughing at the antics of a stray puppy. Lily followed more slowly, feeling as if every eye in the courtyard must surely be upon her.

Though she now realized that many of the castle folk were more than suspicious of her identity, she was unnerved. What mattered was that Tristan did not wish for Sabina to know the truth. That meant Lily would go on as before. It was her only opportunity to be so close to Sabina, her own daughter, whom she had come to love so very much in such a very short time.

Even though she had not recovered the memory of bearing the child, she knew Sabina must be hers. Remembering how Tristan had touched her hair, and the tender and passionate emotions that gesture had aroused, made Lily realize there was little chance that he was not telling the truth about everything.

Her yearning gaze fell upon that small dark head a few steps in front of her. Her child, her Sabina. The ache in her chest told Lily how greatly she would miss her.

"Lily," the little one called out, running back to her. She took her hand, bouncing in excitement. "I have something to show you."

Lily's heart contracted as always when she looked into those ingenuous gray eyes. Such a love of life the child had! Tristan had given her that—Tristan and his family.

Lily knew that if she was honest with herself, she had to admit that she would not want her with anyone else. Without even a memory of her own child, she would not have been a proper mother throughout the past three years.

That Tristan had no patience or consideration for herself was another matter entirely. The ghost of the idealized love they had once shared was a hard taskmaster. It was impossible for him to accept Lily as she was now. And though that might hurt, she had no way to change the last three years, to be the girl he had known. She could be no one but herself, and she was just coming to know what 'being herself' meant.

"Lily," Sabina repeated, obviously growing impatient with her preoccupation. She tugged on her hand to get her attention.

Lily put aside her painful thoughts to focus on the child. "What is it, dearest?"

"I can show you something." Those gray eyes sparkled like wet silver.

Lily was awed by her beauty and the sheer wonder of just looking into those eyes, but she tried to behave as normally as possible. "Then show me, love."

Sabina peered about them, moving forward with stealthy intent. "Come, no one is looking."

Lily could not help laughing softly at this new game, though she did her best to disguise the sound with a cough. She knew that Sabina's imaginings were very real to her.

Sabina led her to a small stone shed at the far end of the castle grounds near the outer wall. All along the way the little one cast careful glances about them to see if anyone was watching. At the entrance she stopped and stole another look about the courtyard, putting her finger to her lips gleefully. Lily smiled and followed when she ducked inside the structure.

It was no more than a storage shed. Along the walls were several narrow bins of different grains, and a stack of hay. More hay was strewn about the floor, but there was no obvious reason as to why this place would be their destination. Lily was just wondering what Sabina would do next when she went to the far end of the structure and squatted down to swipe at the hay covering the floor.

Going over to her, Lily said, "What are you about now, poppet?"

Sabina grinned up at her. "I am showing you the magic tunnel. You go down into it and come up on the outside."

With a frown Lily looked more closely and saw that the child had uncovered a portion of a door in the floor. Suddenly Lily realized just what it was she was being shown.

It was a secret route out of the castle. Surely Sabina was not supposed to tell anyone of this, for it would be meant for use in only the direst of circumstances. As calmly as she could, Lily said, "How did you know about this, dearest?"

Sabina grinned widely, her pink lips pursed with pride. "Da showed me. And I remembered."

"Did he say that you must keep it a secret?"

Sabina nodded, frowning. "He says it is a family secret. You are family." She beamed up at Lily again.

Lily could not help being touched by this pronouncement, but she was not family. Gently she said, "Sabina, it would be best if you did as your father asked you and kept the secret. You really should not show this passage to anyone."

Sabina frowned once more, this time with puzzlement. "Even you, Lily?"

Lily nodded emphatically. "Even me. You should not tell anyone unless you ask your father's permission first."

Sabina shook her head. "Do not worry. I need not ask for you, Lily. Da loves you. He says it is good to share secrets with those you love. Just like he shared the secret with me."

Lily's heart contracted with the unexpected pain

these words brought. Quickly she said, "We must go from here now, Sabina, and we cannot come back. First, though, you must promise me that you will not tell anyone else about this without asking your da. Even if you think he...loves them."

Sabina seemed to sense Lily's heightened emotion and take it seriously. She nodded her dark head. "I promise."

Hurriedly Lily led her back across the castle grounds. And all the while, she tried desperately to deny the misery she felt at Sabina's mistaken assurances that Tristan loved her. But it did little good. For some reason she cared far too much about whom Tristan loved.

"Tristan."

Hearing his name, he looked up from the drawing of the mount for the shield and saw Marcel standing in the doorway of the library. Tristan had been working on the drawing since speaking with Genevieve. He told himself that the work was pressing, that it must be finished soon. Yet in some part of himself, Tristan knew that he simply must find something besides his own painful thoughts of Lily and his hopeless love for her to fill his mind.

But his welcoming smile died aborning when he noted the angry expression on his brother's face. Having no clue what could have brought on such animosity, Tristan stood and moved toward him. "What has happened, Marcel?"

"What Genevieve told me about you and Lily—is it true?"

Tristan looked at him closely. "Genevieve did not

come to you in complaint, of that I am sure. She would never do so.''

Marcel looked at the floor. ''Nay, she did not. I...we are friends.'' His angry gaze then met his brother's. ''Genevieve and I have spent much time together since Lily arrived. She never said to me that she was unhappy, but I thought that she must be. How could it be otherwise? Today her distraction was even more apparent. I guessed that Lily had something to do with it and pressed for an explanation. Genevieve admitted very little and even that little grudgingly.'' His eyes softened. ''Genevieve would say nothing ill of you. It is I who am furious on her behalf. Why would you hurt her for this Lily?''

Tristan frowned, studying Marcel, who seemed almost too protective of Genevieve. The thought that suddenly entered his mind was too preposterous. He pushed it aside. Marcel was the most excitable of them all, the most apt to erupt in anger or pleasure. Tristan took a deep breath and let it out slowly. ''I acted rashly, yes, without thinking, but I did not intend to hurt her, though that has been the outcome.''

''You are right to take the responsibility upon yourself.'' Marcel added, ''So it is true about Lily then.''

Tristan shrugged. ''You want to hear me say that Lily is Sabina's mother. Very well, Lily is Sabina's mother.''

''No, Tristan, that much I had seen some time ago. I mean is it true that she is nobly born, that none of us must know of her identity because she is leaving Brackenmoore and wishes to keep her ever having been here secret?''

So Marcel had been aware of Sabina being Lily's daughter, too. Just hearing his brother say the words was difficult for Tristan, for he realized how very foolish he had been to think no one would know. He nodded as he replied, "Yes, it is true. Lily is nobly born and yes…she is leaving.…" He looked down at his hands, fighting an overwhelming wave of sorrow. "And yes, she does wish to keep the fact that she has been here secret."

Marcel rushed on, seeming oblivious to his pain. "And is it true that Benedict knew the whole time?"

Again Tristan nodded, and Marcel exploded in anger anew. "How could either of you have done that to Genevieve? She is the most beautiful, loyal, loving woman. What could have possessed either of you to shame her so?"

Once more Tristan was shocked at the vehemence with which the words were spoken, surprised at Marcel's accurate, but undeniably idyllic description of Genevieve. He tried to answer with sensitivity, to concentrate on calming his brother. "Has Genevieve told you that she is shamed? She said nothing of such to me, but led me to believe that she understood what we had done."

Marcel blushed. "Nay, she did not say as much, but how could it be otherwise? She is just so good and decent that she does not wish for you to feel you have hurt her." He put his palm to his chest. "It is I who cannot sit idly by and allow this to go on."

Tristan turned away so that Marcel would not see the pain in his face as he replied, "It will not go on. As I said, Lily is leaving. She has written to her father, and the letter has been sent this very afternoon."

Marcel seemed somewhat mollified by this, though there was still a trace of something that Tristan did not recognize in his dark blue gaze. The words Marcel spoke, "It is for the best," brought him enough anguish that he could not even bring himself to try to understand why his brother was acting so strangely.

Tristan answered despite the tightness in his throat, "Aye, I suppose you are right."

Finally some of Tristan's pain must have penetrated Marcel's outrage, for he came close to the table, his gaze darkening with a hint of sympathy. "I...I am sorry, Tristan, for whatever happened between you. We all thought that she was dead. To learn that she is not is, well, shocking, to say the least. If only it had turned out differently, then you and Genevieve would not have become engaged...." He had a faraway look in his eyes, then drew himself up. "But there is no way to turn back time."

Looking away, Tristan replied in a whisper, "Yes, and there is no point in bemoaning it. We must all go on as we can."

Chapter Twelve

Tristan had not had a good morning. He had realized after speaking to Marcel the previous afternoon that he must also talk with his other brothers. Marcel should not have had to come to him. It was up to Tristan to face what he had done.

Thankfully, Kendran had taken the news about Lily much better than Marcel. Though he was young, he also had suspected that she was Sabina's mother.

Tristan had hoped that the astounding resemblance between mother and daughter would help Lily to see the truth. Not to have realized that others would see it seemed ridiculous now.

Once the interview with Kendran was over, Tristan had gone to Benedict, who was working in the library. His brother seemed not in the least surprised by anything that had occurred, yet he did not chide his brother. Instead he leaned back and propped his fingers together, saying, "Well, this is what you wanted—for all the secrets to be out—and mayhap it is for the best."

Tristan sat wearily across from him. "Aye, it is what I wanted. But to what end?"

Benedict looked at him closely. "I see how much this has affected you, brother. I hope you will no longer try to deny that you love her. And I believe, no matter what she might say, that Lily is also in love with you."

Tristan shook his head. "On that score you are wrong. She does not love me. She would never leave us of her own free will if she did. Even to aid her family."

Benedict shrugged. "Believe what you will, Tristan. The fact that she is willing to go is a mark of her love, in my estimation."

There was no way Tristan could make his elder brother understand the way it was between him and Lily. He would not even try.

Benedict spoke again. "What will you do now?"

"Wait for her father to come for her. What else is possible?" He was aware of the defeat in his own voice, but could not summon the energy to hide it.

Benedict watched him closely as he stated, "I have but one bit of advice, and it is yours to take or leave. Do not avoid her. Face your feelings so that you can come to terms with them before Lily is gone. For both your sakes, try to understand why she is doing this, however misguided you believe her to be."

Tristan returned his searching look. "You have never been in love, Benedict, do not know how it would feel to have the woman you love choose to follow the will of others rather than be with you."

"That is true enough, and it is unlikely that I shall ever love that way. When I marry it will be to provide the best mistress for Brackenmoore, the best mother for its heir." There was resignation in his tone, and

Tristan realized anew what a burden the lands and title must be.

Yet mayhap 'twas better never to have loved the way he loved Lily. The loss of that love caused more pain than any man should have to endure.

Tristan did not wish to accept it, but he could not help wondering if there was some value in Benedict's advice. His brother was not one to offer such without due consideration.

Could it be true that Lily was not as wrong here as he believed? Could it be his own misery that made him see the situation as he did?

Perhaps he must face her, spend time with her, to discover just what the truth might be.

Thus it was that he entered the kitchens some time later. He stopped upon the threshold, a fond smile curving his lips in spite of his pain as he heard the trill of childish laughter. He followed the sound to find Sabina and Lily seated at a table near the hearth.

Maggie had told him that they would be here.

Both Lily and Sabina had their hands buried in dough. The bowl of spiced apples nearby made it obvious that the two of them were in the midst of making a sweet pie.

He stood there for a long moment, enjoying the sight of his daughter and her mother, their black hair mingling as they bent close. If things had been different, if he and Lily were together, such a sight would be common.

But they were not together. Lily was leaving.

At that moment she looked up, as if sensing his presence, and her easy smile died. An expression of wariness replaced it.

Tristan tried to repress the regret that rose inside him. He had not wanted her to feel wary of him.

Luckily Sabina also glanced up at the moment, her face beaming as she saw him. "Da, come and see. Lily is helping me to learn to make a pie."

Tristan smiled, albeit stiffly, and moved toward them. He looked down at his daughter's doughy fingers as she held them up for his inspection. "Where is Genevieve? Did she not wish to help?" he asked. He had not fully accepted that Genevieve had not been hurt by what had gone on, especially after she had ended their engagement. He wanted her to feel that her relationship with Sabina was to continue as it had always been. He had made an effort to speak easily when mentioning Genevieve. He saw that he had failed miserably when he saw Lily's face take on a pained expression.

Maeve was the one who replied. "Lady Genevieve has gone down to the village to call upon master mason Jack and his family."

Tristan could think of nothing more to say about Genevieve. All he could think of was that it was difficult to see Lily, after all they had done and said. One moment they had been making love as if they two were the only ones in all the world. And in what seemed the next instant, all hope of their ever being together was gone like so much dust.

He did not know if he would be able to do as Benedict had advised. How could he be near her and know she could not be his?

Yet that was exactly what he knew he must attempt to do—until she was gone. The thought was even more disturbing than the previous one.

* * *

Lily could feel Tristan standing there, his blue eyes fixed upon her. She could not have failed to note his deliberate mention of Genevieve.

He could have saved his breath. She needed no reminder that Tristan was bound to another woman—another life.

What other reason could he have for coming near her? All that could be said had been, and still he refused to understand her.

When Sabina turned to her and said, ''What is next, Lily?'' it took a moment for the words to penetrate her agonized thoughts.

''Lily?'' The child's tone was insistent.

Shaking her head to clear it, Lily forced herself to attend what she was doing. Remaining too aware of Tristan's dark scrutiny, Lily showed the little one how to roll the dough out to create a pocket for the filling.

Even though her hands quivered more than Lily would like, no one else seemed to take note and the pastry was soon finished. Lily turned to Maeve with a fixed smile. ''Could you please see that this is baked now?''

Maeve came forward quickly. ''Certainly.''

Sabina eyed her closely. ''You will bring it back?''

Maeve ruffled the little one's black locks. ''I will do you one better than that, my young lady. You shall have it with your dinner.''

Sabina settled back, appeased. She turned to her father. ''You shall have a bite.''

He came toward them, and Lily felt the heat of him as he bent to give Sabina a kiss on the forehead, saying, ''What a generous girl you are.''

Sabina's smile widened farther.

He smiled back at Sabina and Lily's heart pounded

in her chest. She gave a silent sigh. It had ever been that way when he smiled at her, even the first time. And immediately as that thought entered her mind, so did a vision—a vision of a slightly younger and more carefree looking Tristan. More images bombarded her—a green meadow, brightly colored banners, stalls filled with food and merchandise, young folk from all walks of life. A beribboned maypole, the sound of laughter, including her own...the strange but wonderful touch of lips on her own for the first time....

She gasped aloud, rising unsteadily, reaching out for she knew not what. But there was nothing there and she swayed, putting her hands to her head as the images continued to rush forward. She was besieged by them, pummeled by them.... Herself and Tristan seated on a rug before a fire, both of them naked and unashamed; him bending forward to kiss the slight mound of her stomach, whispering sweet words of love to her and their child. And more—her parents' angry faces, her own tears, her bedchamber at Lakeland, long empty days spent staring out the window in desperation... The letter she had given her nurse, escape in the darkness of night, Tristan's arms holding her close. Feeling safer and more alive than ever in her life...then the pain that had come unceasingly, and Tristan's loving eyes, his gentle voice telling her that he would take care of her and the babe...that she must only believe in him—in them.

Lily opened her eyes and found that she was lying in Tristan's arms. His face, bent over her, was filled with fear. "What is it, Lily? What is wrong?"

She could do no more than whisper, "The memories have come."

Tristan spoke to someone she could not see, and she could only assume that it was one of the other women who had been in the kitchen. "Lily is ill. I must take her up to her chamber. Please, keep Sabina here." The next thing Lily knew she was being carried from the room, her face pressed to his chest.

She knew not how much time had passed before she felt herself being lowered to a bed, for the memories had not ceased but continued to pour in. They were not only of herself and Tristan, but also of other times, other people, including her dear grandmother, Sabina.

Tristan bent over her, his beloved face creased with anxiety. "What have you recalled to make you so ill?"

She could only gaze up at him for a long moment, reveling in the sensations of love, belonging—and yes, passion—that continued to swell inside her in wave after undulating wave. Completely overcome by the sensations, she raised her hand to his lean, muscled cheek, a gesture she now knew she had made many times before.

He watched her, and she could not fail to see the hope and fear that warred on his handsome face. "What is it? Pray speak, what have you remembered this time?"

She felt the tears that clouded her vision, but made no effort to hide them. "You, Tristan, I have remembered you—us."

With a gasp of elation he crushed her to him in a grip that nearly drove the breath from her body. Yet she knew nothing but joy in the act. He drew back slightly to rain hot kisses on her face, and she sighed with happiness. His voice was husky with emotion as he whispered, "My God, Lily, you know me." He held her back then to look into her eyes. "You really know me."

She nodded, the tears wetting her cheeks. "Yes, Tristan, I know you, don't know how I could have ever forgotten." She laughed aloud in elation. "So much of it is coming back to me! Even now I am seeing faces, hearing voices. I am sure that there is more, much more, and not all joyful, but it is so much better than the empty blackness I have known for the past three years."

He gazed at her for a long, long moment, his blue eyes glistening even as they asked a silent question. With the memory of her love for him rolling like the ocean inside her, it was a question that Lily could answer only one way.

She raised her mouth for his kiss.

Tristan needed no other invitation. He kissed her deeply, relentlessly, demanding her very soul.

And Lily gave it without thought of restraint or holding back.

When he turned her to him, she raised her arms to wrap them around his neck. Her eager fingers buried themselves in the hair at his nape, and she gave a silent cry of joy at having the sense of doing just this same thing at another place, another time.

She dragged her mouth from his because of a need to say his name—revel in the familiarity of it. "Tristan, Tristan, Tristan." A sob escaped her on the last utterance.

He laughed huskily, joyfully. "Lily, my Lily."

An unmistakable gasp sounded behind them. Eyes growing round with horror, Lily looked past him and saw that Maeve stood in the doorway.

At the same moment, Tristan spun around and stood. "Maeve."

The head woman seemed unable to move for her shock, her gaze fixed on Lily as she sat up on the bed.

Quickly Tristan went on. "This is not as it might seem. Lily is my—"

"I became far too familiar due to my feelings of illness. Forgive me, pray. I will not forget my place again, my lord." She cast him a glance of warning from beneath her lashes.

His face like a marble mask, he motioned for the head woman to go. Maeve obeyed immediately, though she did send a last bewildered glance toward Lily. Tristan paid her no heed.

He stood staring at Lily for a long moment that seemed to drag on for an eternity. Lily thought she would surely go mad, before he whispered hoarsely, "So nothing has changed."

She tried her utmost to explain, saddened by the coldness of his face. "Though I am so very grateful to have regained my past, our past—dear heaven, the memory of giving birth to my own babe!—it cannot change what must be done. Both of us have obligations that make anything else impossible."

He shook his head. "I had thought that I could try to understand your position, but I cannot. I cannot pretend to realize what could make you leave the child you have only just found in order to protect the man who locked you in your rooms to keep us apart."

She held out her hands in pleading and regret. "I am so very sorry, Tristan, I see now why the memory of all that we once were is so very dear to you. Yet I cannot allow myself to be swayed by that tender memory. My choice is not only in aid of my father. I now know that you were right in what you told me of his actions. My father is not a bad man, but weak and fearful, and Mother is ever wont to follow his lead. I simply wish you could see how he has changed. I believe that all their care of me after the accident was by way of showing me the love that they had never before been able to display. It is true that because they tried too hard they ended in nearly smothering me, but they did try, and desperately. That change of heart has earned them both my pity and loyalty.''

Before he could reply, she went on. ''What I do is also for Sabina. It is the love I bear her—bore even before I remembered she was mine—that makes it clear that I must leave her. She has a right to a peaceful life, a mother and father. You and Genevieve can give her that, have done so already.''

He opened his mouth, but no words came. Clenching his hands together at his sides, he turned and left the room.

In spite of Benedict's advice, Tristan knew he could not bear to be with Lily. Not after what had happened that afternoon six days gone by.

It had been all he could do not to tell her that he and Genevieve were no longer planning to marry. Yet he would not do so, even if it weren't for his promise to Genevieve. Although Lily remembered the way it had been for them, she had made no mention of loving him now. If she stayed it must be because she loved him. He now knew he could settle for no less.

What had proved less difficult than he expected was trying to explain himself to Maeve. That wise soul had nodded her head the moment she saw him and said, "I expected to see as much sooner or later. Coming upon you just came as a shock to me, since Lily seemed so ill only moments before in the kitchen."

Tristan shook his head. "It was not as it seemed. Lily is leaving Brackenmoore very soon."

"Leaving! Leaving her little one? How could she do so when she loves her so dearly?"

Tristan could only throw up his hands. "Is there one man, woman or child in the keep who does not know?"

Maeve shrugged. "That I do not know, my lord. But I am sure there must be several folk who have not taken the time to look at them. I, on the other hand, have known you young lads since before you were weaned. I see *all* that goes on here, ofttimes before those involved even realize what they are about, and I speak of more than Lily."

He frowned, having a difficult time taking an interest in her chatter with this tight band of misery about his chest. "What are you talking about, Maeve?"

She raised her gray eyebrows high. "Ask my lord Marcel, if you wish to know."

The words made no sense whatsoever. Tristan's life was in such a state that Marcel would need see to his own troubles for the moment. Tristan felt even more confused and tormented when Maeve added that he had best do something about talking Lily into staying for her own good.

Lily looked down at the encamped army with horror. They had erected their tents at the edge of the green strip around the castle walls. They were well out of firing range, but close enough to have their presence felt by all inside Brackenmoore.

It had been Genevieve who had come to Sabina's chambers to tell Lily that the army was come and she must keep the child in her rooms while the castle prepared for possible siege. She had left again without another word, but her gaze had clearly indicated that she was certain the invaders were here because of Lily.

Lily had thrown on her cloak and run through the keep. One of the guards in the courtyard had seen the horror on her face and offered some information. He had told her there had been little warning, barely time to get the villagers in behind the castle wall before the army arrived. It had not helped that the weather had suddenly turned very cold and the lowering sky gave a clear threat of snow.

She hurried to the battlements with all haste, hoping against hope that there was some mistake. There was not.

That the army's colors were not her father's was readily apparent when Lily first looked out over the wall. They were Maxim's.

Lily was unable to meet the gazes of the four Ainsworth brothers, who stood along the battlements studying their enemy with four equally foreboding visages. Why had her father told Maxim of her whereabouts when she had so earnestly asked him not to?

If she had realized he might, she would never have sent that letter. Her father had not been able to understand her wish to keep this from Maxim, thus avoiding disaster, a disaster such as was now happening with Brackenmoore under siege.

It was her own fault that this had befallen them, but she could not regret coming to Brackenmoore. Doing so had given her back her life. She had been prepared to go to Maxim, knowing as she now did the whole of her past. She had felt she would be doing so as a whole woman, with her own history clear in her mind and heart, no matter that it was achingly painful to go.

Now she had no notion of what might happen. Would Maxim still want her or was he simply bent on revenge? And even if he did, she feared she would not fare well beneath his hands. She would be willing to suffer, however, if it would make him leave without making war upon these folk.

There was little hope of any outcome other than catastrophe. She could not wish ill upon her father, but neither could she hope for a victory on his side. The people at Brackenmoore had come to mean too much to her in her short time here.

She looked over at the four brothers, who had made no move to speak to her. They seemed so engrossed in their conversation that they appeared not to even notice her presence. As she watched, it was clear that they were about to take their discussion into the keep.

She knew she had to do something, say something. Taking a deep breath, she moved to stand before Benedict as he passed. He stopped, looking down at her in mild surprise and suspicion. "Lily."

Tristan spoke up quickly. "I will deal with her, Benedict."

She cringed at the stiffness of Tristan's tone. He had not so much as come near her in the days since she had regained her memory more fully. Those days had been marked by a loneliness and regret that could not be measured, in spite of her determination to enjoy the precious moments she had left with Sabina. Lily could not allow herself to look directly at the man who so filled her every thought, but concentrated on Benedict, who was shaking his head.

"Nay, I wish to ask her a question," the baron said. His blue eyes seemed to burn into hers. "Did you deliberately betray us?"

Tristan interrupted then, and Lily was shocked and—dare she admit it to herself?—pleased by his words. "I can assure you, Benedict, that she did not. I am certain that she bade her father come in great discretion to collect her."

Lily did not waver from meeting Benedict's gaze. "I did indeed bid him come alone, though I am willing to accept all responsibility for the fact that he did not."

Benedict watched her for one more long moment, then turned to Tristan and bowed. "I would take your bond for her as I have from the beginning, brother, but I, too, believe she speaks true."

She took another deep breath. "My lord Ainsworth, please accept my apology for the ill I have done you all. I beg your permission to leave the keep. If I go out to them mayhap they will go away."

Benedict looked at her, his gaze assessing. At last he shook his head. "I appreciate your offer and the sincerity behind it, but I cannot allow that. They have made no demands, nor have they shown themselves. Until we are clear on what they are even about I will not risk anyone, including you, Lily. Your blood runs through the blood of my own niece. That makes you one of our own."

When she opened her mouth to speak, he stopped

her. "Please, Lily, I will hear no more. This situation is no longer about you alone. No one may make war upon Brackenmoore without being made very sorry that they have done so."

He then stepped around her and continued on his way. His brothers followed, each one so tall and certain and maddeningly stubborn. It was only as they slowed to take the steps to the courtyard that Tristan glanced back for one brief instant.

His gaze was as bleak as a stormy sea. Then he was gone and so was the impression. For why would Tristan feel thus about her?

Tristan strode into the library with grim intent. That Benedict would send for him to come immediately when there was an army camped outside the castle walls did not bode well.

It was especially worrisome in the face of the fierce winter storm that had finally broken that very morning. With each hour that passed, the sky summoned more flakes to spill upon the earth.

When Tristan saw that both Kendran and Marcel were seated on benches placed around the table, he faltered briefly before moving forward.

It was only as he came near them that he noted the man seated at Benedict's left. He had both hands wrapped around a steaming mug, and if his red nose and cheeks were any indication, he had until recently been out in the cold.

Benedict looked up at Tristan with a smile of welcome, albeit an austere one. "Please come in, Tristan. You should hear this."

Tristan moved forward and seated himself beside Kendran. "What has happened?"

Benedict turned to the man. "This is Alfred. He is a cousin to our Maeve. He has learned something that he felt might be of interest to us here, and I thought you, Marcel and Kendran should hear it from his own lips. If you are ready, Alfred?"

The man nodded. "Yes, my lord. I was at the seaport of Hywell. I met a man there in an inn near the docks. He was well into his cups when I happened to sit down next to him. I believe that was why he was so free with his tongue." His face took on a dour expression. "No man would betray Maxim Harcourt lest he was beyond reasonable caution."

"Maxim Harcourt. Where can this be leading?" Tristan asked. He knew he was being ill-mannered, but he was near the end of his reserves of composure. Things had been difficult enough without the previous day's addition of Harcourt's army. "His army is without as we speak. That he means us harm is no secret."

With deliberate patience Benedict said, "I think you will see where this is heading soon enough, brother."

Alfred went on. "This fellow told me as how Lord Harcourt meant to attack Brackenmoore Castle. How he had sent his army to sit outside the keep in order to fool you all, but that he and the girl's father meant to surprise the bastard who had stolen his bride away by creeping up on the seaward side of the keep when no one was watching."

"On the seaward side!" Kendran gasped. "But that is sheer madness on our coast at this time of year. Mother and Father lost their lives in that winter sea."

There was a very long silence as each of them remembered just how terrible that time had been. How it had taken weeks for the sections of the ship to stop washing ashore. How the bodies had never been recovered.

It was Tristan who spoke first, his grief making his voice even harsher than it might have been. "Coming by sea is very likely something the knave would do without compunction, being a madman. Anyone else would care for the danger to his men if not himself." His lips thinned in disgust. "But we must be sure." Tristan faced the messenger with open skepticism. "Are you very certain of this, Alfred?"

Benedict spoke up with impatience. "How can we question that? Was he not forced to sneak into the keep in the midst of a storm in order to warn us?"

Tristan took a deep breath and let it out slowly. "Of course, I ask you to forgive me. I am driven beyond myself by the events of the last day. I did not mean to imply that I do not believe Alfred. I just do not see how this maneuver can benefit them even if they do manage to accomplish it. They can no better breach the castle from that position than any other."

Alfred offered, "The man in the inn—the one I told you about—said that the army was coming to distract you from their true purpose of attacking on the seaward side with their ship's cannons, and to keep you from running once the ship did arrive."

"Keep us from running?" Kendran shouted with indignation, leaping to his feet.

Benedict stood as well, casting his younger brother a quelling glance. "I thank you for bringing this information. I would ask you to go down to the hall now, where Maeve will be eager to talk with you and serve you a hot meal." The man got up and went to the door. Benedict halted him briefly. "I welcome you to stay until it is safe for you to leave. You have the protection of Brackenmoore and the deepest gratitude of myself and my family.''

Alfred nodded. "I thank you, my lord. I will stay." He then left.

As soon as he was gone, Kendran muttered, "The bastards. Ainsworths run from nothing and no one."

"Yes, yes, that is true, brother," Benedict agreed, sitting back down. "We will not run, and 'tis surely a coward's thought that we would ever do so. But we must think about what we should do. We have the other occupants of the keep to consider in open war. Not to mention our own loved ones—Sabina, Genevieve...Lily."

Tristan raked a hand though his hair. "This would explain why the army has made no real attempt at attack. Those first halfhearted volleys could have well been meant as nothing more than a display to distract us from the fact that they have done nothing."

Benedict nodded. "I believe you are right there. I think we must take all this information to heart." He scowled deeply, his black eyebrows meeting over his straight nose. "It is so very like Harcourt to attack from behind."

"What are we to do then?" asked Marcel, who had kept his own counsel until this moment. His resentful glance was directed to Tristan. "This threat has been brought to all we hold dear without our even knowing it was coming. Like the rest of you, I have no doubt that we are well able to counter it. But at what loss, Tristan?"

Benedict interjected before Tristan could. "Do not quarrel with Tristan now. We are best served by making a united front as we always have, Marcel."

Obviously these words broke the dam of feeling

within Marcel, for he stood, his tone cold. "In the past we have always been united in what we faced. This time the decision to bring this upon us was made without our consent."

Tristan cried, "Hold now, that is not—"

Benedict stopped him with a raised hand. "I will deal with this, Tristan. That is quite enough, Marcel. Tristan did not bring this upon us, nor did he act alone. I knew what he was about and gave my blessing. That is my right as baron of these lands. If you have any difficulty with *my* decisions, you must bring that to me." He paused, then went on deliberately. "I feel you act out of a personal grudge of your own in this, Marcel. At least Tristan has been honest enough to admit where his interest lies."

A long silence ensued in which Marcel stared at Benedict, his eyes filled with torment. At last he spoke, his voice barely above a whisper. "I am a landless knight."

Benedict held that gaze with unwavering determination. "You are what you believe yourself to be."

Marcel gave a cry of anguish and stalked from the room.

Tristan spoke into the resulting silence. "What is going on? Maeve made some very cryptic remarks concerning Marcel as well. Do you both hold some knowledge that I do not?"

Benedict shrugged. "You have been too occupied to see. But now is not the time to discuss. It must be dealt with when this crisis is past."

Tristan knew that Benedict was right. The immediate danger must come first. But he was determined to have it out with Marcel when all was done. He loved his brother and could not help agreeing with him on one thing. "He is right, you know. I should not have put everyone at Brackenmoore in danger by my own selfishness."

Benedict shook his head emphatically. "You did what was right. You came to me. You were under no obligation to do more. You are allowed a small measure of privacy in your own life, Tristan, though we all live beneath this roof. A risk was taken, one I was fully aware of and was prepared to take. The consequences are my responsibility, if anyone's. But I see no purpose in sitting about and belaboring who is to blame. We must plan our defense."

He saw that Tristan was still looking at the door through which Marcel had gone. "You must give Marcel some time. As I said, he is fighting a demon of his own just now. But he will come around. He is your brother and will see that he must right his own mind before he can make sense of anything."

Chapter Thirteen

Lily listened to what Tristan told her with a gasp of horror. "How could they say such a thing?"

Tristan had no answer for that. He watched as she went to the window, staring out on the swiftly worsening storm. He had not been alone with her since the night she had recalled her memories. He would not be here now, having asked one of the servants to take Sabina down to the hall, if he did not feel that he must tell Lily about her father and Maxim Harcourt. Even in these circumstances it was difficult not to notice the way the light disappeared into her hair as if absorbed by her, the way her gray gown fell about her tall, slender form with such grace.

She shook her head in confusion. "But it is snowing. Would they not be mad to attempt such a thing in this weather?" She swung back around to look at him hopefully. "Perhaps your man was mistaken or deliberately being misled."

He did not wish to tell Lily just how dangerous the trip by sea was. Tristan shook his head, saying, "We do not believe that he is mistaken." He paused for a long moment before continuing. "I know, Lily, that it is not pleasant for you to learn that your father would be involved in such a thing.''

She faced him, calling on his respect as she admitted, ''Yes, I love my father, but as I have told you, regaining my memories has revealed to me that he is not a man of...strength.''

Tristan was not deaf to the sadness behind the words. He knew that he could no longer delay in telling her what he had only realized after the storm had continued to worsen throughout the day. He took a deep breath. ''There is a possibility that it might well cost him his life. The danger on this stretch of coastline is very real. As you know, it is the very reason for building the signal tower.''

The sudden pain in her eyes confirmed that what he was planning to do was right. Lily loved her father no matter what he might have done. It would hurt her deeply to lose him.

She put her hand to her midriff. ''Is there any chance they could have changed their minds because of the storm?''

Tristan went to her, though he knew that there was nothing he could do or say that would soften the blow of what he must tell her. ''Nay, they were to leave the port at Hywell at dawn, and according to the information given Benedict, the sky was clear there as late as last eve. Barring a complete transformation of conscience, which I can assure you has not taken place, there is really no possibility that Harcourt would change his mind.''

Lily turned to him, her eyes wet with unshed tears. ''What am I to do?''

Tristan held out his arms, unable to stop himself. No force on earth could have prevented him from doing so in this moment when she had need of him. She came into them, her form soft and yielding in her sorrow. He found himself whispering against her silky hair, "I am sorry, Lily, so very sorry." And he was, for many reasons, but mostly because she could not love him.

There was an unmistakable quaver in her voice as she said, "Then there is very little hope that I will ever see my father again?" Her question made it obvious that she had misunderstood his words. He realized there was no point in explaining.

Tristan held her away from him, his eyes meeting hers. "Perhaps there may be something…"

She looked up at him, her gaze incredulous. "But what can you do? It is too late to stop them from coming."

He shook his head. "I will not speak of it now. The decision is not mine alone. Shortly, my brothers will be meeting with me in the library, where we will not be overheard. I wish for you to be there as well."

She stared at him for a long moment, then nodded, her gaze hopeful. "If anyone can think of a way to help my father it is you, Tristan."

He released her, stepping back. Holding her like that, seeing the trust in her eyes, made him wish for things that could never be. He made no rejoinder, only prayed that there would be time to put his plan into effect.

His three brothers were already in the library when Tristan and Lily arrived. Tristan looked at the others seated about the table and knew that he had to convince them. And before it was too late.

He realized that by lighting the tower he would, at best, be saving the life of the man who was coming to take Lily away from him. By not doing so, he would be condemning not only Maxim, but also Lily's father to a near certain death.

Taking a deep breath, Tristan said, "It is my intent to light the signal tower in the hope that Maxim Harcourt's captain will be able to safely come to shore."

The room exploded in outrage.

"What?"

"Are you mad?"

"Tristan, do you know what you ask of us?"

He went on, not answering their comments. "There is more. I will have need of help in getting the reflective metal shield in place. I would appreciate your aid—" he looked at each of his brothers' faces in turn "—but I will understand if you do not feel that you can give me assistance in this. I have endangered all here by my actions as it is—"

Lily interrupted him then, wiping a hand across her horrified eyes. "You cannot do it, Tristan."

He looked at her, so dear and familiar, yet never to be his. His love for her was like a river of pain in his blood as he asked, "How can I do otherwise? You would never be able to forgive me for not trying to save your father, and neither could I forgive myself." He turned back to his brothers. "Well, what say you?"

Benedict stood. "You are my brother, Tristan. How could I do aught but help you when I know that what you propose is the only honorable course? There are more folk than Harcourt, or even Lily's father, aboard that ship."

Tristan bowed. "As ever, you have my love and thanks."

With a cry of despair, Lily swung around and ran

from the room. Tristan's heart throbbed in reaction to
her distress, but he could not call her back.

He knew how responsible she felt for what was
happening. His own guilt in the matter twisted like a
vise in his guts.

Benedict looked to Marcel and Kendran, who had
remained silent after their initial outburst. "Well,
shall we get to it then?"

Kendran stood with a grim nod.

Marcel was slower to react.

Tristan felt his angry stare and met it directly, saying, "I will not mark it against you, Marcel, do you
wish to hold back from this. Your feelings are justi-
fied, and I will ever call you brother in words and in
my heart."

Marcel's anger crumbled before his very eyes.
"Ah, Tristan, you know I cannot hold myself back
from helping you no matter what has happened. And
as Benedict says, there are others upon that ship. I
will come."

Tristan felt his heart swell with emotion. They
would stand together as they had since their parents'
deaths, not only brothers but friends and allies.

Lily ran to Sabina's chambers, refusing to shed the
tears that threatened. She must try to master her own
emotions now. It was because of her own inability to
act as she should and leave Brackenmoore that all of
this had come about.

Genevieve was there with Sabina, and it was no
great task for Lily to read the anxiety in her gaze as
she stood, coming toward her the moment she opened
the door. Her voice was deliberately calm, but this
was obviously in deference to the child who played

near the hearth. ''I know you have met with Tristan and the others. That means they are planning something.''

Lily did not attempt to deny it. ''Yes.'' Quickly she told her about the enemy ship sailing toward them in the storm, and the fact that her own father was aboard.

Genevieve gave a gasp of shock. ''What will they do?''

Lily faced her honestly. She was done with trying to prevaricate. It had all been in aid of protecting herself, at any rate. ''They will light the tower in the hope of guiding the ship to shore.''

Genevieve did not appear surprised by this news. Clearly she knew the brothers well. Scowling thoughtfully, she said, ''The shield is not yet in place. In this storm the signal tower is not likely to be of great aid to them without it.''

Lily did not waver in her gaze as she admitted just how much the brothers were willing to do to save her father. ''Tristan and the others mean to put it into place now.''

Genevieve gasped. ''In this weather?'' She paused, then added, ''Marcel as well?'' There was no mistaking the fear in her voice as she said the last.

A light of understanding suddenly dawned in Lily's mind, though she had no time now to examine it or what it might mean to herself—to Tristan. She went to the chest and took up her cloak as she answered, ''Aye, all four of them have gone.''

Genevieve came after Lily, putting her hand on her arm as she began to put the cloak around her shoulders. ''What are you about, Lily?''

''I am not sure, but I must do something, Genevieve. I am responsible for everything that has happened here. I can not sit idly by and wait for the outcome.'' She faced the other woman with determination.

Genevieve seemed to see that she would be able to do nothing to change Lily's mind on this. She said only, ''Tristan will not be pleased.''

Lily shrugged. ''Then that is as it must be. I will not cower here out of fear of his opinion.''

She knew that Tristan would indeed be angry if he knew that she planned to go out to the signal tower, for she realized that was what she must do. Thus she had no intention of telling him until she got there. He would surely be too occupied to concern himself with her then.

Lily realized there was very little she could do by way of aid, but she could not remain here safe and warm in the keep when Tristan and his brothers were out in the storm trying to save the ship. It would not be right.

To her utter surprise she felt Genevieve's arms close around her. The younger girl spoke earnestly. ''God go with you, Lily.''

Lily simply stood there for a long moment, then she returned the embrace with more feeling than she would have thought possible. ''I...thank you, Genevieve. I shall never forget your kindness to me.''

With that she turned and hurried from the room.

She went straight to the kitchen. There she found Maeve directing the kitchen maids in the preparation of the evening meal. It would certainly be more work with the influx of villagers who had been forced to come in because of the siege.

She turned when Lily stopped at her side, her smile

weary but welcoming. "Is there something you need, Lily?"

Lily nodded, wondering if the head woman would be so pleasant if she knew that Lily was the cause of all this upheaval. "Aye. I have need of a container of warmed wine, some fresh bread and some cheese, if that is possible?"

Maeve nodded without hesitation, obviously responding to the authority in Lily's tone automatically. "I can get it for you immediately."

Moments later Lily was leaving the kitchen, a flask of warm wine and the food in a woolen bag that she held firmly in hand. Her next task would be to gain the outside of the castle wall.

Lily knew that she would need to be careful in leaving the castle. She did not wish to be taken by Maxim's men, but was certain the inclement weather would disguise her activities.

That was indeed the case. As soon as she had passed through the postern, without the guards, who stood nearby, seeing her, she breathed a sigh of relief. The camp at the edge of the clearing around the castle wall was hardly visible through the curtain of falling snow, and she could make out no sign of movement. It seemed the men were just waiting out the storm until their master's arrival. Though they must be concerned on that count, considering the turn the weather had taken.

Lily did not even think of using the tunnel. That was very likely the way that Tristan and his brothers were leaving the keep. Under no circumstances did she wish to meet them there. Not only would she be forced to explain how she had learned of its existence, she would also be sent back to the keep forthwith.

But she had not gone many feet from the gate before she felt a trace of anxiety on her own account. The snow was coming down quite hard and visibility was not good.

Taking a deep breath for courage, she pulled her cloak more closely about her and started off. Her father was out on the rolling sea in this storm. What she would face in gaining the tower would be of little danger in comparison.

The farther she got from the dark and comforting shape of the castle behind her, the less Lily was sure of her bearings. Though the snow was not yet deep in the open, it was beginning to drift about every obstacle, no matter how small. The wind drove the falling snow into her face with a stinging force and whipped her cloak about her wildly. She held on to the hood, knowing she must protect her eyes in order to maintain any sense of direction, for becoming completely disoriented in the white of the sky and ground could prove far too easy. It was only when she focused on the pounding throb of the sea before her that she was able to feel she was consistently going in the right direction. Once she reached the edge of the cliff it was simply a matter of turning to her left and following along it.

She knew it was not so very far to the tower, yet the journey seemed to take a very long time. It was with a vast surge of relief that she finally saw the dark shadow of the structure appear on the horizon ahead of her.

She quickened her pace, not letting herself think about what Tristan would say to her when she arrived. For she was quite aware that it would not be welcoming.

* * *

Tristan and his brothers had had no problem creeping away from the castle. They told no one else what they were doing. By unspoken assent they had decided that what they were about to do need not involve their folk.

Even if by some stroke of fate they were able to get the shield in place, then light it in a timely fashion, and the captain of the ship was able to see it, who knew what Maxim would do? Knowing what they did of his character, it was not unlikely that he might still wish to see his revenge played out. Tristan did not want any of the castle folk to feel that they must give aid to the very men who meant to attack them.

If it were not for Lily's father being on that ship, Tristan was quite sure he would never have suggested this. Maxim Harcourt was a poor excuse for a man, in his view, and the world would not be slighted by the loss of such a one. But Lily's father *was* on that vessel with him. And Lily loved him.

The brothers had slipped through the secret passage with no one the wiser. As they had tramped through the falling snow, none of them having anything to say, he had been glad that he had asked that the shield be delivered to the building site rather than the castle. It would have been near impossible to get that out of the gate without the encamped army seeing them.

Not that Tristan was afraid of them. He felt an intense inner urge to go out there and challenge the whole lot of them to personal combat. But that would gain him nothing but death. And to expect anyone else to enter into such a fight with him was completely unfair.

Tristan looked over at his brothers, each lost in his own thoughts as they trudged along. He would exercise restraint now at all costs and do what was right by his family, who had stood by him in spite of his foolishness.

When they reached the tower, Tristan stopped. "The shield is inside at the base of the tower. We can use the ropes to pull it up from the outside or we can try to maneuver it up the stairs, where we will be in out of the snow. It is heavy, but not so heavy that we could not manage. The problem would be with its awkward length."

Benedict looked up at the falling snow. "I am not afraid of a little more snow."

"Nor I," answered Marcel.

Kendran laughed with a youth's enthusiasm for life. "I am with the rest of you." He held up his hands. "This weather is actually quite invigorating, don't you think? Besides, the four of us would look quite graceful all crowded together on that narrow stairway, grinding elbows here and toes there." He stumbled about awkwardly, starting as he pretended to bang each body part.

Tristan could not help laughing with him in spite of himself. Marcel and Benedict joined in, and as a hush fell among them again, they exchanged brotherly nods. Tristan smiled. It was impossible to keep castigating himself with such men at his side.

He shrugged. "Let us to it then." And he led them inside to get the shield.

It was as they were actually pulling the shield up the side of the structure that Tristan felt Kendran grow suddenly still, without letting go of his rope. Bracing his weight against his own rope instinctively, Tristan looked up, wondering what was the matter, and saw his brother staring at something behind him.

Swinging around, Tristan felt a wave of shock run through him at seeing Lily standing there. He blinked, thinking that he must surely be imagining things.

Yet there she stood, her defiance and determination apparent on her so dearly beloved face.

But the fact that he loved her did not stop Tristan from feeling a rush of intense irritation. "What are you doing here?"

Lily stiffened at his tone, obvious outrage tingeing her own voice as she replied, "I came because I had to, Tristan. All of this is happening because of me. How could I sit in the keep knowing the four of you were out here in the storm?"

Tristan's anger drained from him instantly. He understood far too well her feelings. He shrugged. "There is really nothing you can do to help."

She held up the bag containing the flask of wine and the food. "I brought this. The wine was warm when I left, though I'm sure it isn't now."

Kendran spoke up beside him. "I, for one, am glad to have it no matter what the temperature."

Tristan gestured to indicate the ropes they held, then the shield, which hung high above them. "We must see this finished first," he said. "Benedict and Marcel will wonder what is going on down here. And it is growing dark." He knew he did not have to tell her that once it was dark the men on the ship had very little hope of negotiating the waters along the coast without the guidance of the signal light.

That knowledge made him speak to her with gentle care. "Please go into the tower, out of the weather, until we are ready to go up to the top and mount the shield.''

Lily nodded, and he was glad of that, for he did not wish to be distracted by any worry for her. Their task was dangerous. One wrong move could see the cumbersome metal fall and crush them—or her.

Yet as she turned to go in, he stopped her. ''Lily.''

She swung around to face him, her expression still defiant.

He smiled, loving that willful part of her, along with every other aspect of her person. ''Thank you for bringing the food and drink.''

She smiled in return, her face so lit with happiness that his heart turned over in his breast. ''It is my pleasure,'' she replied, before swinging around to run into the tower.

It was a moment before Tristan was able to still his racing pulse enough to return to the task at hand. Only Kendran's knowing laugh brought him to his senses. Looking up into those blue eyes, Tristan shrugged. ''What can I say to you, my brother? She has only to smile at me and I am as an unschooled lad. I love her.''

He was not encouraged by the expression of sadness that suddenly replaced the amusement in his brother's eyes.

Tristan turned away, concentrating on the work at hand. There would be time enough in future to worry about his troubles with Lily.

Some hours later, Tristan wiped at the band of sweat on his forehead. With continued effort, he and Kendran had managed to keep the fire going throughout the night. Benedict and Marcel were to take another shift at dawn if it was required.

With each passing hour, Tristan was more and more glad that he had sent Lily back to the keep with them, for it began to look less and less as if the ship would manage to find the shore. Even in this storm, which had developed into the worst Tristan had ever seen, it should have come along some time ago.

He looked out into the darkness, seeing the pelting snow illuminated by the reflection of firelight in the temporarily mounted shield, and shook his head.

Yet not much more time had passed when he thought he heard a sound from the beach far below, a sound that was not connected to the pounding waves and driving wind. It was a sound very much like the scrape of oars against rocks.

He listened very carefully, and then finally, the sound came again. It was followed by a faint shout of triumph.

He and Kendran looked at one another and ran to lean over the short wall. They could see nothing, but more noises came to them. It seemed that someone had arrived at their shore. Tristan could only hope that it was Lily's father.

More minutes passed, and Tristan was just wondering if he should go and investigate himself when there was another shout from below. He went to the edge and heard a male voice cry, "You there, is this Brackenmoore?" It was obvious from his tone that the man thought he was addressing an inferior.

Tristan shouted back, "Aye, it is Brackenmoore."

The man called out, "I am Maxim Harcourt."

Tristan answered discreetly, well aware that he and his brother were here alone. "I am glad to hear that, my lord. We heard that you were coming and lit the fire to guide your way."

There was scornful and bitter laughter from below. "I wish for you to tell your master that I thank him for the aid and that for his trouble I will happily kill him quickly rather than make him suffer as I had planned. His folk, on the other hand, will feel the full force of my revenge. The wrong he has done me cannot be appeased in any other way. He will have my answer to his insult in the morning."

Kendran gasped and opened his lips to shout down to him, but Tristan covered his mouth with a firm hand. Clearly Harcourt could see nothing but their silhouettes in the glow of the fire. It would never occur to him that the Ainsworths themselves would be manning the tower. And that suited Tristan well enough at the moment. They were two unarmed men against a troop, however weary, and the bolt at the entrance to the tower would not hold against determined men. He would not see his brother's life end so abruptly.

He called down, "Aye, my lord, I will tell him."

With that he heard them move away from the base of the tower.

Lily shook her head in disbelief. "How could he do this after you saved their lives?" How could her father allow it? But she knew the answer to that question. He would not have the courage or the manpower to make a protest.

Tristan wiped a weary hand across his face. "Clearly the only reason he did not kill us was that he wished for us to bring the message that he would attack in the morning. I have no doubt that he would have gotten the message to the keep in some other way had he known who I was. You have no idea how much I wanted to kill the bastard myself in those moments when he stood at the bottom of the tower and told me just how great his retribution would be.''

Kendran stood. ''We should have killed him.''

''Do not be ridiculous, Kendran. I would never spend your life so cheaply. What could the two of us do against an armed troop, no matter how wet and cold they might be?''

Lily put her hands to her head. ''I should not have come back to the keep with Benedict and Marcel. You could have given me to him and this would all be over.''

The glance Tristan sent her way was exasperated, but he made no rejoinder. He instead looked to Benedict, leaving Lily angry at his disregard of her solution.

She spoke directly to Benedict, who was sitting with his hands propped under his chin. ''I could go to the encampment now. Surely he would leave you all alone if he had me. Perhaps he did not clearly understand that the tower was lit in order to aid him?''

Tristan cast her another glance of exasperation.

Benedict gave her a look that was very much like the one she had received from Tristan. ''There is nothing to be gained in that, Lily. It is Tristan he wants now. He has said as much. Your sacrifice would be for naught.''

Lily clenched her hands in frustration. She would get no further by arguing with these obstinate Ainsworth men.

Benedict shrugged. ''There is nothing more to be

done this night. He will do nothing until morning at the earliest, and not even then, should the storm continue to rage on as it is."

Tristan stood. "You are right, Benedict. We had best all find our beds. The watch will alert us to any untoward action on Harcourt's part." His knowing gaze went to Lily. "I will tell the watch that they must alert us to anyone attempting to leave the keep."

Lily stiffened. None of them, it seemed, had any sense in this. She turned and hurried from the room.

She was halted on the stairs by Tristan's voice. Lily did not know what more he could possibly say to her. She turned to him with her head held high. When she saw that his expression was filled with regret, she wondered at it.

Tristan spoke quickly. "I realize that you feel a need to do what you think is best in this, Lily. I concede that you have the right to do so. As you told me, your life is your own and I have no more right to oblige you to do my will than anyone else. When this is all over you may leave Brackenmoore without argument."

She took a step closer to him, his soft tone of voice making her believe she might be able to make him see reason. "By then it may be too late. I do not want anyone to be hurt more than they already have been. I love—" her voice caught "—Sabina, would have no ill come to her ever."

His reply did not encourage her. "It is possible that Harcourt knows all, not only about us but about Sabina. What think you such a madman as he would do to the woman who has wronged him by bearing another man's child?"

She faltered, then raised her chin. "I will tell him

the truth, that I did not know of what I had done when I said I would marry him.''

''Your father did.''

She took a deep breath. ''That is upon his head. Not mine.''

Tristan shook his own head. ''I cannot allow it. I…would never forgive myself if any ill came to you. Can you not see that? Can you not see that I cannot allow the mother of my child to put herself at such risk to protect me? Nor would any of my brothers.''

''Heaven save us from the Ainsworth pride and obstinacy,'' Lily cried, throwing up her hands in despair. She then turned and ran up the steps, leaving him standing there. But as she went, Lily began to realize that she was not only angry, but moved by the care she was shown by this family. She could not let these maddening, honorable and overprotective men bear the brunt of her own mistakes. Furthermore, she did not require their acquiescence to act. She knew what had to be done, and needed no more than to find the courage within herself to do it.

A sharp stab of regret pierced her breast at the knowledge. It was regret that she would be leaving so very much behind her—leaving everything that mattered to her, the only true sense of belonging she had ever known.

Sabina.

Tristan. And with him she left all hope of love or passion.

She paused in her headlong rush as a thought prodded at the edge of her mind. Yes, she would leave all passion and love behind with Tristan, but she was not yet gone.

What harm would it do to anyone if she took just

a small piece of happiness and yes, pleasure, with her when she went? What Genevieve had inadvertently revealed about her feelings for Marcel had left Lily with the certainty that she would be hurting no one with what she was about to do.

She felt a sweet twinge of longing take her as she raised her head and went on toward Sabina's chambers. The babe was sleeping soundly, and soon everyone else would be as well.

Lily closed the door and dropped her cape to the floor. There was no hesitation in any of her actions. Her mind was at peace. She had made her decisions and would live with the consequences of them. But there was one gift she would give herself before she left.

Tristan.

Slowly she moved toward the bed. The room was rosy with the light of the fire, and she had no trouble finding her way.

When she bent over him, Tristan opened his eyes. Lily did not give him any time to speak; she leaned over and put her lips on his.

He gave just the briefest start before his lips softened, and he reached up to hold the back of her head with one hand while the other sought the curve of her waist. Lily sighed against his mouth, not even realizing until he welcomed her so very completely that she had been afraid he might not.

A shiver passed through her as he lifted her up to lay her across the expanse of his bare chest. She ran trembling fingers over his biceps, realizing as she did so that his physical strength had always had the power to thrill her. As a girl, she had loved the sense of being protected it gave. Now Lily reveled in this difference between him as a man and herself as a woman. No longer did she feel the need to hide behind another's strength. Now she had found her own, and it had given her the courage to take this moment. And take it she would, without demur.

His eyes met hers in the glow of the fire. "I can hardly believe that you are real."

She traced her hand over his lean cheek. "I am real, Tristan."

He stretched up to kiss the curve of her breasts above her gown. She closed her eyes, delight shivering through her as he whispered huskily, "Have you learned that Genevieve has refused to wed me?"

She was not completely surprised, given what she had surmised about Genevieve's feelings for Marcel. "You should have told me."

He smoothed his hand over the silky curtain of her hair. "I wanted you to come to me of your own will and for no other reason."

She looked at him closely, yearned so very much for… But nay; Lily knew what she had to do. Yet she need not think on that now. This moment belonged to her.

She leaned over him and sighed. "No more talk now, Tristan." Then she put her mouth to his, kissing him until she felt her own heart pound, her blood sing.

When Tristan groaned and moved to roll her over onto the bed, Lily resisted him, shaking her head. "Nay," she whispered softly. When he looked at her in question, she sat up and reached for the hem of her night rail.

Tristan watched, barely breathing as Lily pulled the filmy gown over her head and dropped it on the bed.

His gaze traced her face, each feature so delicately beautiful and beloved. It then dipped lower to take in her perfect form, those raspberry-tipped breasts, so white against the midnight curtain of her hair, so firm and lovely. Then on he roved to her narrow waist and gently flaring hips, before his eyes settled once more on her face. He felt his breath quicken as he saw that his perusal had caused her own lids to grow heavy in response.

Lily's pulse raced at the desire in Tristan's eyes as he looked at her. She ran her tongue over suddenly dry lips. Again he reached out for her. But Lily felt a need to explore him, to pleasure him and thus herself.

Tristan was confused by her actions but acquiesced as she gently, but insistently, pushed his hands away. When Lily leaned over and placed her soft mouth, then her hot tongue against his chest, Tristan gasped, his hands twining in the silky fall of her black hair as it spilled across his body.

Again he moved to bring her down to the bed beside him and again she drew away. She continued to kiss him, her mouth leaving a trail of fire on his flesh.

Tristan was drowning, lost in the waves of fiery sensation engendered by her velvety tongue and lips, every fiber of his being urging him toward fulfillment. Yet he forced himself up out of that downy darkness of desire, knowing that if he did not he would be unable to control his release for another moment.

His hands found her delicate shoulders, and this time he would brook no rebellion to his intent. He drew her beside him, his mouth covering hers, plundering that dewy softness.

Lily's head spun, and she felt herself melting into

a sea of pleasure. She had so enjoyed Tristan's reaction to her caresses, had so reveled in his unmistakable delight, that she had not wanted to stop. Yet when he kissed her this way she had no power to think of anything beyond her own response.

As he laid her down upon the bed and leaned over her, she reached up to hold him to her, to bring that knowing mouth back to hers. He did not comply, but whispered, "Nay, little temptress. 'Tis my turn now."

Lily had no words to reply, for the instant his mouth found the tip of her breast she was suffused by heat. The more intently he suckled the more it grew, spiraling down to settle in flickering ripples of delight that licked upward from her lower belly to set her every nerve afire.

His hands dipped down to cradle her hips, fitting the curves as if formed to do so, lifting her gently against the hard length of his manhood. Her head fell back at the sweet easing it brought to the aching core of her. But even as it eased her, the gentle pressure made her yearn for more and she arched against him more fully, desiring above all things to have him slip into her heated flesh.

Tristan knew what she wanted, because he too felt the very same drive to complete their union. Yet he wanted this moment to last forever, wanted to draw out their loving to a fine point of passion.

When she wriggled beneath him he chuckled, a husky, sultry sound that made her flesh tingle, and held her still.

Her fingers curled in the thick hair at the back of his head, and she rolled her own head from side to side, gasping in complete abandon, "Please, Tristan, do not tease me so. I need you."

That pleading voice brought him to the last of his strength. He could deny them no more. He drew back, then forward, slipping into the warmth of her body in one perfect motion.

Lily sobbed out his name. "Tristan, Tristan. I love you," she cried.

He froze in place, his heart contracting as he looked up into her eyes with both shock and inexpressible longing. "You love me?"

She met his gaze directly, her gray eyes dark with passion and yes, love. "Yes, Tristan, I love you, love you as you are now, as you were when we met, have always loved you."

He closed his eyes and his heart seemed to explode with the force of his emotions, filling his chest with a warmth as bright as the sun. He looked down at her, feeling the intensity of his love pouring from his own gaze. "I have so longed to hear those words again."

The impact of the words sang through her blood, bringing each nerve in her body to vibrant life, making the fire at the joining of their two bodies burn all the hotter. She arched beneath him. "Then take me, my love, take me to paradise with you."

Tristan gave in to that sweet melding of flesh, lost all sense of himself as being separate from Lily. He was in her and of her, riding pulse upon pulse of ever-increasing rapture. "Lily, my sweet Lily," he whispered against the dampness of her forehead, and she reached out to hold him more closely to her with her arms and long slender legs.

Lily met his every thrust with equal measure, losing herself, drowning in the wondrous delight of their union as the sensations grew to an excruciating peak of urgency. And then the pinnacle was breached, her body convulsing in rapturous shudders of delight. Joyously she lost herself in Tristan, taking in his breath, his scent, his very essence as he stiffened above her and she felt the spill of his seed inside her.

Tristan sighed, rolling onto his side, pulling Lily with him, unable to release her from arms that had ached too long to be filled with her softness.

He wanted to talk, to tell her how much she meant to him, how glad he was that she loved him.

Dear God, Lily loved him.

He wanted to make plans for their future together. But the knowledge that she loved him had released such a dam of emotions and pent-up regrets that it seemed to sap him of every ounce of his strength. God, how he had fought his anguish at losing her.

He closed his eyes, his hand twining in the silkiness of her hair, the same three words repeating in his wearied mind. *I love you, I love you, I love...*

Chapter Fourteen

Driven to accomplish this deed before she lost her courage, Lily slipped from Tristan's bed. He seemed so very deeply asleep that she was tempted to touch her hand to his beloved cheek one last time, but she dared not. Drawing herself up, she turned away from him and hurried back to Sabina's chambers.

Silently, she went to the child's bed, her hungry gaze drinking in each feature of that so dearly loved little face. Her own tiny daughter, who would grow to womanhood without her. Lily put her hand to her aching heart. Dear heaven, she had not known it would hurt so very much to go.

Quickly then, before she lost all courage, she crossed the room and dressed in the black velvet gown and white underdress, as they were the warmest of the ones Genevieve had given her. She then threw on the cloak and left the room for the last time.

Her heart felt so tight in her chest as that door closed that she thought it might surely stop beating from the pain. But it did not. She called on the memory of Tristan's love, which burned like a torch inside her. It made following through with her decision bear-

able. She would be worthy of the love he bore her,
even if it meant that she would suffer for it for the
rest of her days.

It was right that she should be the one to act here,
to set things right. Too many of her years had been
stolen by the whims of others. Be her decisions good
or ill, they would be her own.

The snow muffled her footfalls as she made her
way through the castle grounds. But she had no need
to concern herself with that at any rate. All the men
she could see in the light of the flares burning along
the castle walls kept their attention fixed without.

Her pain at leaving Tristan and Sabina had kept
Lily from concentrating on her own anxiety about
what Maxim might say or do. But now that she was
on her way, that worry was fast turning to real fear.

She tried to tell herself that thinking this way
would serve no purpose. She had to remain calm and
in control of herself if she hoped to convince Maxim
of the truth—that she had come here of her own will
and that he need take no revenge upon those inside.

But that did not make the dread disappear.

It was made even more powerful by her feelings of
apprehension when she pulled open the secret door
and looked into the blackness beyond. Dear heaven,
but it was dark down there, dark and damp, if the
smell that rose up from inside was any indication.

She had not been able to risk bringing a light with
her.

For a moment Lily balked. She did not know if she
could make herself go down there into that all-
encompassing darkness alone.

Yet did she not have to, for the sake of all the folk

here who had accepted her without question? For the sake of her own daughter?

Taking a deep breath, she started down the ladder. Once she had gained the bottom, Lily was surprised to find that the smell was not quite as bad as she had feared.

Staying close to the wall, she started off, hoping that there would be few twists and turns to confuse her.

As she went on Lily realized that if there were any twists or turns she might well be in serious danger of becoming lost, for she could see nothing. She had never been afraid of the dark, but this was beyond darkness, so enveloping and deep that she could not even see the shadow of her hand before her eyes. It did not help that the air inside the tunnel soon began to seem musty and close, making breathing almost an effort.

She did not stop, telling herself that she must go forward, must find the end of this labyrinth. On she trudged, her fingers sliding along the uneven surface of the wall. She closed her eyes, summoning up Sabina's dear little face, and kept going.

It was some time later that she realized that the air had become crisper again.

She moved on with more enthusiasm, sensing that the end of her goal was near. When at last she found herself stepping out into the snow-covered forest, Lily breathed a deep sigh of relief. She raised her head and took a deep breath as the snowflakes fell upon her upturned cheeks. She, Lily, had done it. With no help from her parents or Tristan. She was capable of standing on her own two feet.

That thought drove her to continue on to the encamped army. Facing Maxim was something she had to do, no matter what the outcome.

Lily gained the camp with no problem; its location was known to all in the keep. She circled the edge until she located a tent that was larger than the rest. Quickly she went to it and ducked inside.

Maxim sat at a table, writing on a sheet of parchment. He continued to write with a distracted wave of his hand. "Put it over there and go."

Lily stood where she was, unable to say a word.

As the silence went on, Maxim looked up with an angry grunt. "I said…" But the moment he saw her his eyes widened beneath straight gray eyebrows. For what seemed a very long time, he simply sat there staring at her as if she were a mirage.

She took a deep breath.

That seemed to break the spell, for he stood and rushed toward her, his expression unreadable. Yet the tight grip he took of her shoulders told her something of his feelings, as did the harsh tone of his voice when he spoke her name. "Lily, how did you come here?"

Remembering that she wanted to gain Maxim's acquiescence to her wishes, Lily tried to stand still beneath that grip. She told herself that he was upset, and rightly so in his own mind, but his thumbs were digging into her collarbone quite painfully. She could not help trying to shrug loose from his grasp as she said, "Maxim, please, you are hurting me."

He heeded her not all, for his reaction was to shake her roughly. "I said, how did you come here?" He stopped shaking her to look behind her. "Did Ainsworth bring you?"

She tried to reason with him, to get through the anger. "He did not bring me. I came on my own. I knew that I had to talk with you, to explain what had happened.''

He laughed bitterly. "Explain! Is there aught you can say that will take us back to the beginning? Can you erase all that has occurred since the moment you left the inn?''

She took a deep breath and let it out slowly, trying as much as she was able to have patience with his rage. "You know that I cannot do that. But I can tell you that no one here meant you any insult then, nor do they now. Can we not just take our leave and allow them some peace?''

A sudden and unexpected calm descended upon him, and if Lily had been any less distraught, she would have questioned it. As it was, she simply listened with hope as he said, "So that is why you are here—to tell me that none here mean me any insult? To ask me if we cannot just go on our way and leave them in peace?''

She peered up at him, her gaze filled with optimism. "Yes, that is what I wish above all else. You will have my undying devotion all the rest of our days together if you will heed me in this.''

He stared at her for one long, incredulous moment before he exploded in another spate of fury. "Little fool that you are, Lily, you can not actually imagine that is possible.'' He made a sweeping gesture with his free hand. "All my men know that I have come here to rescue my bride, the bride they have been scouring the countryside for these past weeks.'' His scathing gaze raked her. "Do you imagine that your wishes would outweigh regaining my own honor? Not now, nor ever, will any woman mean enough to me that I would simply walk away from such a slight.''

She shook her head, aghast not only at his anger, but at his total lack of concern for herself or anyone else in this matter. Clearly he cared for nothing but his pride.

Never had she thought he would take her suggestion easily. She had felt it would take persuasion on her part, but she had not thought anyone could be this hateful, this self-centered.

Tristan and Genevieve had been right about him all along. And she, fool that she was, had been suspicious of their antagonism, in order to absolve her father of any conscious wrongdoing in giving her to such a man.

She could no longer do so. No one who loved her—as she had thought her father did—would ever do something so thoughtless, even in order to secure his position at court. She could not withhold her anger, which was made stronger by her disillusionment. "You are despicable. If only I had not had to regain my memory in order to—"

It was her father who interrupted her. She could hear the fear in his voice as he said, "You have regained your memory?"

Lily swung around to face him, realizing they had not heard his entrance in the heat of their discussion. "Yes, Father. I have regained my memory."

Regret and sadness colored his gray eyes, and for a moment she felt sympathy for him as he said, "Then you now know…you have seen…?"

She nodded, rubbing a weary hand over her brow as she said, "Aye, I know all." She cast him a warning look. She had a sinking suspicion that her father was speaking of Sabina. Lily did not wish for Maxim to know of Sabina, not for her own sake but for the child's. Something told her this man would not wish her babe anything but ill.

But it seemed that Maxim was as clever as he was evil, for he turned to her father. "What does she now know? What has she seen?"

Her father looked at his hands, then back at the other man. Lily willed him to remain silent, yet he did not. Robert Gray started forward, his voice pleading. "Maxim, there is something I must tell you. I know that you bear these Ainsworths much ill will, as I do. Yet they did save our lives by lighting that tower, and there is a child involved. Lily's child and my own grandchild."

Lily cringed as Maxim exploded in rage. "A child, you say? Lily has borne a child to one of these Ainsworths?"

Robert Gray backed away from him in genuine fear. "Maxim, I know that you are angry, and you have a right to be. But it was some years past and the memory of the man, as well as that of the child, had been utterly wiped from her mind. I did not imagine…did not think—"

"You did not think indeed! Can you even wonder that I would want the leavings of such as they?" Maxim swung around to face the horrified Lily. "You, whore, will pay for this insult to me. Too many know of my engagement to you to draw back from it now, and I can manage to comfort myself with your wealth. But no one must ever know of this child."

She ran to him, grasping his arm as she pleaded in desperation, "Nay, I will never tell a soul. I meant it when I said that I would leave with you and never look back. We have kept my identity a secret from all here."

He shook her off, his face as cold and emotionless as granite. ''Even if that was true, the Ainsworths know. I will not afford them that.''

She looked at him in dawning horror, realizing that his hatred for the Ainsworths had driven him past all reason. ''What will you do?''

He leaned over, his burning brown eyes as menacing and evil as anything she had encountered in her most terrifying nightmare. ''No matter how long it takes I will burn this castle to the ground. Not one stone will I leave standing.''

''No,'' she sobbed, her heart breaking inside her. ''My babe.''

The words seemed to only make him more cruel. He went to the door and called out, ''Guard!'' A man entered and bowed deeply, his gaze never meeting his master's. Maxim spat. ''Take her and her father to his tent and make sure they remain there until I say otherwise.'' The man bowed again without raising his eyes.

Lily knew there would be no hope in securing the aid of one so cowed. She did not look at her father, knowing he would be of no help, either. She moved toward the door of the tent without another word.

Maxim halted her briefly. ''*Lady* Lily—and I want you to know that I use the term loosely.'' When she met his gaze, he smiled with cold pleasure. ''You had best find some rest, my dear. I would not have you miss any of the festivities that will begin at dawn.''

''Tristan!''

Tristan woke to the insistent sound of his own name. Even with the fog of the first deep sleep he had had since the accident three years gone by clouding his mind, he reached for Lily. He reached for her and found emptiness.

His confused gaze alighted on Genevieve, who stood beside the bed. He shook his head to try to clear it as he peered about the chamber. "Where is Lily?" He had no concern about what his words might reveal to the other woman.

Genevieve answered hurriedly. "That is why I am come, Tristan. Lily has gone."

He bolted upright. "Gone! What can you mean?"

She wiped her honey-gold curls back from her forehead, her eyes haunted by fear. "She has left the castle."

Tristan leaped from the bed and began to pull on his leggings, completely oblivious to the girl's presence. "I will have the head of whomever is on watch."

Genevieve put a hand on his arm as he raised it to tug on his tunic. "There will be no need for that. She did not go by way of the gate, Tristan. She left through the tunnel."

Incredulity made his eyes widen. "The tunnel. By God, how could she even know of its existence?"

"There I cannot help you," she told him. "I know only that she was aware of it and that she has gone by way of it."

"God's blood," he shouted, sitting down on the edge of the bed as he jerked on his boots. He then stood. "You are sure of this, Genevieve? There can be no mistake?"

She shook her head. "No mistake. From the upper window, as I was coming from the privy, I saw her go into the shed. She was naught but a dark shape against the snow, but I felt it was Lily. I went to

Sabina's chambers to make certain that I was not in error. She was not there. I then came directly here and she is not here, either, though from your reactions I think she was.''

Tristan faced her. ''I will not apologize for that.''

She faced him with affection in her gaze. ''There is no need, brother of my heart. As I am beginning to understand, love has its own order.''

He put his arms around her, giving her a tight hug. Genevieve pushed him away quickly. ''Lily has put herself into the hands of a very dangerous and selfish man. She may be in grave peril. You must not delay.''

Tristan reached for his sword. ''If he harms one hair on her head, Maxim Harcourt will pray for death long before it comes to him.''

Lily paced the floor of the tent. She had nothing to say to her father, who sat on his bed, his hand clasped to his head.

Unexpectedly he spoke into the stillness. ''Lily, I have no words to tell you how very sorry I am for all of this. I should not have spoken of the babe. I thought that doing so might make him understand.''

She could not keep the fatigue and frustration from her voice. ''Did you, Father?'' She met his regretful eyes.

''Aye, I did. But I now see that I have made many errors. You must understand, Lily, that I had no notion of just how unscrupulous Maxim could be.''

Her brow arched, and he had the grace to look away. ''Oh, 'tis true enough that I knew he was not above underhandedness,'' he continued. ''But you must believe that I did not know how far he would go. Even when he decided to attack the keep after they had lit the signal fire in order to aid us, I did not think…'' His eyes focused on hers, pleaded for her belief in what he was saying. ''It was not until he said that he would burn down the keep with your child inside. Then I knew.''

Lily moved to sit down beside him. ''I do believe you, Father. But I must tell you that you could not have been so blind to Maxim's true nature lest you wished to be.''

He blanched. ''I cannot deny that what you say may well be fact.'' He looked at her more closely. ''You are different, daughter. There is a strength in you that I have not seen for a very long time.''

She shrugged. ''Before, I was a headstrong girl. I have grown to be a woman in the last weeks, Father. My illness delayed that process, but it has finally come, and rightly so.''

He nodded. ''I see that now. Your mother and I, we did not aid you in that. We just felt so guilty over what had happened—your running away, the accident….'' His eyes hardened. ''Those Ainsworths had left you to die there alone. We thought it was for your own good that we kept the truth from you.''

Lily stiffened. ''Benedict believed me dead, and Tristan and Sabina were so very ill that he was afraid—''

''Sabina!'' Robert Gray interrupted. ''So it is a girl child, and the lad called her after your grandmother.'' There was no mistaking the amazement in his voice.

Lily nodded. ''He knew that was my wish. He is a good man, Father, and one I would happily spend my life with if I had not thrown it all away by coming here this night.''

He put his hand over hers. ''I was wrong to expect

you to marry Maxim. Although I was not aware of the extent of his dishonorable nature, I did know that you did not love him. I would not ask that of you again.''

She looked at him with determination as well as compassion. ''And you must understand that I would no longer obey. I was wrong to meet Tristan without your consent, but I loved him. You could have tried to take that into account rather than deny me from the beginning. Even an hour ago I believed I should help you, although my main concern in coming to Maxim was to ask him to leave without harming those I love. I have realized that I did not make your troubles, Father, you did. To continue to protect you would only keep you from seeing that.''

He looked at the ground. ''I believed York would be defeated. We could not make an alliance with an Ainsworth.''

She took a deep breath and stood. ''Yet none of that is of any importance now. I have ruined all hope for any of us. For with Tristan and…Sabina gone—'' she could no longer withhold a sob ''—with them dead, my life would have no purpose or hope.''

Utter frustration brought her to her feet, and Lily began to pace once more. If only she could think of some way to rectify the situation.

She had made a terrible mistake in coming to the camp. Why had she not listened to Tristan when he had told her that Maxim would not heed her?

Because in spite of everything, she had not wished to face the fact that her father could knowingly give her hand to one such as he. In truth, nothing could have prepared her for the pure evil of the man. Now she had only served to put all at Brackenmoore to death.

Tristan dispatched the guard with one quick thrust of his sword. He knew Lily had to be inside the tent: it was the only one with a guard posted at the entrance. Other than that there was very little activity in the camp, apart from the three watchmen who had been set to patrol through the night. The storm had begun to die down somewhat, but it was by no means over, and Harcourt must feel that he was safe from assault as long as it went on.

Silently Tristan moved to the door of the tent. He could hear no sound coming from inside. He took a deep breath. If he was wrong, he walked into certain disaster. If he was right, Lily was inside. On that chance he had to act.

In one fluid motion he flipped open the door and stepped inside. His gaze came to rest on an older man seated upon the bed.

An instant later, his attention was drawn by a joyous gasp to his left. Lily stood there smiling like the very sun, a torch in her hand, ready to strike. "Now this is a strange welcome from the woman who loves me," Tristan said pleasantly.

She lowered the torch and ran to him as he dropped the tent flap in place and strode forward. "I feared you might be one of them. Oh, Tristan, I am so glad you have come. I should have listened to you from the start. Maxim is so mad with rage that he would not hear me. We must leave this tent now and warn everyone inside Brackenmoore, for he means to burn down the keep at dawn."

Immediately Tristan's teasing expression turned serious even as he clasped her to him with his free arm. In the other he kept his sword ready. He looked to the man on the bed. "I take it you are Lily's father?"

She answered for him. "He is, Tristan, and we must take him with us, for he has been held prisoner here with me for deigning to say that Maxim has gone too far."

Tristan gave a brief nod. He was glad that Gray had come to his senses in the end, but he could summon no true respect for the man. "Let us go then and quickly."

Even as Lily's father stood to join them, there was a shout from outside. Tristan's brow knit. From the sounds of it, he was fairly certain that the watch had discovered the fallen guard. "I am found out. There is no time to lose."

As he moved to the tent opening, Maxim Harcourt stepped though it. His face immediately twisted in a cold smile. "Ah, Ainsworth, how very good of you to come and afford me the pleasure of killing you by my own hand. I did so regret the lack of intimacy in burning you alive. You and your whelp."

Tristan rushed at him with a shout of rage. "Bastard." His sword clashed loudly upon Maxim's, who had barely raised his own in time.

Lily shouted, "Tristan, have a care."

Even before he could land another blow, several soldiers raced through the tent flap. They grabbed Tristan from behind.

Rage rushed through Tristan's blood as he tried to break free from the four men and failed. "Fight me, you bastard," he screamed. His burning gaze fixed on Maxim with hatred. "Are you afraid of me then, that you must set your lackeys upon me? Can you not face me as a man?''

Maxim scowled darkly. "I am not afraid to face you, Ainsworth. You are as nothing to me."

"Then prove it before your men by meeting me here and now." Even in his anger, Tristan could feel the excitement from the soldiers. Though he was obeyed without question, Maxim Harcourt was clearly not a man who was loved by his retainers. He ruled by power and intimidation, and Tristan had just brought his position into question.

It seemed that Maxim was well aware of this, for he glanced about the faces of his men, then shrugged with studied indifference. He waved a hand. "Release him." He then turned to Tristan. "Make ready, sir. I would not have this prove too simple."

Tristan stood tall as the men backed away. Perhaps he had gained them nothing by this. Maxim was not likely to allow him to kill him even if it did mean calling on his men. But Tristan would have a place to expend this great dark rage that burned inside him like the fires of hell. And perhaps he would put a rent in the fearful hold Maxim had over his troops.

He didn't wait for another invitation, but charged the other man. Perhaps if he acted quickly enough, he thought grimly, he *could* manage to kill the blackguard before anyone could stop him.

But Maxim was ready for him and countered the blow.

Tristan set to in earnest, feeling out his opponent. He realized after a few moments that Maxim was quite proficient in the art of swordsmanship. He was, in fact, very skilled. There was a coldness and precision to his technique that had likely proved quite formidable in many a contest. With his conceited swagger and superior expression, he managed to give the impression that he was somehow toying with Tristan.

But he was not better than Tristan. And he was not fighting to protect those he loved. Tristan began to note that sometimes there was just the slightest hesitation before Maxim recovered from a blow to his left side.

On they fought. Tristan watched, waited and worked his way around to that oh so slightly vulnerable left side.

And just as he was ready to strike, praying with all his might that the blow would do enough damage to kill the man who had come to destroy his family, there was a sharp cry from outside the tent.

Maxim called out to his men, not pausing in his attack, "Go and find out what is amiss."

They ran from the tent just as total chaos seemed to erupt, if the cacophony of noise from outside was any indication. Tristan realized that his brothers must be attacking the camp.

For the first time, he saw anxiety enter his enemy's eyes. Maxim called to Robert Gray, "Get your sword, man."

Lily cried, "No, Father, do not help him."

The older man shook his head. "There is no need for you to worry, Lily." He looked to Maxim. "I will not aid you in this, nor in anything in the future. You were prepared to kill my grandchild without compunction."

Maxim looked to Tristan, who smiled and said, "Make yourself ready."

Maxim ran at him then, slashing downward in reck-

less anger. Tristan was prepared for him. He thrust
upward and met flesh. Maxim stumbled backward,
dropping his sword as he tried to pull Tristan's blade
from his belly. He fell to his knees, his shocked gaze
going to Tristan's. He then toppled and lay still.

Tristan stepped backward as Lily ran to his side.
"Dear God, Tristan, you have killed him."

He held her tightly for a long desperate moment,
then drew back. "I have killed him, but we are not
out of danger yet. Even if those are my brothers' men
outside, I must somehow get you safely from the bat-
tle."

Tristan turned to Gray. "Are you with us?"

"I am," he answered, taking up his sword.

Outside, Tristan saw that the sky had begun to
lighten on its path to dawn and the snow had nearly
ceased falling. But it was still fairly dark in the camp,
and the many small battles that raged throughout appeared as dark pockets of turmoil against the white
of the snow. It was obvious now, as men continued
to come down the hill from the keep, that Benedict's
army had indeed attacked the camp.

Tristan could only assume that Genevieve, bless
her, had alerted them.

He kept hold of Lily's hand as he led her through
the fray, hoping that perhaps they could make it out
of the embattled camp without mishap. If he could
get Lily into the tunnel, he could return to help end
the fighting.

Though she held on tightly to him as she moved
along at his side, she did not cower. Her bravery did
not surprise him, and though he knew it was what had
gotten them here, he also knew he would not change

one hair of her head. He loved her, body and soul, without reservation.

It was as they reached the outskirts of the camp that they were beset by two of Maxim's men. Tristan wondered what they would do if they knew their master was dead, but had no time to discuss this as he leaped forward, putting himself between them and Lily. While he engaged one, Gray took on the other. The fighting was short-lived.

Tristan stepped back from the fallen man and shook his head. He'd had enough of killing this day. He drew Lily with him to a higher point on the rise above the camp, raised his arm and shouted loudly, "Harcourt is dead. I invite you to lay down your arms."

A moment later a voice nearby took up the call. "Harcourt is dead. Lay down your arms."

More voices echoed the same words. And then Tristan heard the dull clatter of swords being dropped to the snow-covered ground, along with shouts for quarter. As more voices joined in, he saw his brothers appear from the fray. One by one they came toward him, to stand looking down at the gathering as Benedict's soldiers moved to surround the invaders.

Tristan had not realized how worried he was that something might befall one of his siblings until the three were standing there beside him. He held out his hand to each in turn. "My brothers. You have my thanks."

Benedict spoke for them all. "We were only looking after our own." He threw his arms about Tristan and then Lily. "Praise God, you are both well."

She drew back with bright, tear-dampened eyes.

Tristan laughed, feeling tears start to his own eyes

at his brother's acceptance of Lily. "I have not even had opportunity to do that yet."

He took her in his arms, his mouth finding her eager one, amid shouts of encouragement from his brothers, including Marcel. Then Tristan drew away, telling Kendran, "Please take Lily and her father to the keep. I will come when we have finished here." He looked to her father. "There are several matters that need discussing."

Lily and her father waited in the library. It was less public than the hall, and she did not wish to take him to Sabina's chambers, as the child would still be asleep, though he had expressed a wish to see her. Lily was not averse to this, but felt it must wait until Tristan gave his consent. She felt a strange sense of unreality about it all and was not sure what would happen now. Did Tristan want them to spend their lives together or did he wish for her to remain here as Sabina's honored maid, as he had once suggested?

They were served warmed wine and food. Maeve was clearly pleased at the fact that Lily was well. When Lily introduced her father, Maeve said not a word, though she did cast him a long look. Lily told her no details, having decided that it was not her place. Tristan would explain all, or not, as he desired.

Tristan arrived after what seemed an eternity, though Lily knew it had not been so very long. She rushed toward him and he took her into his arms, his lips meeting hers with not only joy, but ill-suppressed passion as well.

Lily felt her body respond to Tristan's as it always did, in spite of the fact that her father stood by, in spite of the fact that her future here was uncertain.

Passionate was the way things were between them, the way they would always be.

Her father spoke up hastily from behind her. "We will return to Lakeland and arrange a wedding. All here will be invited."

Lily turned from Tristan and spoke with unwavering determination. "You speak too soon, Father. If he will allow it, I will remain here at Brackenmoore, be it as Tristan's wife or not."

Tristan swung her around to face him, his eyes hot on hers. "If I will allow it! I want nothing more than that you should be my wife and the mother of my child—of all our children."

Happiness swept through her in a cleansing tide, and her face flushed with warmth and happiness. "I love you, Tristan Ainsworth, and there shall be as many children as you desire."

She raised her own mouth as he bent to kiss her, but her father's voice halted him. "What of Lakeland? What of your heritage? Maxim, God rot him, would have looked to Lakeland upon my death, if nothing else."

She faced her father with resolve as well as compassion. "Can you not see that my place is here with Tristan and my child?"

The older man reached toward her. "You are my child, my heir."

Slowly she took his hand. "I am your child, but I am a woman now and you must accept that. I love this man, who has no reason to feel any obligation to you or Lakeland." She took Tristan's hand in her free one. "I also love my daughter, who needs me with her."

Tristan spoke up then. "Perhaps, Lord Gray, there

is a chance of beginning again. Perhaps in time we will come to know one another as we should have in the beginning. Perhaps then we will come to some terms concerning the lands you hold so dear.''

The nobleman looked at him, his eyes filled with amazement. ''You would offer this, after all I have done?''

Tristan shrugged. ''You are Lily's father, and no matter what has occurred, I know she bears you much love. No more do I fear that you can take her from me. Her choice is made, and I am not so poor in spirit that I cannot share some small bit of my own happiness.'' His shining gaze met Lily's and her heart filled to bursting as he went on. ''For there is so very much of it.''

Lily let go of her father's hand and turned to the man she loved. Tristan was correct—no matter what happened, he need never fear that she would ever go from him again. She looked into his eyes. ''I am yours, love, now and for always, body, mind and soul.''

He bent and whispered into her ear, ''Let us away to a more private place, my love, where I might take advantage of the promise in those words.''

Her troubled gaze found his as she whispered back, ''What of Sabina, Tristan? What shall we tell her?''

''Why, that we are to be married and you will be her mother, that she has grandparents. Time enough to worry about the rest when she is slightly older.''

Lily bit her lip in anxiety. ''But will she understand when she is older? 'Tis all so unbelievable.''

''Pardon my interrupting.'' A voice came from behind them.

Lily spun around to see Genevieve in the open

doorway. She held a smiling, pink-cheeked Sabina in her arms, and when she saw that she had their attention, she continued, "Maeve told me you were here. I thought the little one should meet her mother and her grandpa."

Lily looked to Tristan, who was smiling as widely as his daughter. "That is a fine notion. Bring her to me." He took Sabina in his arms and turned toward Lily. "Sabina, how would you like for Lily to be your mother?"

The smiling Genevieve then sailed off again as the child beamed like the very sun. "I love her to be my mother." She held out her chubby arms, and Lily took her into her own, her throat catching on a sob of sheer joy as she breathed in the soft warm scent of her child.

Lily was pulled from this moment of indescribable joy by her father's voice. "She is so very beautiful, Lily. So very like her mother. God forgive me for the wrong I have done you."

Seeing the tears in his eyes, she knew that there was indeed hope for salvaging a relationship.

"May I, please?" As her father held out his arms for the child, she allowed him to take her.

Tristan wrapped his arms around Lily once more as Sabina looked at the man who held her. "Are you my grandpa?"

He nodded gravely. "I am your grandpa." His gray eyes glistened. "And you have a grandma as well."

Sabina clapped her hands. "Where is my grandma?"

As Robert Gray spoke with the child, Tristan turned Lily in his arms and kissed her gently, tenderly. "You see, Lily, she will understand." He smiled into her eyes. "By the time it is necessary to tell her all, she will see that I love you more than my own life. She will believe the story we tell is true, for nothing less could have kept me from making us a family—kept me from you." He touched her hair with a trembling hand. "I lost you in the winter and it was in winter that I found you again. You are my winter lily, now and forever. Nothing will ever separate us again."

Her gaze held his. "May I take that as your pledge?"

His voice held a promise of all the love and devotion she would ever need. "Upon my life you may."

And she did.

* * * * *

Harlequin® Historical

After the first two sensational books in award-winning author Theresa Michaels's new series

July 1997

THE MERRY WIDOWS—MARY #372

"...a heartbreaking tale of strength, courage, and tender romance...."
—*Rendezvous*

and

February 1998

THE MERRY WIDOWS—CATHERINE #400

"Smart, sassy and sexy...one of those rare, laugh-out-loud romances that is as delicious as a chocolate confection. 4☆s."
—*Romantic Times*

Comes the final book in the trilogy

July 1999

THE MERRY WIDOWS—SARAH #469

"Extraordinarily powerful!"
—*Romantic Times*

The story of a half-breed single father and a beautiful loner who come together in a breathtaking melding of human hearts....

You won't be able to put it down!

Available wherever Harlequin books are sold.

HARLEQUIN®
Makes any time special ™

"Don't miss this, it's a keeper!"
—**Muriel Jensen**

"Entertaining, exciting and
utterly enticing!"
—**Susan Mallery**

"Engaging, sexy...a fun-filled romp."
—**Vicki Lewis Thompson**

See what all your favorite authors
are talking about.

Coming October 1999 to a retail store near you.

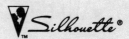

 **HARLEQUIN®**
Makes any time special ™

COMING NEXT MONTH FROM

HARLEQUIN HISTORICALS

DON'T MISS THESE FOUR GREAT TITLES AVAILABLE NOW!